CONSPIRACY

HAS

A NAME

JASON MINICK

CONSPIRACY

HAS

A NAME

ARCAM

jasonminick.com

Published by Jason Minick

ISBN: 978-1-9996620-0-4

Cover design & interior formatting: Mark Thomas / Coverness.com

DEDICATION

To my wife, Emma, and my amazing children,
Lucy, William and Sophie - who have tolerated my writing passion,
and who have supported and encouraged me
in spite of all the time it took me away from them.

This is for you. x

CHAPTER 1

As he began to regain consciousness, the doctor felt his body reverberate in reluctant harmony with the rumbling suspension, perpetually unforgiving as the mobile prison thundered to its mystery destination. His eyelids refused to open, and the cerebral effort exacerbated the thumping in his head. With huge exertion, they peeled apart by a couple of millimetres to reveal a blurred environment. Regaining the use of the nerves, he blinked involuntarily and began to survey the scene as objects moved in and out of focus in synch with the rumbling. To his left, one full-size and two miniature bodies lay deathly still. A tall, slim figure wobbled in the seat at the very end of the long, dirty white metallic interior. After another pulsation deep inside his cranium, his auto-focus momentarily revealed the features of a male. The man had his back to the double metal doors, and sat watching the scene within. The contented smile seemed paradoxical to the doctor, considering the automatic rifle that he held in a relaxed two-handed grip.

This was not Doctor O'Hara's normal routine. He should have been in the surgery, preparing for the day ahead. He couldn't remember how the alternative schedule came about, but he knew that it hadn't been of his own free will. He ventured to test his jaw muscles.

"Who are you? What do you want?"

The voice seemed to emanate from elsewhere, nevertheless the croaky oration was a manifestation of his thoughts, as it echoed in the tin shell that surrounded them.

The smile remained on the high cheek-boned, weathered face, introducing a thin gap that unveiled a glimpse of yellow incisors within the dark stubble. The doctor found their abductor's lethargic manner most irritating. Taking another glance at the still bodies beside him, it seemed out of context to him that his wife and their offspring appeared so peaceful. The sedatives had been powerful.

"For heaven's sake, who do you think we are? We have nothing – where are you taking us?!"

The query tailed off into a slight shriek and the doctor became stirred by his own words. His ire grew further at the impassive reaction of their captor, and he coughed as he wobbled to his feet.

When the scruffy figure spoke at last, his voice had the distinctive twang that was indigenous to the area.

"Doctor, I know this is difficult for you to accept right now, but you and your family are among the lucky few. All will soon be revealed."

"What?!"

The doctor's normally mild demeanour was almost completely overcome with anger.

"You've been specially chosen, Doctor. You're being rescued."

Dr O'Hara was disturbed by the quixotic suggestion of

the words and immediately judged the man with the firearm to be irrational. His next decision was impulsive by his own standards, but motivated by despair, he made his move without hesitation.

After checking his family again, he corrected himself as he wobbled off balance and charged towards the armed guard. The reaction was swift and brutal. The guard remained composed as he sharply swung the butt of the rifle across the face of the incoming attacker. As the greasy-haired man twisted sharply, the last thing O'Hara noticed was the short ponytail as it whipped across the side of his tensed neck, just before the darkness descended. The top half of his torso flew backwards as his feet left the ground, and their steel enclosure sounded like a gong as the back of O'Hara's skull connected. The ringing metal continued to reverberate as his body slid to the floor. The doctor was already unconscious as his assailant bent his lanky frame to administer another dose of sedative.

CHAPTER 2

Jasmine snuggled up to her father and listened intently as he read *Peter Rabbit* to her, with his usual under-stated enthusiasm. The same story they had read together a thousand times. Until two years ago, the young girl's bedtime routine had always consisted of a story from mummy and then daddy. Now her father held both roles. The little plump arms remained locked tightly around his neck, until the sound of soft rhythmic breathing accompanied the relaxation of the muscles in the girl's body. He withdrew a strong arm from around her and gently positioned the fair head on the pillow, before administering a tender kiss on her forehead and drawing the duvet up, so that it covered her bare arms.

The mobile telephone could be heard warbling in the lounge as the kettle completed its task and the switch clunked back to '0'. He poured the steaming water onto the tea bag, so that the *Peppa Pig* mug was full to within a centimetre of the brim, before wandering unenthusiastically in the direction of the sound.

He noted the name on the display as he lifted the phone: 'Gibson'. One corner of his mouth turned upwards slightly as he touched the green handset symbol.

"Hello Chief, are you missing me?"

"So sorry to disturb you at this hour, Jack. How was the holiday? I trust you and Jasmine had a nice time?"

"Really good thank you, but I think she's looking forward to Sarah coming back in the morning. Apparently, she's better than me at cooking."

"Ha! Well if those cakes that you brought in last month were anything to go by, then she has a point."

"Fair enough. How can I help anyway, John?" He stroked his chiselled, stubbled jawline, before running a tired hand through the unkempt lock of brown hair on his head. The caller paused for an unnaturally long sigh, before departing the small talk.

"As I say, my apologies for the hour. I know you're back in the morning, but I wanted to give you some advance warning."

"Sounds ominous already, John."

"I'll brief you tomorrow, of course. I need to assign you to a new case, but unfortunately it's not local, Jack. Our provincial colleagues down in the South West need some support with a case. Basically, I need you to travel to Somerset for a few days."

"Ah right, I see. The case being?"

"A spate of kidnappings. It's been going on for the past two months. There seems to be a pattern apparently, but no clear motive. Listen, I know you don't want to be away, and you don't have to explain the reasons to me, you know that, Jack. But this request has come from on high. They have asked for our top detective."

"Shucks, John."

"Not flannel, Jack. You've been asked for in person. Can you come and see me as soon as you get in tomorrow? You'll be fully briefed then. I just wanted to let you know about the location."

"Sure. How soon?"

"Immediately."

"I see."

"Sorry, Jack, this has come from nowhere. But the Home Secretary himself is expecting an update on the appointment tomorrow. Come in tomorrow morning, then take the afternoon off with Jasmine, to sort out personal arrangements. I'll tell them that you'll be there on Tuesday?"

"See you in the morning, John."

"Thanks, Jack. I'll leave you in peace."

Jack Robson completed his brew in the kitchen, which had taken on a dark tan colour by now; just as he liked it. After adding a delicate splash of milk, he returned to the living room with his hot nightcap and settled into the armchair. He placed the mug on the coffee table, adjacent to the classic novel that he had intended to complete that evening, so that the image of daddy pig smiled at him, beneath the text 'Best Daddy in the whole world!'.

His gaze was directed towards the large flat television screen that he never had any use for, unless it was displaying a Spurs match. It was the large framed portrait photograph that his eyes had settled on. He thought to himself how much younger he looked in the picture, standing proudly with his stunning bride, and, despite it being less than a decade old, how his world had utterly changed since the snap had been taken by one of the wedding guests. Both he and Isabelle had preferred it to any of the professional photographs. His eyes rested on the serene bride that stood beside him inside the distressed white picture frame and he sighed.

"Sorry, honey. Comes with the territory, but you always knew that. I'll make it quick and she has a blast with Sarah anyway."

He wiped a droplet from the corner of his eye as he allowed himself to indulge in what had become his daily purgatorial routine of recollection.

They had both gasped in awe of the scene beneath them as the mountain grew even more majestic, the closer they got. The layer of snow at the top had come to define the image of the Welsh mountain. From the air, the view was better than any postcard and the perspective so unexpectedly different from the year before, when they had both stood on the mountain itself after an impressively fast climb. Like many accidents, the irony of the cause wasn't obvious until cold reflection after the event. The weather system that had been responsible for creating such a spectacular scene, before giving way to the clarity that allowed the helicopter trip to proceed, had returned with a vengeance. Isabelle had pulled the small digital camera from her pocket, remembering that she had promised their little two-year-old daughter a photo of the very top. The camera flew across the floor of the chopper as the whirling wind took a firm hold of them in its fist and spun them in a random, chaotic course. The aircraft began spinning towards the mountainside. Isabelle was the first to react as the pilot screamed over his shoulder, "Evacuate!". This hadn't featured in Jack's planning for their fifth anniversary weekend. He checked his pocket to ensure that the eternity ring was safe as his wife dragged him to the opening and they leapt together. He had just fallen through a layer of cloud as he heard the explosion. The erupting fireball confirmed the cause of the bang. He hadn't seen whether the pilot had jumped. Jack's landing was hard, but paled into insignificance compared to what followed. He was desperate and exhausted after searching for nearly an hour. He discovered the horribly twisted form minutes before the rescue helicopter arrived on the mountain. It seemed so cruel and almost deliberate that the storm, having discharged its objective, died as soon as it had taken its victims. By the time the rescue crew arrived to join him on the mountain, he didn't want to survive.

The same regression took place every night in DCI Jack Robson's dreams, although occasionally Jasmine was on board the helicopter. The constant was Jack as the helpless survivor.

It had always been Isabelle who had the adventurous spirit. Jack was no shirker when it came to physical activity or indeed moderate excitement, but his wife actually loved, even craved the danger. A true adrenaline junkie. He had discovered that soon after they became acquainted as fellow newcomers to the detective branch. It had taken Jack months to muster the courage to invite his colleague out for dinner, accepting the assistance of the patented 'Dutch courage' on a branch social event to finally stick his neck out. He was both delighted and relieved when she had accepted the offer, and when he gave her the honour of selecting the venue for what he had hoped would be a romantic encounter, he was unable to suppress his shock when she revealed she had been looking for a companion to complete a two hundred-foot bungee jump that weekend.

Isabelle had always encouraged him to take risks, on the basis that it helped one in the management of fear. Despite driving himself along in her slipstream, far outside his comfort zone, Jack had never felt that relief, but, like many other things, he hadn't ever opened up to his wife about them.

Even after having their one and only child and leaving the force to concentrate on her new maternal duties, Isabelle never lost her thirst for danger. If anything, the need for it had intensified, and she was candid that her immense pride in her husband was tempered with a degree of envy, when he was promoted to Detective Chief Inspector. The truth was, Jack would have been happier to have stayed at home with the child, while his wife pursued her dreams, but he would certainly never have dared to admit that to her.

Jack Robson had built quite a reputation in his first five years and his powers of deduction and downright thoroughness had made him an instant star. He would never accept that he had any special talent for the job, merely that he was neither a lazy bastard like a lot of the so-called experienced staff, nor a dedicated desk-junkie like most of the population of bright young things.

He necked the lukewarm tea and abandoned the mug on the coffee table. His body ached for sleep, so he decided to retire for the evening, but not before calling into the small pink bedroom to indulge in another soft embrace of his sleeping kin.

CHAPTER 3

Jasmine sat on the small travel case, giggling as her father gave another tug on the zip to get it started. Sarah smiled in reluctant acceptance.

"I just can't believe you've got to go away on your second day back Jack. It's as though the branch has closed down and done nothing while you've been on holiday. Couldn't someone else have been sent?"

He continued to look at the child and smiled, doing his best to conceal his true feelings.

"Well, for some reason, they've asked for daddy, haven't they Jazzy!".

The little girl jumped into his open arms and he turned to face the young woman, who had done so much to try to fill the chasm that had been detonated into their lives two years ago. She had always been close to them and had been hit as hard as anybody outside of the immediate family by the tragic death of her lifelong friend. She was the same age as Isabelle, to the day, which was what had first brought them to one another's attention all those years ago, during the first year of primary school. She was the only possible choice for Isabelle as her maid of honour, and on her wedding day most of the guests agreed that she probably blubbed more than the mother of the bride had. Jack had always got on like a house on fire with her too; they had even shared a rather flirtatious relationship until the passing of Isabelle. That no longer felt appropriate to either of them and the innuendos had stopped, but they had remained close. It wasn't that Jack had stopped noticing her elegant figure or the healthy complexion of her pretty face, but the guilt he felt at such moments of weakness served as a constant deterrent for allowing those feelings to surface very often.

Jasmine loved Sarah like a big sister, and it was only natural that she had placed such a degree of trust in her, given the altruistic way her substitute mummy behaved around her. She understood that Sarah would sacrifice just about anything for her well-being. Jack knew it too. The understanding between them was unspoken, but Sarah had been with him and Jasmine from the moment he returned alone from the tragic excursion to Snowdonia, and she had been so strong for them, despite her own broken heart.

"I think they believe that my experience fits with certain details of the case, that's all. I'm just going to help out for a short while, just to assist with making a breakthrough, hopefully."

Sarah suspected that it wasn't the full story, but she also knew not to probe. Jack had spent all morning at the branch headquarters, getting the full details from the Superintendent. He had been asked for personally, by the Home Secretary no less, whose path he had crossed just over a year earlier. In the spring of the previous year, the Super had been asked to assemble a small team of his best detectives to provide support to the counter terrorism branch. It might not have been public knowledge, but within the inner establishment the case was high on the agenda, due to its potentially inflammable outcome. The Home Secretary had known DCI Robson by name, ever since he had been the one to make the breakthrough that led to the subversion of a sophisticated plot. A plot that had been designed to bring the heart of government to a standstill. Typically, it was Jack's thoroughness and dogged determination that enabled them to uncover the London-based cell that had been poised to strike. The intelligence community hadn't been able to supply the answers on that occasion and it had been good old-fashioned detective work, largely on the part of DCI Jack Robson's, that had uncovered the perpetrators in the nick of time. Since that moment, he had carried the burden that came from possessing knowledge that few others did. And it was expected that he would carry that knowledge to the grave.

But the case in Somerset wasn't similar. Jack perceived that his sudden secondment was down to the embarrassment that the kidnapping incidents were causing the law enforcement community. People were being snatched seemingly at will along a forty-mile stretch of coast in the South West, and the poorly staffed provincials had no idea where to start looking. Added to this was the fact that a highly respected military and political dignitary resided in the area; which typically had the indisputable effect of bumping up the prioritisation of the case. A case which would have generated focus anywhere, but with a powerful constituent in the area, the depressingly low resources were never going to be tolerated for long.

"You don't mind though, do you darling? You're going to teach Sarah how to make our amazing cheesecake that we had last week!"

The little girl took her cue and produced the dutiful smile of a good-natured child being instructed that they are happy about something. Jasmine's ability to cope was not childlike. Doubtless her survival mechanism had been tested, but she had continued to develop in her mother's model. Jack had decided that that had to be proof of some kind of gene theory, because it certainly wasn't a consequence of his example. At the tender age of four, she was also acutely tuned into her father's emotions and responsibilities and never questioned his commitments.

CHAPTER 4

It was approaching midday on Tuesday when Jack breathed a sigh of relief, as he crossed the mouth of the river Avon and the motorway sign indicated that he was approaching the junction for Portishead. It had been a frustrating drive and the rows of caravans reminded him of his childhood holidays and the pain that had to be endured to allow oneself the luxury of sleeping in a field and taking cold showers for a week or two.

He would have liked to have spent a little more time recuperating after checking into his hotel, but that would have to wait until after his appointment. He arrived fifteen minutes early for his 14:30 meeting at the vast site that housed the Avon and Somerset constabulary headquarters, and was given directions to the department that he needed.

The contrast between his normal place of work and this new, temporary base couldn't have been more pronounced. DCI Robson had almost forgotten that it was possible for a place of work to reveal human habitation and felt almost envious seeing the eclectic combination of desks that, instead of being totally barren, contained paperwork, items of stationery and permanently stationed desktop computers. For the first time since he could remember, he didn't feel the onset of anxiety in the pit of his stomach that occurred whenever he entered the London base. He wasn't sure why he got that feeling. Perhaps it was the fact that the idea of sleek minimalism seemed in such contradiction to the natural world. But the concept had evidently not yet been embraced in Somerset, and Jack already considered it a more enriched environment for it.

As far as he could tell, everyone was engaged in activities that were familiar to him, but without the senseless intensity that arose from the notion that every second mattered. The conversations in progress seemed to be amiable rather than feigned out of necessity, yet, still professional. He hesitated at the first greeting of 'Good afternoon', but by the third salutation he had easily slipped back into the phenomenon of polite interaction.

Under normal circumstances, he wouldn't have been phased by the apathetic demeanour of his new boss as he was introduced. However, the atmosphere of the station had disarmed him of the defence mechanism that seemed to be ingrained in most inhabitants of the capital, which would normally have suppressed any expectations of conviviality. Robson was annoyed with himself for blushing in front of the PA as she introduced him to the Superintendent. Evidently it was considered acceptable by the criminal investigation department in Somerset to reject the offer of a handshake. He followed the broad, jacketed shoulders into the office marked

'Superintendent Thorpe'.

He registered the faint odour of cigar emanating from the Superintendent's clothing, as Thorpe eased his bulky torso into the swivel chair behind the solid-looking oak desk. DCI Robson decided against waiting for the invitation to sit and moved to help himself. He only became aware of the petite blond out of the corner of his eye as he turned to sit in the chair. The radiant young woman wore a figure hugging ensemble of dark trousers and turtle neck top. She smiled and looked at the new arrival with intelligent eyes.

"Good afternoon, Chief Inspector. Can I interest you in a coffee?" She already held the opaque jug full of steaming coffee and had begun to pour before Jack answered.

"Yes please. Just black, thank you."

"This is Inspector Emma Wilson," offered the Superintendent, in a decidedly unenthusiastic tone, although it seemed that whatever had prevented him from acknowledging Jack's existence minutes earlier had begun to subside.

"Pleased to meet you," said Robson as he forced his eyes to lock onto hers, resisting the temptation to study her form in closer detail, as she leant across to place the cup and saucer on the desk in front of him. Evidently, she had no need for make-up, allowing her healthy, pale visage to be totally unveiled. Her hand felt soft, yet seemed unusually strong as Jack accepted the offer of a handshake and she took the seat beside him, holding her tiny knees together so that her lap formed a delightful heart shape.

"Emma's been recently seconded to the investigation. I'm not sure how much you know, but it's become quite a hot potato."

Robson now noticed the smoker's gruffness in the agrarian inflection as the Superintendent spoke.

"The case is causing a great deal of unrest in the local area and we are now under immense pressure from all quarters to show progress. To speak of which, I was just receiving a summons to see the Chief Superintendent as you arrived. He wants an update in person, so I'm going to have to leave you in Emma's capable hands."

The chair beneath groaned in relief as the Superintendent stood and collected his laptop case from somewhere beneath the desk.

"Welcome to the team, Jack. I'm told that you were given very little notice. But we welcome your support. We are expecting you to lead the investigation from here. You will take over as the senior investigating officer. Let me know if there is anything you need."

DCI Robson and Inspector Wilson watched the large man wearily depart his office, carrying with him the tangible burden of expectation. He stopped briefly at the door and looked back at Jack.

"And I apologise for the frosty reception. We believe there was another kidnapping yesterday, Emma will fill you in on the details. As you will soon discover yourself, we are under intense pressure to start delivering on this case. I'll catch up with you both later."

Robson followed Inspector Wilson's lead and took a sip of his coffee, allowing her to break the ice.

"He is glad that you're here."

Tiny dimples appeared beneath her pale cheekbones as she offered him a slightly apologetic smile.

"Hmm, if you say so."

"But at the same time, it is rather a poisoned chalice. On the one hand, we are being supplied with a much-needed resource for our understaffed enquiry, but politically it simply adds more fuel to those that believe that the poor man can't cope."

He noticed that her voice did not possess any of the West Country inflection of her superior officer, as he inhaled another breath of sweet-scented perfume.

"How do you see it?"

"In both contexts. The Super has been leading the investigation personally, such is our resource shortage. I'm nearly as new to this case as you."

"Oh?"

"I was reassigned to this last week." She responded to Jack's facial expression. "It's not quite as chaotic as it sounds. From what I've seen so far, the chief has been typically meticulous in the investigation to date, but there is simply no clue as to what has been motivating the snatches. Anyway, more of that later. Let me introduce you to the rest of the team."

Her walk was not entirely feminine, but that did not detract from the attractiveness of her subtly curved form as she led Jack out of the Superintendent's office and into the open-plan section. He was introduced to four people sat in a huddle around a computer monitor, which was displaying a map of a coastal region. Inspector Wilson introduced them to the new DCI individually, before the gathering dispersed, leaving them with the sharp-looking inhabitant of the desk. Sergeant James

Matthews minimised the map and brought another file up onto the screen. A list of names ran down the screen, with brief details against each row:

1 – *Emily* **Jameson**. *(22).* *Primary school teacher. Dennis* **Marcher** *(Fiancé) (27). Plumber.*

2 – **Hudson**: *Mark (38) (Sports Coach) and Janet (36) (Electrical/ Electronic Engineer). Two Children: Zac (8) and Francesca (6).*

3 – **Whitstable**: *Max (46) (Orthopaedic Surgeon). Sylvia (47) (Plastic surgeon).*

4 – **Bertrand**: *Duncan (29) (Psychologist and language expert). Jacqui (26) (Humanist and yoga teacher).*

5 – **Janson**: *Dave (38) (Carpenter). Karen (37) (Owns dress-making business). Two children: Matt (9) and Katie (6).*

6 – **Reeves**: *Phillip (44) (Writer and Author). Juliet (49) (Journalist). Two Children: Lois (10) and Lenny (7).*

7 – **Alexander**: *Malcolm (32) (Builder/Architect). Justine (30) (Scientist). One child: James (8).*

8 – **O'Hara**: *Darryl (46) (GP/expert practitioner in alternative medicines). Julie (43) (Dental surgeon). Two children: Lola (11) and James (9).*

"These are the victims to date," explained Sergeant Matthews, as he adjusted the thick rimmed spectacles on his nose, before scratching his scalp and disturbing the scruffy, long blond hair. Robson interrupted the young man's discreet examination of the athletic female torso on his left.

"When was the first?"

"A little over two months ago. It's been just about one per

week ever since, in the order listed there. It's got us chasing our tails, to be perfectly honest."

DCI Robson pretended not to notice the irritation on Inspector Wilson's face following the crass use of cliché, and continued.

"That looks to be a broad spectrum of the community. Are there any obvious connections between these people?"

"Nothing, apart from the fact that they've all taken place within about a forty-mile radius, mainly concentrated around the Somerset coast and the Quantocks."

"Are there any prevailing details shared by the victims?"

"Well, you can see for yourself that the kids are all of approximately the same age group. But apart from that, nothing obvious. It's as per your original observation – they appear to be from just about the whole range of the community, both in terms of occupation and social standing."

"Anything extraordinary about the only child, this one?" Robson held his forefinger close to the monitor screen, just beneath the entry for James Alexander.

"Well, actually yes."

"Go on."

"He's an outstanding musician. Aged eight, he's been awarded a scholarship at the Royal College of Music."

Jack nodded slowly, and his bottom lip protruded slightly, as it always did when pondering some news that piqued his interest.

"And the most recent kidnapping was yesterday, I understand?"

"Yes sir, or some time over the weekend, we can't be sure

yet. As with the others, we're not sure about the exact timings. Both the O'Haras were in surgery as normal last Friday and the children went to school. The alarm was raised Monday late morning, when it became apparent that not only had the kids not turned up at school, but neither of the parents had shown for work."

"How far is it to the home of the most recent victims?"

"About an hour, sir. We've actually just arrived back, but forensics are still there. They should be finished at the house this afternoon."

"It's Jack by the way. Has anything of interest been uncovered?"

"Nothing. Just appears that the house was abandoned in a hurry. Another vanishing act. Their passports and wallets are still in the house. The family car is still on the drive. Although it looks like another vehicle had been at the house, judging by the tyre marks in the gravel. "

Wilson was ready for the next question before it left her new colleague's lips.

"Can we go and join them?"

"Follow me." She gave a faint smile as DCI Robson nodded farewell to the small team of detectives, before turning his gaze back to address the Sergeant.

"Do you think you could acquire a list of all patients for both the O'Haras, James?"

The young man's eyes indicated that he was pleased to see the new senior investigating officer taking an early lead. "Sure. We're just waiting on that to come through."

"Okay, and also a list of clients and business associates for the others?" Jack felt the need to establish how much background work this young group of detectives had carried out, but he really hoped that such basic elements of information gathering were either already underway or had been completed.

"Daisy has been compiling that – we should be able to have it with you in a couple of days."

The Sergeant nodded to the lady in the corner of the open-plan office with the neat appearance, who responded with a professional-looking smile.

DCI Robson followed Inspector Wilson out into the car park, carefully feigning an interest in the surrounding environment, instead of the slender neckline that was revealed as she skilfully tied her fair hair back while they walked.

CHAPTER 5

Wilson's driving seemed to epitomise the confidence that had been evident to Robson from the second he made her acquaintance. He also had a hunch that the sparkle in her eyes pointed to a remarkable character.

The small talk had only lasted for the first twenty minutes of the journey. In her cordial manner, she had explained that she had been in the CID for a mere two years. She was one of the new generation of recruits in the police force. A high-flying graduate who had passed the inspector's examination within three years of joining, and was prepared to relocate from her home in Yorkshire to snatch the opportunity of an inspector vacancy in the criminal investigation department.

In many ways, her profile was typical of that which riled many of the longer-serving, seasoned officers. Another fast-tracked world beater, running before she could walk. Jack thought to himself how her appearance no doubt helped to soften any animosity. He had never considered himself to hold patriarchal tendencies, but felt mildly ignorant for his silent speculation. Her demeanour did not suggest that she was not up to the role and Jack had already noticed that she seemed to emanate composure and perhaps even a little wisdom.

He judged it to be too early to get into private details just yet, having already noticed the lack of jewellery on her left hand as it firmly gripped the wheel.

"So, what about witnesses?"

"Nobody has seen a thing. We've interviewed the neighbours, naturally. The trouble is, as James was suggesting, we don't really have a precise time for any of the kidnappings. All we have to go on are two separate sightings of a white van, in locations that may have coincided with the times of the kidnappings."

"Were they all taken from their homes?"

"Again, we can't be certain. But forensics have found a few prints and DNA that is common to all of the homes."

"What about the families?"

"They all seem distraught. And perplexed – there is no motive apparent for any of the cases."

"Money?"

"Some of them are relatively affluent, but not all. None are what you would describe as super-rich."

"Are you sure the cases are linked?"

"No."

The bluntness of her honesty took DCI Robson by surprise and the silence that followed was only disturbed by the rumbling tyres, as they opened up a distance from the bus they had overtaken on the single carriageway seconds earlier.

"A frustrating case."

"Frustrating is certainly an apt description. Quite understandably, the local community is becoming increasingly anxious. There is gathering momentum for the chief to quit. The local MP stepped in to request assistance from the Met. So it's politically hot, hence the sudden summons."

"Sounds like a stay of execution to me."

"I think it's fair to say you represent the last throw of the dice, as far as Thorpe's longevity in the job goes."

They had left the main trunk route and now wound along the minor roads, gliding through the Quantock hills. Jack watched the craft in the glistening Bristol Channel to their right, forming a picture-perfect backdrop to the stone houses and taverns. The tranquil scene yelled at the incongruity of the events that he had been sent to investigate. Unlike the constantly alive city that was his usual habitat, there was no sign of crime on these streets and the visible habitation spoke only of middle class apathy and peaceful retirement.

He watched the caravan travelling in the opposite direction, as it was pulled by a family hatchback complete with roof-box, ensuring that the family could bring almost their entire domestic belongings with them. The sight reminded DCI Robson that they were just entering the season during which the area didn't only accommodate permanent residents.

Their winding ascent was immediately followed by a long downhill section, and on their right the sea was lost behind another field of glowing rape. The livestock on their left reinforced the countryside image. The Signs for a cider farm and steam railway were shortly followed by a larger one, welcoming them to Williton. As they approached the most built-up area they had encountered in the last ten miles, Inspector Wilson took a sharp right instead of proceeding along the small high street.

After passing another handful of charming residences adorned with thatched roofs, the settlements became fewer. A red brick house stood proudly in contrast with the little thatched cottages that they had admired earlier. Overlooking the channel and with enough land to accommodate an orchard and large front lawn, it spoke of affluence. As they drew into the stony driveway, Robson noticed that further dwellings existed in the immediate area, mostly further down the hill, and possibly a convenience store in the other direction.

The gravel cracked and popped beneath the tyres as Wilson swung the car around and parked adjacent to the white Land Rover with blue and yellow checks. The only other vehicle at the property was a small white van, where a man in white overalls was in discussion with the uniformed owners of the Land Rover. The greying, balding man in the overalls raised his hand in a greeting as they got out of the car, and Inspector Wilson approached him, smiling.

"Hi Bob. How's it going?"

"Greetings Emma. It's the same old story I'm afraid my dear, even the door handles are clean on this one," he lamented while blatantly scrutinising the new arrival.

"This is DCI Robson. Jack, meet Bob Jefferies, our lead forensic investigator."

Bob evidently didn't require further explanation, giving a seemingly sympathetic grin.

"Hello sir, you've come to rescue us from total embarrassment I understand?" The wrinkles spread across the large round face as he smiled and removed the glove from his right hand.

"Or come to share in it perhaps."

Jack took Bob Jefferies' outstretched hand in a firm shake and decided to get straight down to business, rather than invite further scrutiny from the disgruntled locals.

"Pleased to meet you, Bob. So, nothing of significance here?"

He had never felt comfortable with formalities, especially not if he was in danger of being an object of reverence. Jack assessed the forensic scientist to be at least twenty years his senior, which compounded his uneasiness with being called 'Sir'.

"We might once again pick up common DNA traces, I dare say," the older man extended a gloved white arm to point at the gravel, "and you can tell that these tyre marks aren't from the family saloon over there. More like a four by four, or even larger, like a van maybe."

Wilson gave a frustrated nod, while DCI Robson continued.

"Has anyone spoken to the neighbours yet?"

The forensic team leader deflected the question to the DCI's new colleague.

"I believe that Emma's, or should I say, *your* team were engaged in house to house calls this morning."

His new partner obliged.

"If you can call them neighbours. The nearest are about a hundred yards along the coastal road. James interviewed them this morning, but nobody saw a thing."

"Aren't there more homes further along the road?"

"Possibly – this is my first visit too."

She responded to Robson's raised eyebrow. "Thorpe had me in a brainstorming session yesterday, preparing himself for the Chief Super's latest attack. And today he wanted me to stick around for your arrival."

He nodded impassively, disguising his true feelings and fixed his eyes on Bob again.

"Mind if we take a look inside?"

"Be my guest, we're just about done."

Jefferies led them both between the wooden portico and through the open front door, not noticing that DCI Robson had paused to examine the structure more closely while the other two proceeded ahead of him. After several seconds, he heard voices inside. Evidently Emma and Bob had met up with the uniformed officers again and hadn't noticed that their new colleague wasn't behind them. He paused in the porchway, examining the discreet electronic device that had been attached to the apex of the decorative oak porch.

When he eventually caught up, Inspector Wilson and Jefferies were stood in the modest hallway, apparently humouring the local bobbies as they gave their expert analysis on how the crime was committed.

"Must have been known to them," declared a tall, overweight constable.

"No sign of disturbance," agreed his eager, younger sidekick. They bade farewell as Bob confirmed that they were finished for the day and that he would take care of sealing the property on their departure. Another man in white overalls followed the officers outside, evidently loading the van as his boss stayed to assist the new arrivals.

"Doesn't seem to be any sign of a forced entry at the front; what are the other entrances like?" Wilson enquired.

Jefferies patiently escorted DCI Robson and Inspector Wilson around the house, so that they could witness the same thing that both he and the rest of their team had earlier. Jack indicated towards the front entrance as the three of them returned to the hallway.

"Has anyone checked the CCTV footage yet?"

Bob stopped himself from a condescending response, noting that the DCI's demeanour suggested that the question had perhaps not been asked out of naivety.

"I don't believe any cameras have been found at the property?"

Robson took them both out to the porchway and pointed at the corner of the inverted 'V'. Jefferies appeared slightly irked, seemingly wary of the new DCI, but Inspector Wilson, squinting, spotted the faint red LED in the corner of the woodwork and stepped out onto the driveway to see the tiny lens pointing down. "My goodness, that's rather discreet."

"Isn't it just? They're all the rage in London I believe. Helps people find out who their friends really are."

The older man still cast a slightly frustrated figure as he listened, with his hands on his hips, to the other two discussing the invisible device. Emma offered assistance, and standing on tiptoes, she pointed her forefinger as close as she could get to the device.

"Looks like there's a little wireless camera in there."

"Well I never."

Bob's assistant now joined them to see what could have demanded such attention on the front doorstep, and attempted to rescue his boss's pride.

"I'll find out where the data is being stored; there's a laptop in the study, I'll see if I can get into it."

Robson and Wilson left the young assistant to massage his boss's ego a little more and went back inside to inspect the upper floor. Ten minutes later, Jack was standing pensively on the generous landing. Emma joined him, having examined the last of the bedrooms; evidently that of a young girl, the walls covered in pink and white hearts and the white wooden furniture decorated with similar emblems of love. There was an array of dolls lying around on the floor, each with pristine figures and long glamorous hair styles. Emma noticed how each doll was effectively a mini version of the equally plastic ladies that were presented in modern female magazines. Jack was more interested in how the girl apparently still played imaginative games, despite being into double figures and wondered if Jasmine at eleven, would still resist the constant temptation to resort to mundane electronic devices, providing a constant feed of mindless trash. Wilson spoke first.

"It just looks like they dropped everything and left." Robson nodded in agreement.

"It does indeed."

"There doesn't appear to be any sign of a physical altercation," she continued. "It almost gives the impression that they left the house of their own free will, albeit in a mighty hurry."

In the downstairs study, Bob appeared to have regained his dignity and was standing over his younger colleague as he sat at the desk and searched the hard drive of a laptop.

"Any joy?" asked Emma.

"Nothing yet, but if it's here I'll find it," assured the young man. "It never ceases to amaze me the way people don't bother to use password protection."

Choosing not to disclose that he didn't bother with IT security himself, Jack suggested taking advantage of the kitchen facilities. All three accepted the suggestion of refreshments.

Emma took another look at the cereal bowls on the work surface in the kitchen and the large milk container that had been left out of the fridge, while Jack filled the kettle at the sink. Whatever had caused the O'Haras to depart was ostensibly more pressing than completing their breakfast. She let DCI Robson try the switch for the fifth time before taking pity and deciding to step in. Jack was mildly amused at the pleasure she seemed to derive from the situation, as she silently operated the switch on the wall socket. He quickly diverted his attention from her unintentionally seductive smile and decided to concede defeat to the kettle as it still refused to operate.

Wilson walked across to the door and tried the light switch. The spotlights in the ceiling remained extinguished. DCI Robson was happy for her to take the lead, not being particularly handy himself, as she trudged into the ground floor toilet and pulled open the fuse box.

"Nothing's tripped in here," she declared and raised her voice so that the men in the study could hear. "Bob, have you used the house electricity today?"

Bob was walking towards her as she approached the study.

"No, why?"

"Because it doesn't seem to be on."

She continued into the study as she spoke and looked over the young man's shoulder at the laptop screen. The symbol in the bottom right hand corner of the screen indicated 15% battery life and confirmed that the device was not charging, despite being plugged in. After trying the lights and TV in the living room, she announced to the others that the house seemed to be without electricity.

"I wonder if any other houses are affected?" asked Bob.

"Let's find out," she responded. "I noticed there was a distribution box out in the street, at the end of the driveway."

With that she paced out of the house and towards the front gate. Jack and Bob followed.

Jefferies was already pacing down the road to check with the nearest neighbour, as Wilson and Robson both stood at the green, waist-high enclosure. Jack was the first to notice the elderly couple walk towards them, both slightly bent as they struggled up the hill.

"Hello, dear." The lady seemed pleased to encounter another human being.

"Good afternoon, madam. Sir," replied Jack, as Emma continued to examine the box for tampering.

"Are you not finished my love? You look smarter than the others I must say!" The lady addressed Emma directly now, forcing her to raise herself from the green housing.

"Sorry, madam, what do you mean?"

"*Others* did you say?" added Jack.

"Yes well, my wife means you people were here yesterday weren't you?" The conversation seemed to have awakened the crooked man's gregarious nature.

"Has your electricity supply been interrupted over the last couple of days?" Emma tried to tease a little more detail, although it was clear that it wasn't going to be difficult to get them to talk.

"No, hasn't affected us luckily," said the man. "Don't know what they were doin'. Seemed a bit cagey if you ask me. Folks these days are so rude, nobody seems to want to be sociable anymore."

"All right Rodge, get off yer blinkin' high horse!"

The lady placed a wrinkled hand on her husband's portly midriff, in a subtle gesture of authority.

"You say they were here yesterday?" Emma's voice had a gentle, patient tone. "What time would that have been?"

"Yeah, we walked past these two blokes, just here weren't it, Marge?" Marge nodded enthusiastically, while her husband continued. "We takes a walk to the paper shop about half-nine every day, you know, once all the folks have gone to work and school, so it's a bit less busy. But we were a bit earlier yesterday, because I had a doctor's appointment at half-nine, see, probably about eight.....ish?"

Marge's zeal spilled over.

"It's his only bloody exercise. He just sits in his chair the rest of the day. Only reason he's here now is coz he hasn't got no bread left for 'is breakfast in the mornin'. I told him he'd 'ave to come too. That's why he's looking so bloomin' grumpy!"

Emma was keen to avoid the comment becoming a catalyst for bickering.

"Oh I see, what company were they from?"

"Well like I said, they hardly bleedin' spoke. They had a white van parked up on the curb there di'nt they marge? Didn't see any markings on 'im though."

Marge nodded.

"Yes Rodge, were a white van, definitely. No writin' though."

"Just had their heads in that there box. They've sent the professionals out now then have they?"

"Something like that. Well we should be all back to normal now. Glad it didn't affect you both anyway."

Jack judged that they had now extracted all the information likely to be useful from the eager couple.

"Not at all me 'ansum, we'll leave ye both to it then."

After allowing the couple to take their leave in their own time, the next person to walk up the road was known to them.

"Bob, do you think you could get this cover open?" Emma asked, looking at the worn green housing.

"I should think so. The next house along the road hasn't noticed any interruption to the electrical supply over the past few days by the way. I didn't go any further."

"That's okay," answered Jack, "it's becoming apparent that this might be a local fault."

Bob quickly returned from his van with a small T-shaped tool, which he inserted into the hole in the door of the green cabinet and gave a half turn. The door stuttered open after a firm pull and the three of them leaned in at the row of switches that sat above the neatly secured bundles of wiring. Jack concentrated on blocking out the sweet smell emanating from the bare portion of white neck to his left, as Emma reached out to the only switch in the row that was in a different position to the others. They moved a few paces to the right, so that the driveway to the O'Hara's property was in view, and observed the Victorian style lanterns either side of the portico glow a dim yellow, sensing the early spring onset of dusk. The lantern style light also came on above the front porch of the O'Hara house.

"Somebody deliberately isolated their electricity," Bob said, whilst visibly processing the permutations. "To cause confusion?" he added.

"Well, it's not exactly going to plunge the house into darkness at this time of year, unless it was done in the middle of the night?" Emma's thoughts had become audible. "Besides, Marge and Rodge have just informed us that someone was working here on Monday morning."

Jack remained silent.

"Why would they do that? Almost as if they wanted to alert the O'Haras?" said Bob.

After an infinitesimal silence, Jack spoke.

"No, to give them a reason to enter the house, invited."

CHAPTER 6

The grainy CCTV footage had apparently been digitally enhanced for their second viewing, but as they watched it being projected onto the wall of the small briefing room, DCI Robson considered it to be no clearer than the images they had viewed on the laptop screen the previous day.

Robson, Wilson and Thorpe watched two men transfer four seemingly lifeless figures, one by one, on what looked like a field stretcher. The still bodies were hauled into the side entrance of a long wheelbase, white van, which had been parked so it obstructed the view of the front door of the house.

The techies had failed to get a legible close-up of the vehicle's registration plate from the frozen image. The best they had was two very hazy mugshots. Both assailants appeared to be dressed in official-looking uniforms consisting of blue overall trousers and cream polo shirts.

The first man had a closely shaved, watermelon sized head, which sat on a frame that must have exceeded six and half feet.

The officers watched the film unfold in silence, as the man wrapped a shovel-like hand around the frame of the driver's side door and pulled it shut on himself. The wiry man that entered the rear of the van through the side door looked small in comparison to his comrade, but using the front porch of the house as reference, they all agreed he probably surpassed the six-foot mark himself, with no distinguishing features apart from tattoos evident on both forearms. They couldn't decide whether a moving dark spot was caused by the poor quality recording, but it seemed to sway, as though perhaps a ponytail wobbled from side to side as the thinner man moved. Thorpe broke the ponderous silence with a jolt of reality.

"The forensics team have drawn a blank as usual." For all the promise of this new lead, a visual lead no less, they were no closer to identifying the perpetrators. "We can't get the bloody reg clarified it seems."

"Sir," responded Wilson, "the electricity company that the O'Haras were with have no record of anybody being on duty in that area over the past few days, nor any record of a fault being reported."

"Tell me," Thorpe made a steeple with his fingertips as he continued probing, "if the electricity supply was isolated, how is it that we are viewing footage from the CCTV system?"

Wilson held the Superintendent's gaze for a moment, before answering.

"The camera had its own battery back up sir, quite a neat little product really, motion activated too. At first, we thought we weren't going to get anything, because the communication to the wireless hub had been interrupted by the power outage.

But it turns out that the camera has its own internal SD card, which stored the footage that we've just seen."

"So, if they'd had their electricity cut off in the morning, as your current hypothesis would have it," said Thorpe, "then why would it go unreported? And more to the point, what fucking relevance does it hold?"

DCI Robson had seen senior officers buckle under pressure before – perfectly competent, sometimes even gifted, in their earlier career. The political bullshit almost always served as an obstruction to the free-minded creativity needed to inspire a lead out of apparently nothing. He attempted to uphold their theory.

"Sir, they wouldn't have had to call the electricity board if, say, the electricity company had already called them to inform them of the fault."

For the moment, Jack seemed to have found the valve to the pressure cooker. The redness in the Superintendent's face faded subtly and his shoulders fell back to their quiescent state, submitting to gravity again. His brusque manner remained however.

"How do you plan to proceed, DCI Robson?"

"We've had the O'Haras phone records examined."

"And?"

"We've eliminated most of the calls on each of their mobile phones and the landline. All incoming and outgoing calls are accounted for, barring two."

It was simple protocol; thoroughness, covering the angles. Leave no stone unturned, the mantra of any detective worth their salt. He had been assured by the young team of detectives, or 'Thorpe's babes' as they were known in some quarters, that the same check had of course been carried out for the previous victims. Jack requested the data anyway, informing Sergeant Matthews that it wasn't personal, but it was often productive to have an independent eye review old, otherwise discounted evidence.

The Superintendent continued to hold his gaze, clearly waiting for any snippet of information that would endorse the relevance of this line of enquiry.

"The O'Haras received a call on the landline early on Monday morning. The area code was Porlock. Apparently, it turns out to have been from a phone box near the harbourside."

Thorpe chose not to interrupt the silence and a little edginess seemed to creep back into his manner. Robson took little notice as Thorpe rubbed a large palm up and down his wrinkled face. Inspector Wilson, however, was more tuned into such indicators, and sought to address what appeared to Jack to be a simple lack of faith on the Superintendent's part. She understood that the boss was looking for specifics. Robson, already growing tired of the capitulating attitude, welcomed the interruption.

"Also, sir," she said, "an incoming call was answered on Mrs O'Hara's phone about half an hour later. The call was from another mobile."

"Belonging to?"

"A certain 'Barry Searle', who, we think at this stage, resides in Porlock."

DCI Robson studied the deep-set, unreadable expression on the Superintendent's face. He concluded that the man had reached the point where he rejected any twinkling of hope.

Wilson judged that Thorpe, being a local man, was accessing his own A-Z, of which he was once immensely proud. Indeed, when she was first introduced to her new boss some eighteen months ago, one would have got the impression that he considered his memory of people to be his greatest achievement in life. She offered him a potential key to the ageing vault.

"His family have been based in Porlock for generations sir – a long line of fishermen. Although he seems to have broken the mould and served in the military. That's all we know so far."

The Superintendent blinked as he lit a fat cigar, apparently oblivious to modern smoking laws.

"So you don't know what he's doing these days?"

"Not yet sir. We're about to go and pay him a visit."

The Superintendent shuffled his large frame towards the window to provide an escape route for the cigar fumes. While the sweet-smelling tobacco continued to fill the room, DCI Robson and Inspector Wilson both felt relieved to see signs of the Super returning from whatever dark place he had been residing in for most of their briefing. Doubtless the nicotine fix helped, but his voice even seemed to contain a positive edge again.

"Okay good, please do, and keep me updated."

"Of course, sir."

DCI Robson turned to leave.

"Just before you go, I have to make my daily call to the Chief Superintendent and then hold a press briefing. Given the unfolding events of the last twenty-four hours, I could really do with a brief report from you. It doesn't need to be comprehensive."

Robson tried to conceal antipathy from his expression.

"Sir, with respect, we ought to move fast on this, can the paperwork wait?"

"Sorry Jack. I have the local and national press camped outside this station morning, noon and evening. The Chief Superintendent calls me for an update twice a day, despite the fact there never are any, so that he can convey the same report of sweet-fuck-all on to the commissioner for further onward distribution. It's politics, but that doesn't make it avoidable I'm afraid. I can get the local bobbies to trace this guy's locality with immediate effect, so all the prep will be done for your visit."

CHAPTER 7

Dr Darryl O'Hara woke in a firm but comfortable bed. The first sensation was the dull aching inside his head. Instinctively, he placed a palm at the source of the thud. He withdrew his hand abruptly at the unfamiliar texture of the skin surface. He ventured again, this time with both hands. As his frayed senses fought to shake off their numbness, the doctor finally evaluated that his head had been bandaged. He looked around to observe that the scene was not entirely unfamiliar, at least not in terms of the people who populated it. It was definitely his wife and children who were sat just a few metres away at the table, but he found himself disturbed by the gormless fashion in which each of them mechanically consumed the fare before them.

The environment was certainly alien. It seemed to be about the size of an average family hotel room. The bland decor was partly rescued by the fact that each wall had been adorned with a piece of art. The open door in the corner of the room revealed a modest sized en-suite, which is where the similarities with any ordinary lodging ended. The lack of windows and peculiar pipe-laden ceiling prevented their new dwelling from having any real sense of comfort. It still felt like incarceration. He wondered how long he had been in his stupor, and allowed his bleary eyes to wander until a second door came into focus. Intuition told him that the windowless metallic portal did not offer them the freedom of the outside world.

CHAPTER 8

Thorpe was in the process of delivering a verbal torrent down the telephone as DCI Robson and Inspector Wilson arrived outside his office door with their hastily prepared report. His distinct West Country accent had a default volume that was higher than most, a consequence of many years spent delivering briefings, and yelling, Jack suspected. The conversation could be heard despite the closed office door.

"What do you mean you can't find him? There aren't many fucking places for him to hide in a fishing village. I want him in this station within the hour!"

The phone bounced on the wooden desk, as the handset was slammed back into position. Robson chuckled inwardly as he considered going in and asking if that had been the Chief Superintendent. Evidently, he hadn't completely hidden his thoughts from view as he noticed his new partner directing a disapproving frown towards him.

"Sorry." He couldn't think of an excuse for smirking and so

decided not to try.

They both hesitated outside the glass door, as they watched the Superintendent through the blinds. Thorpe was slumped at his desk, supporting his head with both hands, completely covering his haggard face. Thorpe's secretary entered the office reception from the door marked 'Ladies' and cast a questioning look when she first noticed them hovering outside the Superintendent's office door. Her expression quickly displayed a comprehension of the situation, as she moved close enough to see beyond them through the window blinds, at her boss in his all too familiar perturbed state. Inspector Wilson swiftly took up the opportunity. "Louise, I don't suppose we could leave this with you? We seem to have arrived at a bad time, but the boss wanted this."

She offered the report to the mature, well-kept receptionist. "Of course."

"I don't suppose you know the cause of his mood?" Robson asked.

"I'm afraid not. The call went directly through to him."

"Okay, well I think we got the gist from here really. We don't need to disturb him anyway, if you could just see that he gets the report."

"Thanks Loo," added Emma, as they left to join the search for their only potential lead, not noticing that Thorpe had now raised his head from the desk and watched them depart.

Thorpe grunted as the report was placed on his desk in front of him. Louise waited while he continued to stare at it, waiting to see if there would be any requests for her. The Superintendent finally raised his creased forehead to look his secretary in the eye.

"I'll be leaving in ten minutes Louise. The Chief Superintendent wants me to deliver the report in person again today."

His loyal assistant looked at her boss with pitiful eyes.

"Okay Christian, let me know if you need anything."

He watched her neat and tidy form leave the office. She paused and gave him an affectionate smile, before closing the blinded door.

CHAPTER 9

As they weaved between the stationary motorway traffic, they were both grateful for the flashing blue light and siren. The motorway was jammed with those taking the opportunity make an early getaway for the Easter bank holiday.

The flashback hit Jack out of nowhere, as they always did: it was three Easter breaks ago. He and his young family had sat for hours, in a similar scene to that which they were now racing past on the hard shoulder. He sat in the driving seat cursing every passing moment, while the toddler sat in the back sleeping serenely, doubtless exhausted from the responsibility of ensuring that every cuddly toy, doll and associated accessory had been packed for the journey. To his left, the woman he adored sat in her typical semi-meditative condition. She held his hand and initiated conversation after conversation to calm him. Although he wasn't oblivious to his irrational, childish behaviour, it didn't mean he could do anything to prevent it. He watched himself getting more and more irate until his wife eventually gave up trying to pacify him. He recognised that his petulance might have been partly down to envy of her apparent inner peace. The three-day break had been worth the pain, even though the journey itself had taken a day out of the holiday. The desire he felt to leap back in time and return to the image in his mind tortured him. He remembered how, as the three of them played together on the grass, it was as if nothing else existed. It was a stark reminder of what he had lost, and he knew it was time to forcibly break with nostalgia before the woman beside him in the present noticed the droplets in his eyes. *Focus on the job.*

"I think they might be there for a while yet."

The sound of his own voice confirmed his return to the here-and-now, as they finally veered off the motorway and left the three lanes of stationary traffic. Inspector Wilson maintained a fierce speed along the gradient of the exit road.

"It's not untypical, especially for this time of year."

Her response seemed slightly disinterested.

"I know. Listen, I've been thinking about what happened back at HQ."

"What do you mean?"

"Why hasn't Thorpe set up a base closer to the crime scene?"

Her bottom lip protruded slightly as she shrugged her petite shoulders, while her small hands remained gripped to the wheel.

"It would make sense though wouldn't it? Given that the case revolves around a common area. An area that is over an hour away from the office. It doesn't exactly give us an efficient response potential."

"No, agreed. I'm not sure. Like I've said, I'm a newcomer to the case too. And frankly, my initial observations are quite likely to be similar to yours. The team seems to have been overwhelmed by the attention and, without wanting to be critical, they appear to have lost some of their ability to act rationally."

"Precisely. Take that incident back at the station. We gave him a name for the first time. A name! And he asked for a fucking report?!" The passion in his own voice surprised him. "So it could prove beneficial on more than just one level, if we were to locate the team away from headquarters for a period."

"All right, I'll have a chat with the team this afternoon. We should be able to get something in place after the bank holiday. Were you thinking the whole team?"

"Yes."

He relaxed into the seat a little as his attractive partner expertly handled the vehicle, while maintaining a good speed. As they whizzed past the queued holiday-makers, Jack was pleased that there hadn't been any resistance to his proposal. He had a feeling that with his colleague on board, he wouldn't face too much opposition. No wonder Thorpe was pulling his hair out; apart from present company, these cops were still wet behind the ears. But he was still surprised that the Superintendent hadn't already implemented such measures. That's what pressure does, he thought, as his partner thundered through the red lights and cornered the crossroads with a screech. Thorpe certainly wouldn't resist the idea – besides, he could sell it as progress in the next report.

CHAPTER 10

"Daddy, Daddy!" shouted Ellie. "Come and see, quickly!"

"Okay sweetie, coming, is it a good one?" The young man grinned proudly at the unbridled enthusiasm of his five-year-old. "Daddy's bucket is nearly full to the top now, so we'll make this the last one and then we can take them back to show Mummy."

The father still hadn't spotted the two black mounds that the child had discovered, his eyes instead scanning the area for a rock in the direction of the small pointed finger.

"It's not a rock Daddy. Look, someone's left their boots on the seaweed and they're getting wet from the sea, look!"

"Oh dear, never mind darling, come on let's find one more fossil."

He saw the pair of adult sized black boots on the surface of the seaweed as he carefully circumnavigated the rock pool to get to his daughter, who had clearly decided that she wasn't abandoning her treasure without at least getting to showcase it.

She hadn't noticed the horror spreading across her father's face as he stood rooted to the rock ten yards away, eyes unblinkingly fixed on the dark, soaking wet industrial safety boots.

Unlike her keen-eyed father, Ellie hadn't noticed the discolouring around the boots where they protruded from the seaweed. When he spoke again, she looked up instantly, detecting the anxiety in his shaky request.

"Ellie. Come here now please, darling."

"What's the matter, Daddy?" She began to cry in reaction to her father's tone.

He swept across the area of slimy rocks that separated them and stretched forward to take her by her arm. The pain of the fall wouldn't hit him until later – it was the grim vision that presented itself which terrorised him, as he slipped and landed on his backside a few feet away from the boots. The seaweed in front of him parted with the disturbance, to reveal the ghostly wide eyes of a man beneath the shallow surface. Ellie screamed instinctively as she watched her father vomit over the seaweed.

CHAPTER 11

DCI Robson found the silence in the car uncomfortable. He privately berated himself for allowing his mind to wander off into scenarios that were not entirely related to the job, but his brain had frozen from the effort, rendering lateral and creative thought temporarily unavailable.

The car speakers suddenly interrupted the silence, warbling as they transmitted the incoming call from the phone mounted on the dash in front of them. Inspector Wilson seemed to hardly notice at first as she continued to concentrate on negotiating the undulating country road, which was becoming narrower the further they progressed. She afforded a brief glance toward the dash and placed a slim forefinger to the screen, accepting the call.

"Hi James."

"Hi Em, where are you?" enquired the voice of Sergeant James Matthews.

"Jack and I are just approaching Porlock. We've come to

help track down this guy. Is everything all right?"

"A body has just been discovered, washed up on Kilve beach. You're only twenty to thirty minutes away."

"I think we can leave that one to the constabulary James?"

"They're on the scene. They called us after they salvaged a wallet from the body. The driver's licence is still legible. Obviously, we haven't got a positive ID yet, but ... "

Jack was frowning in exasperation at the young man's procrastination as Emma offered him some encouragement to complete the message.

"Jamie?"

"Sorry. It's just that the licence they recovered from the body belongs to a Mr Barry Graham Searle."

DCI Robson's head fell back in frustration as Wilson switched her right foot one pedal along from the accelerator. The tyres screeched as the back of the car swung by a hundred and eighty degrees to exchange position with the front.

"We're on our way."

CHAPTER 12

DCI Robson paid disinterested attention to the briefing, as the bespectacled young Sergeant delivered the results of his research into Mr Barry Graham Searle. Following the positive identification of the body, this current line of enquiry was now the top priority, given that it was the only lead. Twenty-four hours had elapsed since the washed-up body was discovered on the shores of the pebbly beach at Kilve and they were now assessing the fruits of their bank holiday analysis.

Not only had their new DCI made them work on a bank holiday weekend, but they had set up a new temporary base, an hour away from their usual place of work. And to top it off, St Audries village hall didn't offer the same modern luxuries of the station. Refreshment facilities comprised a kettle, tea and instant coffee, and a hastily acquired fridge.

The small audience in the incident room silently watched Matthews' animated thin, bony arms, protruding from the T-shirt bearing the emblem of a computer game, as he expounded with an impressive degree of enthusiasm. Information gathering was obviously the Sergeant's speciality. However, as they were informed of the deceased man's army background, having refused to embrace the family tradition of being a fisherman, DCI Robson could only wonder at the cruel coincidence that the unfortunate man should meet his maker just as he had come to their attention.

Inspector Wilson demonstrated that she was still paying attention, and enquired about Searle's associates, love interests and family members.

"Never married and both parents deceased."

"Who confirmed the identity?"

"His older brother. The only surviving family member."

Awoken by the sight of Wilson's shapely legs as they protruded from the black, pencil skirt, Jack sat up in his chair.

"So, what was he doing for a living?"

Emma addressed the question herself.

"He was registered as a self-employed maintenance worker. A handyman I guess."

White van man? Jack thought to himself, but concentrated on averting his eyes from her bare, milky-white legs, as Inspector Wilson continued, seemingly having relieved Sergeant Matthews of his briefing responsibilities for the moment.

"The brother is called Jonny Searle. He and Barry shared a house together in Porlock."

"Has he been questioned yet?"

"Only by the local constabulary. Apparently, he was pretty cut up, understandably. The statement is rather bland. He saw Barry early on Thursday morning, prior to work, and everything seemed fine. But he reports that he hadn't seen or heard from him since. That ties in with the pathologist's findings. It appears the father and daughter must have stumbled across the body only hours after he had been killed, at the most."

DCI Robson stood and looked at Sergeant Matthews.

"Do you have an address for Jonny Searle?"

The young man nodded. Jack thought he looked slightly offended by the question.

"Has anyone briefed Thorpe?"

Wilson nodded.

"I spoke with him this morning. You can imagine the reaction. He's in London with the Chief Superintendent."

"Okay, well, shall we go and find Jonny?" He forced his eyes to look into hers, but her legs still occupied his peripheral vision. "I want to know as soon as we get cause of death confirmed."

"Sir, if you could just give me a second." Sergeant Matthews was sitting at his new desk, blinking at the screen of his laptop. "It looks like that might have just come through, I'm just open … oh."

He had the attention of the room.

Wilson recognised the look of her young colleague as he took his time to ensure that he gave an accurate representation of the data before him.

"James?"

He straightened his specs and looked up from the screen.

"Barry Searle was shot in the back."

CHAPTER 13

The main car park for the little fishing village had been consumed by coaches, which were surrounded by elderly tourists. Wilson seemed to find the scene heart-warming, Robson thought, while he cringed at the sight of wrinkled white-topped heads bobbing around cheerfully, each one determined to be the first back onto their respective carriages. The traffic was just starting to build up in Porlock's answer to rush hour, with cars containing tourists and early finishers gradually progressing through the main artery of the little street.

As far as Jack could tell, the town didn't seem to have been affected by the passing of time. The narrow street was lined with fudge shops, gift shops, traditional-looking taverns and hardware stores on either side, bordered by pavements just wide enough to accommodate two walking abreast. He couldn't spot any hint of a food or drink outlet belonging to one of the twenty-first century corporate chains, and there wasn't a swanky fashion brand in sight.

They finally crawled to the end of the high street and the water far below could be seen glistening in the weak spring sunshine as the bay came into view in the distance. The rugged majesty of the coastal backdrop increased as they progressed and left the busy street behind. The view of the shimmering bay disappeared again as they left the village, and continued their descent towards Porlock Weir. The narrow country lanes were lined with luscious green hedgerows, which finally opened out as the gradient levelled off and the bay came back into view, now from a much lower vantage point. The wooden tables outside the Ship Inn were fully occupied by those peacefully enjoying their refreshments whilst watching the sun set over the harbour – an eclectic mixture of gossipers, dreamers, enthused tourists and drinkers.

After a left turn, they climbed steeply for a hundred yards before pulling into a small housing development, passing the sign that announced they had found Weir View. Inspector Wilson stopped the car outside a house with no front garden. Steps led from the gated entrance on the pavement up to the front door of the house, which was strategically positioned at the appropriate elevation to achieve a sea view. Jack surmised that the large bay windows, which formed the common frontage of each of the north-facing houses in the small cul-de-sac, had acted as the primary selling point for people seeking to live by the sea. The home that currently held their attention was the only one in the neighbourhood that had the curtains drawn, in apparent repudiation of this star feature.

They climbed the steps and Wilson knocked at the tired looking-front door with the faded brass number '2' screwed to it, while Jack waited behind her on the top step. Following a few minutes of knocking, at what she considered to be respectful intervals, she lifted the letterbox and peered inside. The dreary carpeted hall and staircase gave no clue as to the current status of the homeowner.

She turned to her DCI and shook her head to indicate that it seemed there wasn't going to be a response. Robson had moved up to the bay window to try to get a peek through the small gap in the curtains.

"Jack … " Emma interrupted from halfway down the steps. "Jack … " Her tone indicated that something of interest had come to her attention.

He looked over his shoulder and then adjusted his gaze in the same direction as his partner's. The shabby-looking fellow approaching along the street didn't seem to be of any significance at first. They both silently watched the man in nautical garb zig-zag clumsily along the middle of the quiet street. At about the fifth stumble against the curb he fell awkwardly and lay sprawled with his top half on the pavement, legs trailing lifelessly into the street. He rose nonchalantly as though it were an everyday occurrence, and proceeded to the gate of number two, blissfully unaware of the man watching him from the top of the steps.

Nor had he spotted the young woman walk to the bottom of the steps to greet him. Inspector Wilson now watched him from close quarters as she stood with her hands resting on the faded wooden gate. The unmistakable scent of stale alcohol attacked her sinuses as it emanated from the pores of the drunken man. She guessed that he was only just in his thirties, but his dishevelled condition added several years to his appearance.

He leant forward and grabbed the gate before his feet had arrived, as though attempting to prevent the house from drifting away from him. He then appeared to brace, as if in readiness for a huge gust of wind. With vacant eyes still fixed on the pavement, he hadn't spotted the young woman step away from him on the other side of the gate, which he had now anchored himself to. Still watching from the top of the steps, Robson found the contrast amusing; the haggard specimen of a man, in desperate need of a retune, hanging on his front gate to prevent total collapse and the striking girl patiently waiting for the man to notice her.

As he dragged his bottom half closer to the gate, Wilson noticed a bottle protruding from a pocket, and the mess down one side of his yellow fishing jacket appeared to be vomit. The powerful aroma indicated it was recent.

"Mr Searle?" asked Emma.

It took a few seconds, and a swig of the bourbon that he had taken from his pocket, to locate the source of the unexpected feminine voice. His head jerked upwards and slightly to the side, as if it had just been yanked by an invisible rope. While he examined the female before him, his face displayed the short emotional journey from confusion to anger, finishing with unmistakable drunken libido. As he attempted to focus his salacious gaze on the beauty on the other side of the gate, the gargling sound that came from his throat was not discernible. Noticing her male companion arrive, the drunken man's mood reverted to anger.

"Wuthafuk," he hiccupped, "yathingyerdoin?"

"Sir," said Wilson, "we're from CID and we were hoping for a chat, if that's okay? We understand it's not great timing, but we would very much appreciate just a few minutes."

"Nah. Nodint'rested. Ta!"

Robson decided to intervene.

"Come on Jonny. You must want us to get to the bottom of this. We appreciate it's still early, but we can't delay if we're going to get to the bottom of Barry's dea … "

"Too late!" The hoarse scream was the clearest elocution produced yet by Jonny Searle, seemingly sobered a fraction by his anger. The slur soon returned. "S'too fockin' … lay … "

He pulled the gate open so that it smashed back against the fence it was attached to and pushed past them both, stumbling up the steps. Robson followed a couple of steps behind, bracing himself for a backward fall. The man was only of medium build, but Jack wasn't entirely confident of being able to carry twelve to thirteen stone of drunken dead-weight. Both detectives felt relieved as he made it over the top step and crashed face first against the front door.

He cast a hostile glance at Jack while fumbling for his keys, before eventually taking aim at the keyhole. The small slot in the door did its best to evade his advance but the key finally engaged and, after giving it a sharp twist, he fell through the opening and laid spreadeagled on the worn hallway carpet.

CHAPTER 14

Jack felt the springs pressing against his backside as he sat on the threadbare sofa next to his partner. Emma subtly flattened a piece of fabric that had risen from the arm as she brushed against it while lowering herself. They watched their reluctant, inebriated host sip at another black coffee that they had prepared for him. Within moments, the man was comatose.

Between them, they observed him in his unconscious state for an hour, as they took turns exploring the residence. Having discovered nothing of significance between them, Jack's frustration took over. Emma had considered his insistence on waiting for Jonny to come round to be futile, but she hadn't factored in the use of a pint of cold water. The reaction wasn't tame, but the profanities had died down after a few moments and more coffee seemed to help smooth things over.

"We're really sorry about Barry," said Inspector Wilson offering the olive-branch while Robson sipped at his second mug of instant coffee. Their host belched and placed his mug down on the stained coffee table. "Jonny," she ventured, as though the eruption hadn't occurred, "we were wondering if you might be able to help us understand a little about your brother's life over the past few months. Perhaps in particular, what he was doing for a living?"

"He didn't work with me." The response was throaty, but clear. The accent was very similar to Thorpe's, Jack thought.

"You lived together though?"

At first it appeared that another volley of abuse was on the way, but something inside seemed to tell him to lower his defences slightly as his shoulders dropped with a pronounced sigh.

"What do you want to know?"

"Was Barry in employment?"

He nodded.

"Self-employed."

"What was his trade?"

"All sorts. Carpentry, plumbing, sparky, gardening, roofer and lord knows what else. Everything except fishing!"

"So, was he picking up all of his work locally?"

"Yep."

"Did he manage to keep busy most of the time?"

"Oh yeah, he were busy all right."

The drunken man's cynicism seemed heightened.

"What about socially – did he have a fixed circle of friends?"

"Yep, Barry were pop'lar. Used to socialise with me and the boys down at the Ship." He paused to deal with the lump in his throat but couldn't prevent the build-up of tears in his eyes. Emma silently handed him a tissue. "Well, he did until a few

63

months ago … ”

Noticing the break in his voice, they patiently waited for him to continue of his own accord.

"He landed a big commercial contract. But he had been tryin' to squeeze in the private stuff too. Bloody fool. I told 'im it were gonna bloody kill 'im … ”

"Take your time Jonny. Would you like a glass of water?"

Shaking his head, Jonny Searle continued.

"Promised 'im at least a year of work, so he didn't have to juggle clients or advertise nor nothin'. Guaranteed work it were, so he said it'd be less stress. Bloody joke!"

"Oh, where was the work?"

"Up at the power station."

Jack looked at them both blankly, awaiting clarification.

"Hinkley?" asked Emma.

He nodded while dabbing his wet cheeks with the tissue.

"Doing what?"

"Who knows? Anything and everything, so far as I'm aware. He just said that they needed him for general work."

"I see. Do you know if he was at work on Thursday?"

"He were at work every pissin' day." Jonny's voice broke again. "Stopped coming out on the boat with me, and I hardly ever saw him on the weekends."

Emma allowed time for Jonny to compose himself.

"Do you know anyone that he was working with?"

"He never really told me anything about it. Before this job, we used to talk all the time. We were close. He was the strong one you know. Typical ex-military, used to knock me into shape. Baz worked hard, they took advantage of that if you ask me. He was my big brother …"

The tear flow increased and began to drop from his cheeks.

"I think we'll leave you in peace, Jonny," said Emma. "We know this is very painful right now, but try to look after yourself, eh?"

Jonny gestured an acknowledgement with the tissue as he dabbed at the tears. Jack found himself feeling impressed by Emma's conduct, but the final question was necessary.

"Jonny, could I just check one last thing please?"

Emma watched from the doorway, having already risen to gently pat the grieving man on the shoulder. Jack responded to her look with a glance to confirm it would be brief.

"Jonny, could you tell us what sort of vehicle Barry drove?"

"White van of course, what else? Bloody great thing too. The neighbours hated it being parked on the street out there. At least they won't have to worry about their precious fucking view being spoilt no more."

"Where's the vehicle now?"

"Fuck knows."

The apparently broken man slumped back, simultaneously blowing his nose into the tissue.

They left Jonny Searle in his armchair, physically and emotionally alone.

CHAPTER 15

Outside the security-guarded entrance on the following grey, uninspiring spring morning, DCI Robson and Inspector Wilson sat in a queue of traffic, waiting to be granted access to the equally prosaic industrial site.

Earlier, Sergeant Matthews had delivered a sufficiently comprehensive briefing on the new power plant. He may have still been a little wet behind the ears, but his dedication to the task impressed Robson, along with his thoroughness, having been asked to do the research only late the previous afternoon.

The locals were, on the whole, familiar with the plant, and Jack sensed that a significant portion of the information had been for his benefit, given that he had never even heard of the apparently high-profile project.

He had learnt that morning that Hinkley C power station comprised a new, state of the art nuclear reactor, replacing its decommissioned predecessor. Having been financed and therefore owned by foreign wealth, it had generated a healthy local economy during the construction stage. It represented a vision of the future – sustainable energy. According to official sources, it was claimed that its legacy impact had included the creation of local jobs, as well as indirectly benefiting the area due to the expertise that it demanded.

It had been too late yesterday for Sergeant Matthews to contact the HR section regarding the employment of Barry Searle. Jack and Emma both agreed to pay a visit straight away, for expediency. Secretly, Jack was hoping to demonstrate some form of progress to Superintendent Thorpe at his return briefing. Inspector Wilson would never have guessed that the newly acquainted DCI was the sort of person to care about other people's impressions; but it was a fact that, despite no longer harbouring any particular career ambitions beyond being able to support his daughter, Jack Robson still retained his professional pride.

Emma lowered the driver's side window to be greeted at the barrier by an overweight security guard, while, inside the security cabin, his sidekick kept his face buried in a crumpled tabloid.

"Can I help you madam?"

She held her ID up to the open window.

"Hello there. Could you direct us to the HR office please?"

"Certainly Inspector."

While handing two visitors passes through the window, he pointed to a bland, modern-looking brick building about two hundred yards in the distance.

"It's straight over the roundabout there and go into the main entrance of that office block. Tell reception who you want to speak to."

"Thank you."

"Pleasure, ma'am."

She sensed her partner's broad grin and glanced at him as she drove off.

"You ok, Jack?"

"Yes, ma'am."

He immediately felt childish, but felt emboldened by the faint snigger that emerged from the inspector.

As they proceeded, they noticed the assembly of large construction traffic in the distance against the backdrop of the sullen-looking Bristol Channel, framed by the grey skyline. Jack looked behind and watched the security guard admitting a large delivery vehicle.

"What are they constructing?" he asked

"I think the distribution capacity is being expanded."

"I see. Maybe that could explain Searle's involvement?" he offered speculatively.

"Perhaps."

The HR reception portrayed an efficient, professional image. Both officers declined the offer of refreshments from the young receptionist, who had now returned to thrashing the keyboard in front of her at remarkable speed. DCI Robson again wondered at the modern office, an environment considered unruly if there was any evidence of hard files on display. The waiting area they sat at consisted of four small but comfortable chairs and a sofa, which together surrounded a circular glass table. He idly wondered if the person responsible for the magazine display on the table had used a ruler to achieve the even spacing within the fan-like composition. He felt tempted to take one from the middle, just to be able to stick around and watch the reconstruction, but, judging by the front cover of the top-most magazine, *Sustainable Energy* wasn't going to provide too much excitement.

They hadn't noticed the softly-spoken receptionist answer the telephone when it buzzed, but she had apparently received confirmation that the HR manager was free and duly invited them to proceed through the glass door labelled 'Thelma Scott-Palmer - HR Manager'.

Inside, they were greeted by a sturdy lady wearing a smile that Jack supposed was a permanent fixture when in company. Her right hand protruded from the sleeve of a conservative, dark trouser suit as she welcomed them both.

"Sorry to have kept you waiting, Inspectors."

"Not at all, Ms Palmer," Emma responded. "We must apologise for calling on you unannounced."

"No need to apologise for that." Her head tilted backwards on its stocky neck as she gave a hearty laugh. "You've just rescued me from a very tricky management briefing!"

Both detectives wore polite smiles and accepted the invitation to once again rest their backsides on a couple of upholstered seats, as the HR manager assumed her position behind yet another neat and tidy desk bearing only a laptop.

"How can I assist you today, Officers? Please call me Thelma, by the way."

"Thank you, Thelma. I'm DCI Robson, and this is Inspector Wilson. We're trying to locate somebody in connection with a local investigation. We understand that he was employed here."

"I see." Her look turned serious and assured, in an effort to prove herself worthy of trust with such delicate matters. Jack continued.

"Could you tell us if you have anyone on your payroll records by the name of Barry Searle?"

"Barry Searle? S-e-a-r-l-e?"

Both inspectors nodded.

"Let's have a look."

She immediately hit a few keys to access the relevant records on her laptop and proceeded to carry out a search of the employee database. A shake of the head indicated the results of the search.

"Hmm, that name doesn't appear to be on our system."

"Does that list temporary workers? Self-employed contractors?"

"It does if they work directly for us. But if they are employed by another contractor then we wouldn't have their details. But I could take a look at the security database, which would list anybody that's ever been admitted onto this site."

"Can you do that from here?" Jack enquired.

"I can indeed, Chief Inspector."

The HR manager operated the keys on the laptop almost with the deft speed of her receptionist. After a short pause, she seemed pleased to be able to supply a more positive result.

"Ah. Here we are. Barry Graham Searle. He still has a valid permit, according to this. In fact," she added, looking above the screen, "he evidently has the highest level of security clearance."

"What does that mean exactly?" enquired Jack further.

"It means he has access to all areas. As you can appreciate, this is not your average commercial site. This facility houses equipment of unimaginable value, and of course, given the nature of the power plant, we have to store some particularly sensitive materials. There aren't very many people allowed access to anything other than their own specific station of work."

"What job is he likely to be doing here, given that level of access?"

"Well I suppose that's quite easy to deduce. It has to be one of two possibilities: he is either a nuclear engineer, or he works for the ONR"

"ONR?" asked Jack.

"The Office for Nuclear Regulation. They have a team permanently based here."

The inspectors both nodded.

"There's something slightly unusual about this though." Thelma frowned slightly at the laptop.

"Go on," Jack encouraged.

"Well, somebody with that level of security clearance is more than likely to be on our books, with the exception perhaps of a few of the highly specialist nuclear engineers. But they would be on our system for health and safety requirements, even if not on the payroll."

"What if he were a delivery driver or a handyman?"

"They wouldn't have that level of access. The drivers have access to the goods inward sector, sure. But that's the limit of their access. And like I say, this chap seems to have been granted unlimited access."

"Where is the regulator based?" asked Emma.

"They have an office adjoining the nuclear facility, so that they can readily monitor both the delivery of fuel and the operation of the reactors."

"Could we go and meet them? Now?" requested Jack.

"Indeed. In fact, I'd recommend it. They ought to be able to clear this up. Goodness knows they're keen on observing access limitations. Any security clearance of the level we're looking at here would have been authorised by them, so they must have a handle on what this guy has been doing. I'll have to get someone to come and collect you though – I'm afraid you won't be able to venture into the facility unaccompanied."

*

The small van arrived to collect them half an hour after the HR boss had put in the request and made the necessary arrangements to extend the boundaries of their visit. The short, five-minute journey brought them a little closer to the channel beyond, and the existence of an additional security point confirmed the stringent access regulations that had been described to them earlier. However, there was evidently an efficient mechanism in place for short-notice access, as a guard presented them with more temporary permits, allowing them to pass through the check-point.

Despite the obvious signs of ongoing construction work, the complex that they had now arrived at was an archetype of modern industry. Large grey towers loomed in the distance and Jack mused at the rapidity with which humankind could accomplish such a dramatic alteration to a landscape. No doubt the newly born, grey giants now encroached on the vista experienced by walkers in search of natural beauty, while they marched across the Quantock hills.

The building they were taken to was consistent with the dull grey of the towers. The windows indicated that this part of the metal construction stood on two storeys, dwarfed by the towers beyond, but still covering a vast footprint. They were led inside through the only entrance visible on that side of the building and were immediately greeted by a slight, conservatively dressed man wearing spectacles. He made what seemed an unnatural effort to smile at them.

"Hello officers. My name's Colin Underhill." He shook both their hands. "Would you like to follow me into the office?"

They passed a door with a keypad on their left, marked 'Authorised Personnel Only', and arrived at the bottom of a stairwell. At the same time, a couple descended wearing high visibility jackets and gave the faintest nod at them as they passed and walked in the direction of the security door behind them.

Underhill led them up the stairs and through a pair of swing doors beneath a sign that stated: 'Her Majesty's Office for Nuclear Regulation'. They nodded at the receptionist as they entered a small open plan-office, and their diminutive host led them into a small meeting room off the main office. They accepted his invitation to sit around the table.

"Human Resources have advised that you would like to ask us some questions, officers?"

"Yes please, Mr Underhill." Emma replicated the nervous man's formal tone.

"It's Colin, please. Oh, I'm sorry, can I get you both drinks?"

He appeared to become a little less aloof. Both officers shook their heads to decline.

"Thank you, Colin, no," Emma continued, "we'll try not to take up too much of your valuable time. To come straight to the purpose of our visit, we are trying to get some information about someone. We believe it's possible that the person in question worked in this establishment. Could you tell us if you know a man by the name of Barry Searle?"

Underhill continued to stare at her, before finally blinking.

"Hmm, yes I think I do."

DCI Robson and Inspector Wilson silently suppressed their desire for more, and instead signalled with their eyes that Underhill still had the floor.

"He's not one of the inspectors, but he has become something of a trusted servant here. A sort of combination of general maintenance man and almost personal assistant to Sir Geoffrey. Having said that, I haven't seen him around for a few days, perhaps a week. Is he all right?"

"Sir Geoffrey?" Robson slightly tilted his head as he looked at Underhill.

"Our boss, Inspector. Sir Geoffrey Charlesworth. The government's senior inspector for nuclear power, he is personally overseeing the operation of this facility."

DCI Robson noticed his female partner nodding in recognition.

"I see. Is Sir Geoffrey here today?"

"I'm afraid not. He is here two or three days a week typically."

"Is he part-time?"

"Somebody of Sir Geoffrey's stature doesn't exactly work core hours. He is often in London in meetings – he has regular appointments with the energy minister. With that and his own personal projects, I certainly wouldn't describe him as part-time."

There was just a hint of condescension in the man's tone, which made Jack feel as though he had been expected to know a little more than he did. It was a feature of the job that had never discouraged him from comprehensive questioning.

"I see. Can you tell us any more about what kind of work Barry Searle does around here?"

"Well, as I just mentioned, he carries out general maintenance duties, which really is all-encompassing I suppose. One day he could be assembling desks for us or installing lighting, the next he is assisting Sir Geoffrey and the inspectors, overseeing a fuel delivery into the reactor facility."

"But he wasn't … isn't, a competent nuclear engineer himself?"

"No, he isn't. But he's a very reliable assistant."

"Can you remember the last time you saw him?"

"Let's see. Three days ago, perhaps?"

"Okay, thank you Colin. What would be the best way to arrange an audience with Sir Geoffrey himself?"

"If you speak to his secretary outside, she has access to his diary."

"Does he live nearby?"

"Yes, he lives at St Audries manor. It's about half an hour's drive away."

CHAPTER 16

Dr O'Hara followed the armed man along a narrow, dimly lit corridor. The doctor thought it a poor effort of a ponytail, barely reaching the top of the man's shoulder blades. It moved slightly to one side as he bent his lanky frame to punch in the entry code. He held the door open, to allow for the reduced mobility imposed by the handcuffs that Darryl O'Hara wore. Although he seemed to have a relaxed physical manner, his eyes held an unnerving confidence, behind which the doctor did not see any scope for negotiation. The man seemed to have total belief in his objective, and despite behaving in a perfectly amenable fashion, the doctor suspected that his captor would undertake whatever action was necessary to fulfil his goal.

O'Hara's initial surprise at finding himself in a medical treatment room was superseded by the sight of a woman laying on the bed against the wall to his right. An attractive girl, perhaps in her twenties, he estimated. That she was unwell was not an estimate. She appeared to be suffering from a fever, and the doctor walked over to her from the instinct of a practitioner of care. As he reached the bed, he could see from what remained visible of her eyes beneath the heavy lids, that she had been sedated. However, that did little to disguise her utter terror.

"This woman is not well," O'Hara declared, casting a concerned glance towards the man that now approached him holding a small key between thumb and forefinger.

"I know, Doctor. That's why you're here."

O'Hara felt shivers along his spine as he took in the relaxed manner of their captor. The clunk of the door made him jump and then experience a brief glimpse of hope, quickly turning to confused fear, as it became apparent that the new occupant was an acquaintance of the man currently releasing his cuffs. O'Hara's mind spun with endless permutations as he surveyed the kind looking lady donning a nurse's uniform. She smiled at the doctor as she approached the bed, as if they were two colleagues in familiar surroundings.

"Ah good. Look Emily, the doctor is here to see you now. Everything's going to be fine," she said, placing a maternal hand around the patient's.

For the first time, Darryl O'Hara noticed the wall-mounted glass cabinets that surrounded them. On closer inspection, he saw that they contained a wide spectrum of drugs. He breathed deeply to control his anxiety, while doing his best to suppress the need to vomit.

CHAPTER 17

DCI Robson negotiated the right-hand turn at low speed, departing the deserted A39 for a steep narrow decline. Immediately, a small medieval church came into view, completing the somewhat surreal, fairy-tale setting before them. They passed the church, which was surrounded by a scattering of giant conifers and willows, and then rounded a corner while still descending. The Severn channel now formed their backdrop, interrupted only by the stunning Georgian mansion before them. Robson smirked ironically as he looked across at Inspector Wilson in the passenger seat.

"He owns this estate?"

Wilson widened her eyes, which served to emphasise their sparkle.

"Oh yes, and the rest."

"The rest? Does he own a lot of property then?"

"No doubt he has properties scattered everywhere, overseas even, I wouldn't know the details. But I do know, as most local people do, that he even has an island within his portfolio."

"Really?"

"Oh, nothing as glamourous as you might be imagining. There are a couple of tiny, uninhabited islands out there in the channel," she indicated with her forefinger, but Jack couldn't see any evidence of islands. "He owns one of them. Steep Holm it's called."

"What does he want with it?"

"He's a keen conservationist. They ran a programme on national TV – nature something or other … "

"Got you hooked then, did it?"

She attempted to conceal her amusement, revealing a playful side that made Jack smile inwardly.

"He's turned the place into a nature reserve, I believe."

"What sort of nature?"

"Flora and fauna, I believe they call it."

"Thank you, Attenborough. What species?"

"Don't know. Lots of trees and birds, and a bit of sea life, from what I remember. As I was saying earlier, Charlesworth is something of a local dignitary."

"Better remember that then."

"Oh, don't worry. He's no elitist."

Robson shook his head as he watched a small herd of deer bound across the road in front of them and race towards the woods up on their right.

When the receptionist had consulted the calendar back at Hinkley the previous day, they had both agreed that waiting another week to meet the head of the ONR would not be acceptable. Progress couldn't come soon enough for their under-fire Superintendent, but Thorpe had seemed somewhat apprehensive at the proposal to go and meet Sir Geoffrey Charlesworth at his home. DCI Robson was mildly amazed at the sense of reverence afforded to him, but was no stranger to the need to keep influential members of the community onside.

He parked the car on the vast gravel driveway at the front of the stately property. No sooner had they slammed the car doors than a formal looking gent approached them from the house.

"DCI Robson and Inspector Wilson, I presume?"

"Yes indeed, how do you do?" Inspector Wilson presented the pristine steward with a courteous smile.

"Welcome to St Audries house, officers. Sir Geoffrey is expecting you. Allow me to show you inside."

Jack stood aside to allow Emma to enter the grand doorway ahead, as they were escorted beneath the tall turret. He followed them towards the entrance, pausing briefly to gaze up at the flag above as it rippled in the sea breeze. The rainbow-like pattern intrigued him as he contemplated how it differed from the default flag of St George, which one might normally expect to be flying at such properties.

Inside, the butler seemed to delay slightly, as if to allow them time to absorb the beauty of their surroundings. They stood inside a large, regal hallway with an impressive antique wooden staircase. After a few seconds, with impeccable courtesy, he led them through another doorway into a large reception room.

"Please have a seat here officers. Sir Geoffrey won't keep you waiting."

The butler glided from the room with a back so straight it

seemed his suit had been pressed with him inside it.

The room was large enough to accommodate two separate, equally spacious seating areas, a fireplace, and a small bar section, complete with a grand piano in one corner. The butler indicated for them to rest themselves in the area adjacent to the large bay window that provided a view of the Channel. Jack and Emma sat at either end of the grand sofa, opposite two high backed armchairs, with a mahogany coffee table in between. The walls beneath the high ceiling were decorated with luxurious wallpaper and were further adorned by huge paintings, evidently of the Charlesworth ancestry interspersed with one or two hunting scenes and an impressive landscape of the manor with the Channel in the background, which seemed to do the estate justice, thought Jack.

Emma observed the way her partner seemed particularly drawn to the artwork, as the door opened again, and the butler entered carrying a silver tray topped with matching pots and fine china crockery. He placed the tray on the table in front of them.

"Tea or coffee madam?" he asked with a professional smile.

"Coffee, please."

"And for you sir?" he continued as he poured the steaming liquid into a cup that appeared to Jack far too dainty to accommodate such heat.

"Same again please, thank you."

The entrance to the room opened as Jack's beverage was poured. A tall, striking figure, moving with an understated elegance, strode into the room. The attire was casual, yet somehow still seemed to indicate status. The newcomer, with his aristocratic poise seemed to have preserved the gracefulness of youth, despite being in his early sixties. He approached them, displaying a charming smile indicating that he was genuinely delighted to welcome his new guests.

Clipped vowels rolled from his cultured tongue with effortless elocution.

"Officers, welcome to my home." He took Inspector Wilson's hand gently, and Robson was surprised at the way she seemingly, momentarily, submitted to the man's alluring charisma. He received an equally friendly salutation, if not quite as chivalrous as that reserved for his partner. Their host moved freely despite a disciplined posture and shook DCI Robson firmly by the hand.

"What a beautiful home you have, sir," Wilson seemed to have broken free of the spell. "We are grateful to you for seeing us at short notice."

"Not at all, Inspector, but thank you kindly. I am extremely fortunate. The estate has been in my family for many generations."

"You do it credit, sir. It's kept so beautifully"

"You're very kind, madam."

Jack felt the requirement for pleasantries had been fulfilled.

"Yes, as my colleague says Sir Geoffrey, thank you for agreeing to see us today. We understand that you're busy and we don't intend to overstay our welcome."

"Please, officers," he took the armchair opposite Emma, "for as long as I have breath, I would not knowingly refuse the opportunity to support the local constabulary. Especially not in the current climate. I do hope that you're making some headway on these blasted kidnappings. Are you any closer to catching the perpetrators?"

"We're making progress sir, just not quickly enough at present."

"Extraordinary business. I hear the case is starting to achieve national coverage now?"

"You could say the profile seems to be escalating, yes." Jack decided to correct the role reversal and become the interviewer. "We are trying to build some information on someone who has come to our attention. We believe that the person in question has recently been in your employment."

"Oh, I see. And who might that be?"

"A certain Barry Searle?"

The lofty man paused for a split second, as if he hadn't expected to hear the name, Jack thought.

"Oh yes, Barry. You are correct. Barry Searle very much works in my employment." He suddenly had a concerned, puzzled look, as though he wasn't sure what to ask next. He perceptibly restrained himself to allow the officers to continue.

Jack returned Emma's enquiring eyes with an inaudible *Not yet*.

"Could you tell us a little about what he does for you?" continued Jack.

"Certainly. But he is okay, I trust?"

"If you don't mind, we'll come to that."

Emma shifted nervously at her colleague's bluntness. However, Charlesworth showed no outward sign of offence, although the concerned countenance remained.

"Of course, I apologise, this is your interview. It's just that

Barry has worked for me for some time now, and is almost a part of the family." His eyes returned to their impassive state as he settled into the story. "Barry is a very reliable worker. I first met him several years ago, when I hired him for some maintenance work – a plumbing repair, if I remember correctly."

Jack gave an interested nod, but did not interrupt.

"Anyway, I recall being so impressed with his work that I decided I'd found someone that I could trust with a job that I'd been putting off for a while – the dreaded kitchen! It wasn't just the quality of his work, you see, it was his work ethic and professional attitude. Six months later, he completed a fabulous job of refitting the kitchen here, and basically became my go-to handyman for anything – from plumbing to electrical work, building and even gardening."

"We understand that you employed him in a more official capacity also?"

"Well, I suppose you could call it that. I dare say that we have become friends – an unlikely pairing, you might say. But we found common ground in our military careers, as is often the case. Have either of you served?"

They both shook their heads and he took the cue to continue.

"Basically, the more I grew to know Barry, the more I trusted him. Trust is important in my line of work, you see inspectors. Much like it is in yours."

Emma took the prompt for interaction and returned a polite tilt of the head, raising the corner of her mouth to confirm that common principles existed between them.

"So, I offered him the opportunity for work at the power station. To tell you the truth, the vacancy didn't even exist at the time. As you no doubt know yourselves, ancillary jobs such as general caretaking are overlooked these days, and we are all expected to provide our own support. I am in a privileged position, in so far as I am responsible for discharging the duties of the regulator at Hinkley, and there is a commercial mechanism in place with the foreign investors that means that we are not subjected to the usual government budget constraints, shall we say."

"According to the HR manager, Barry has been given maximum security clearance, is that correct?"

"That is true, yes. In terms of security, Barry is classed as my personal assistant and therefore he requires the same level of access as me."

"Of course," Jack nodded. "Do you know if Barry was still carrying out work outside of the power station?"

"I don't believe so, except for the odd bits he still does for me personally, of course. We kept him rather busy."

"Would that include any of your personal projects, such as the nature reserve?"

"Oh, you know about that, Inspector? It's my absolute passion, it really is. Yes, Barry has assisted with certain things on the island, mainly ferrying materials across and carrying out minor construction work for me."

"Does he work alone?"

"Overall, yes he does. He wasn't part of a fixed team, put it that way. But there may well have been others working with him from time to time, depending on the scale and nature of the work."

Jack nodded in understanding.

"You must come out and see the island, if you get the chance while you're here, DCI Robson. Both of you."

"Thank you, that's very kind."

Emma smiled to indicate she agreed with the sentiment.

"What about his private life – do you know anything about his social scene?"

"Not really. I know I said we were on friendly terms, but I must confess ninety nine percent of our conversation was connected to the work arena, either directly or indirectly. I believe his brother is his main companion outside of work, though."

"Have you noticed a change in his behaviour at all, recently?"

Charlesworth paused, as if trying to ensure that he gave an accurate analysis.

"Not that I have noticed, no. Although I have been away for a few days, which is why you didn't find me at the plant yesterday."

"Have there been any occasions when he has missed work?"

There was another thoughtful pause.

"I'm not sure such an event would be obvious, really. Barry's job description covers a broad spectrum, which means that, apart from when he is specifically requested to support an activity on a given time and date, he is self-managing." The pause allowed him to return to his own line of enquiry. "I must confess, you have me a little concerned. Are you unable to give me any insight into the cause of these questions?"

The two officers exchanged brief glances of acknowledgement, sealing the silent confirmation that it was time to be frank. Jack took the lead.

"I'm really sorry to have to tell you this sir, but Barry was discovered dead, two days ago."

Charlesworth allowed his lean torso to fall back into the armchair and at first it seemed that an emotional reaction would follow. However, he appeared to immediately snap into military protocol, and regained his composure.

"My god. Do you know how?"

"We're still investigating that. His body was found washed up on the shore. He had been shot."

Charlesworth's face dropped slightly, losing some of its tautness.

"I just can't believe it … "

"Sorry, sir. Hence the questions. We really would appreciate any assistance you could provide in identifying Barry's associates, either in or out of work."

"Of course. Might I just enquire – you indicated at the beginning of our meeting that you were investigating the spate of kidnappings in the county. Do you suspect that Barry's death is in some way connected with the case?"

"We don't know, sir. We'd like to formulate a picture of what he was doing in the last few weeks leading to his death. Tell me, do you happen to know where he kept his vehicle? It hasn't been located yet – we believe it was a white van?"

"I don't, I'm afraid. I must admit, I always assumed that he kept it where he lived?"

Jack began to feel genuine pity for their host. For all his stoic demeanour, the man's distress was palpable.

"All right, I think we'll leave you in peace Sir Geoffrey. Thank you again for your time."

"And hospitality," Emma added, indicating the regal tea set before them.

"Really officers, any time at all. A pleasure meeting you both." His tone became more muted, as though the termination of their meeting would signal the need to confront the awful news that had been delivered. "Notwithstanding the circumstances, obviously."

The butler entered the room silently, as the three of them rose in unison. Jack wondered whether it had been a coincidence, intuitive timing based on experience of typical meeting lengths, or whether he had simply been listening at the door. He waited to receive them at the entrance to the stately room, with well-rehearsed patience.

Jack paused next to a large picture, which at first glance appeared to portray a scene of natural beauty, but the artist had chosen to depict a sinister looking weather system in the background which seemed to threaten the tranquillity. He suddenly realised that he had given the piece more than just a cursory glance and became aware of the other three in the room watching him. Charlesworth seemed particularly satisfied that it had piqued his guest's interest.

"Do you like art, Chief Inspector?"

"Yes, I suppose you could say that. Although I'm no expert."

He studied the signature in the bottom corner of the frame.

"One doesn't need to be an expert to appreciate art, DCI Robson. This one's by a local artist. In fact, most of the pieces I purchase these days are. A work of art may mean something different to you than it does to me. We may both have different interpretations, but it doesn't mean that either one of us is correct or incorrect, does it?"

"I don't suppose it does."

"A microcosm of society, you might say. Too many, alas, including, or perhaps especially, those in power, seem to view issues as black and white, right or wrong. Humankind has lost the ability to empathise and open up to different possibilities."

Neither Jack nor Emma could think of anything to offer to the conversation, which had suddenly become a little highbrow, so both opted to display politely interested expressions.

"I'm sorry, I've started haven't I? And you were only looking at a damned picture. It's just that I believe with a passion in the importance of art, and possibly more so now than at any time."

"I think I know what you mean, sir."

Jack moved to end the meeting, offering his right hand to Charlesworth.

Sir Geoffrey gave them both respectful, yet subdued handshakes, before appearing to slip back into a pensive state.

"Would you show the officers to their car, Carl? I wish you well with your enquiries. I apologise if I've been slightly scatty. The news has been quite a shock."

"That's perfectly understandable, sir. We're sorry to have had to bring you such news. Thank you once again for your time."

After seeing them into the car park, the butler retreated to the house and watched them depart from the grand porch. As he started the engine, Jack noticed the small boat moored at the end of the garden.

"A sailor too? Busy chap," he said thoughtfully as he drove from the estate. Emma nodded.

CHAPTER 18

"He seemed quite upset about the news."

Emma shuffled in the passenger seat to get comfortable as she looked across at Jack, whose attention was momentarily diverted from the figure bouncing up and down on the tractor seat, four cars ahead.

"Yes," he agreed. "Nothing seems to cause a military diehard to grieve more than the loss of a fellow comrade."

"Military diehard?"

"Would you not say so? Stiff upper lip and all that, refusing to submit to emotion."

"Yes, it's just that, in some ways he seems quite removed from the arena of conflict."

"Perhaps, but at one point I thought he was going to salute rather than shake hands when he entered the room."

"He's an ex-military commander – a highly decorated one. He has served and advised the government in some of the most complicated conflicts of recent times."

"You know a lot about him?"

"He's not a particularly low-profile character. But I've been looking at Matthews' research."

"And?"

"He does a lot for the local community. Canvassing for new and improved infrastructure and more funding; even contributing financially himself, I understand. Seems quite a philanthropist actually. He ran a little group of volunteers for a while."

"Doing what?"

"Seems it was like a little community charity. The fourth emergency service for Somerset, as one local newspaper article put it. He's been quite vocal about the need for support in the kidnapping case."

"I see. I'll bet I can guess how Thorpe feels about him then..."

"Not sure really. Charlesworth has been quite supportive of the Super. He's merely been banging the drum about assigning appropriate resources to tackle the case seriously, bending the ear of the local MP et cetera. Anyway, as I was saying, he's a decorated war veteran. No doubt he was always destined for great things, but a significant catalyst for his career progression seemed to be distinguished service in the Falklands. He then went on to become a senior military advisor to the government."

"So how does that link to his position with the nuclear regulator?"

"His position in the government led to his involvement in nuclear research for military purposes. He sat on the Trident committee. That somehow culminated in him being appointed as a UN weapons inspector around ten years ago."

Jack suddenly clicked his fingers as the penny dropped.

"That's where I know the name."

Emma nodded.

"Anyway, he served in that position for just over five years. Then I guess he was considered a natural fit for the position that he now holds. I imagine he grabbed the Hinkley project with both hands, because it's allowed him to return to his family home."

"See out Hinkley and then retire?"

"Perhaps. It seems to have allowed him to focus on other, local interests."

"What's this island project all about, then?"

"A few years back, Sir Geoffrey purchased this small, uninhabited island in the Channel. You can still watch the television show online. The objective of the project is to create a sustainable, natural habitat for birds, wildlife, plants and also sea mammals."

He noted with respect that Inspector Wilson had clearly taken the time to watch the documentary.

"He didn't make it sound as though Barry did anything much outside of the power plant. Do you think it would have required any significant construction or engineering that he could have been involved in?"

"I don't know. It's likely though. The programme showed that they had created watching posts that blended into the natural surroundings. There must also be some basic facilities there for the workers, and of course visitors."

"I think it might be worth trying to catch Barry's brother

again, preferably while he's sober."

Emma nodded, appreciating her partner's inquisitive mind. It was peculiar that it somehow evoked the memory of one of her former mentors in her training. She could almost hear his gravelly voice – *If you're nothing else Wilson, be thorough. Leave nothing unanswered, despite how irrelevant it might seem at the time.* Out of respect for her tutor, she had opted to follow that guidance when many of her peers had not. She had the feeling that the man next to her came from the same school of thought.

CHAPTER 19

The house presented more or less the same appearance as their previous visit, except for the open curtains, which suggested habitation. However, their call was met with the same fruitless silence as before. They both agreed there was an obvious alternative location for the absent homeowner.

The short drive from the house down to the harbour was more successful. The rotund harbour master had pointed them in the direction of one of the boats moored in the row beneath them, on which a figure could be seen busy on deck.

The view of the hunched shoulders beneath the cable-knit sweater did little to confirm the identity of the person on board. They carefully walked along the row of moorings until they were alongside the thirty-foot length of sleek white fibreglass with navy blue trim, which matched the colour of the calligraphy on the side of the hull stating the name of the vessel – *Orinoco*.

As they peered onto the deck, they both recognised the

face as an apparently sober version of the visage that had made their acquaintance two days previously. The facial features were a little less slack, and as the man turned to behold his visitors, his eyes possessed a level of comprehension that they previously had not. He feigned a puzzled expression as he met their gazes, but his eyes had already betrayed recognition and Jack waded in with a greeting of familiarity, slightly impressed that his power of recollection had not been impaired by the brain pickling.

"Morning Jonny, how's it going?"

He nodded, evidently still trying to decide between amicability and deference. Jack read the situation and took the opportunity to steer the direction of their second meeting.

"Hope you don't mind us dropping by. We were a little worried about you after the other day, so we thought we'd call to see how you're getting on. How are things?"

"Yeah, I'm doin' just fine ta. An' I don't need babysittin'."

Jack was not perturbed by their host's attempt at hostility.

"Course not. Do you mind if we come aboard for a chat?"

DCI Robson's demeanour signalled that his embarkation was not dependent on obtaining permission. Jonny Searle pointed to the small set of steps towards the rear of the vessel.

The swell caused by another boat entering the harbour seemed to amplify the slight motion that had been caused by Jack climbing the steps and he flew forward as *Orinoco* rolled the swell. Jonny had been too busy acknowledging the greeting offered by the two-man crew on the other vessel to notice his guest flying across the deck, until he heard the crash. Emma had already arrived to assist by the time Jonny noticed the DCI lying face first with blood pouring from his nose, and his initial hostility promptly transformed to concern as he ran to the aid of the injured Chief Inspector.

After ten minutes of stemming the flow from his numb nose, DCI Robson's pain began to give way to humiliation. Inspector Wilson seemed to be tuned into Robson's vexation and suggested that they get him inside the cabin. She backed off slightly as her partner indicated with his palm that he considered he had received sufficient treatment. As Jonny delivered a steaming cup of tea to both his guests, Jack noticed his uncommonly large hands for the first time. Evidently lined with asbestos, he also thought, and he wondered if it would be possible to sacrifice any more masculinity that day in the name of the job, as he fumbled with the hot mug that had been delivered by his host's left paw.

In light of the situation, Emma took responsibility for striking up a conversation.

"How have the last couple of days been for you, Jonny?"

His eyes became inimical again at what he seemed to regard as superficial concern.

"Just great, thank you. And yourselves? Have you found the person that murdered my brother yet?"

"We're still trying to piece together what work Barry had been involved in over the past few months. We went to meet his former boss yesterday."

A sneer began to form.

"Not Saint Geoffrey himself?"

"Do you know Sir Geoffrey Charlesworth?"

"Everyone 'round here knows him, don't they?"

"Did Barry ever speak about him?"

His short chuckle was loaded with animosity.

"Just a bit." He began to shake his head as he remembered his brother. "Baz spent most of his recent life in the man's company. Seemed to worship him."

"Oh? Do you know why that might have been?"

"Well, obviously I understand that he makes a significant contribution to the community, blah, blah. But I think it was the military connection that seemed to seal some kind of bond between them."

"You don't seem to share in the adoration?"

"Ah, I've got nothin against the bloke. Just made me laugh sometimes when Baz went on about how fuckin' great this guy was, what he had achieved. It just got a bit boring, that's all. Perhaps I've been a little jealous, coz he got to see more of my brother than I did."

The appearance of Jack checking that the blood had stopped oozing from his nose allowed Jonny to escape the melancholy of the moment and he offered the DCI another tissue.

Jack spoke at last.

"Do you think it's possible that your brother could have been working for anyone else?"

"As far as I'm aware, he was, yes. He could never say no to work, unfortunately. That's how he met Charlesworth, just doin an odd job or two for 'im. They ended up hitting it off. He started helping out at Hinkley, and that bloody nature project. Even joined some do-gooder group with the guy."

Jack and Emma both remained silent, sensing that Jonny was in full flow.

"I think he even said that his work on the island and at the power station was winding down, so he was picking up some other stuff again. Still didn't change though."

"What do you mean?" Jack asked.

"I dunno. Baz used to be the life and soul of this whole village, just ask anyone around here. He just seemed so damned preoccupied lately. I couldn't work out where his head was half the time. We began to fall out."

Tears appeared in his eyes again. Jack spoke after a few respectful seconds.

"Did you ever get to meet any of his work colleagues?"

He shook his head.

"Not one. He seemed to close up when it came to his work. Baz could always be like that though – one minute, he's the centre of everything, and the next he's carrying on like he's back on fuckin' parade."

"Have you ever been to the island?"

"Not since Charlesworth bought it. Baz and me used to go out there fishin' when we were young'uns."

"Do you know if there's anyone working there still?"

"No idea. Maybe so."

"It's just that you said you thought that the work had been completed?"

Jack was looking for an angle that didn't reveal to the mourning man that his dead brother was the prime suspect in a kidnapping enquiry.

"Yeah, well that's what Baz said, but he was always heading out there to tinker with something. It's the only time he asked to borrow the boat."

"He used this to travel to the island?"

"On occasion, yeah. When Charlesworth's boat were already in use."

"How would you feel about taking us out to see this island for ourselves?"

"Uh, could do I 'spose. When?"

"Have you got any plans now?"

Jonny appeared less incredulous than the female inspector he had drunkenly admired during their previous meeting. Indeed, after several seconds, the brother of their prime suspect seemed to quite warm to the idea.

"Okay."

CHAPTER 20

The breeze was strong as they left the tranquillity of the bay and the strong current of the Channel could be felt as it gripped *Orinoco*. DCI Robson inhaled the briny smell of the sea as he watched the nautical-looking buildings illuminated by the late afternoon sun, which was gradually descending behind a fluffy white blanket of cumulus above. He stoically avoided allowing himself to become distracted by the serene form of his female partner as she stood on the deck, thumbs casually tucked inside the armpits of her life jacket, while expertly shifting her balance as they cut a path through the swell. Jack had not tested his sea legs since a ferry journey to France a few years ago with Isabelle and Jasmine, during which he vomited for the entire journey. But he hadn't figured on the anxiety. *We're not even in the sky, get a grip.* He straightened his own life jacket and buried his fear.

On the shore, the maritime settlements gave way to sheer cliffs, and while Emma appeared transfixed on the coastline,

Jack took the opportunity to study the natural form some four feet away, appreciating the seductive geometry of her slim upper torso and the way it subtly widened into perfect curves around the hips, before tapering gently into well-defined limbs. He had allowed himself to momentarily enter a trance-like state and couldn't be sure how long she had been watching him, no doubt in search of a reaction to the beauty before them, of the non-anthropomorphic type.

He returned a guilty smile before feigning an instinct to gaze over the starboard side towards the English coastline. Apart from watching the occasional television documentary, he had little interest in the study of ecology, but he felt that had the guy from the Coastal TV programme been in his place right now, he would be waxing lyrical about the clear layers visible on the bare rock face. The predominant colour was rusty red, which ran in distinct mantles above and beneath varying paler shades, doubtless depicting several hundred million years of the planet's history right there on open display.

Jack had just begun to trust his sea legs and considered standing, partly to improve his view, but mainly in an attempt at asserting his masculinity, in response to the gauntlet that had been laid down by his partner. Jonny continued to guide *Orinoco*, carving its course through the strong current of the Channel, as they hit a large swell and it felt like the boat had momentarily become airborne. The sensation of his bowel entering his throat convinced him to remain on his backside, despite the slight humiliation of his partner behaving as though she were merely stood on an escalator. He had begun to regret the decision to accompany Emma on the deck.

As the swell calmed, he took the opportunity to retreat to the more comfortable cabin.

"Just want to speak with Jonny," he shouted over the noise of the engine and increasingly whirling wind.

Emma smiled, then joined him inside the relative luxury of the cabin. The soft upholstered seating seemed inviting to Jack, but needing to keep up the semi-pretence of his motive, he went and stood alongside the skipper.

"How much further?"

Jonny responded by removing a hand from the wheel and casually pointing towards the dark object in the middle of the channel ahead. The pilot was now flanked as Emma stood port side of him and the three of them observed the rock in greater detail as it grew larger. As they got closer, the dark shadows became dominant patches of forestation and plant growth over the grey-rocky foundation.

"Where do we park?"

The response to Jack's question was met with several seconds of silent condescension by his two companions.

"Where that boat's approachin." The grey towers floating towards them in the opposite direction belonged to a huge cargo vessel. "The landing beach is on the southern side, but the tide is too high at the moment, so I'll head for the pier, just alongside. I'll circle round the North to get out of her way first though."

"Sounds like a good idea."

The luscious green flora on the surface of the island was a surprising vision, compared with the impression one had from afar. Jack watched their skipper frown as he studied the dramatic concentration of jagged rocks that protruded from the water, slashing and creating a dirty-white frothy boundary all around them. They drifted within twenty metres of the north-eastern side of the rock.

"What's that?" Jack asked.

"Well, it always were an opening in the rock formation."

"A cave?"

"Yeah, though I don't remember it being quite so precarious. Looks like there've been some serious erosion."

"Have you ever been inside?"

"Course I 'ave." The tone was a reminder that, to Jonny Searle and his family, the Channel represented the streets that they roamed as children, their playground and their park.

"Can you take a boat in then?"

"Have done. Used to dive in there, was always a great spot for conger," Jonny recalled.

"Why's that – d'you want to go an' see?"

Jack felt strangely intrigued at the thought of seeing the famous eel in its natural habitat, having only previously encountered the species in its lifeless, marinated form. His and Isabelle's honeymoon hadn't exactly been restful, but in a rare moment of escape from the action of their Asian tour, he still cherished the memory of one of their most romantic evenings together. The couple had watched the sun set over Victoria harbour, sitting until the early hours eating sushi, while discussing what the future might hold for them, with all the excitement of young newly-weds. Emma graciously humoured Jack's silent affirmation, raising no objection.

Searle reduced the speed of *Orinoco* to a crawl as they drifted within ten metres of the cave. From five metres, Jack had begun to regret his request, as the water slapping the threateningly rocky outlets indicated the treacherousness of the manoeuvre. Jack was again reminded of his late wife as he noticed his partner exuding calmness, as though they were drifting along on a canal barge. As was so often the case when he was with Isabelle, he swallowed deeply and buried his anxiety, as their skipper negotiated the current with an impressive level of expertise. With an instinctive sense of extraordinarily accurate timing, they broached the entrance to the cave, somehow missing the violent breakers that seemed to Jack to have been warning them against coming any closer. Before them, the light tapered abruptly into darkness and Jack instinctively turned his head at the gigantic slap that sounded at their rear, to witness the return of the aggressive breakers, almost immediately after the hull entered the still water of the cave.

The skipper operated a switch and suddenly the majesty of their new surroundings became illuminated. The slimy cavernous shell that they now inhabited appeared transient as it fluttered between dark brown and then the colours of the light spectrum, intermittently spraying around them as though they were inside a kaleidoscope. Had it not been for the obvious man-made construction, the natural mystery of the cave might have held their attention longer. As they approached alongside a large, wide landing jetty, all three surveyed the vast gates up ahead.

Jack prompted Jonny to confirm the bewildered look on his face.

"Do I take it that this isn't quite how you remembered it?"

"Not even close. This must be where they bring in cargo. I guess that must be the store?"

They drew slowly alongside a sturdy wooden platform that contained moorings on their left. A construction of similar width could be seen on their far right, on which an array of cuboid and cylindrical containers had been left.

"Let's take a look, shall we?"

"Jack," Emma could see that the discovery had generated a degree of interest in her partner, "we have no authorisation to go any further, and considering who this establishment belongs to … "

The comment had the desired effect of reminding him of the need to follow protocol. He was acutely aware that it was becoming increasingly difficult not to reveal his suspicions to their water chauffeur. Still, it was with reluctance that he agreed with his partner's sentiments and requested that Jonny returned them to Porlock, instead of continuing with their planned excursion around to the southern landing pier.

The grey waters of the Channel looked even more depressing without the sun's rays to provide a much-needed lift. The air felt distinctly chilly now that the orange orb that had accompanied them on their outward journey had been totally smothered by the thick layer of cloud overhead, as it headed ever nearer to the horizon. Jack noted to himself how, during their twenty-minute spell in the cave, they seemed to have skipped a season and were greeted by a decidedly wintry landscape.

From his standing position, DCI Robson watched the huge rock reduce to a distant black mound in the Channel. Jonny had opened up a generous distance between *Orinoco* and the boat that had been behind them when they departed the cave. It almost seemed that the other vessel had drawn up at the island.

The thundering swell convinced Jack to take up one of the empty seats. He used the time to meditate on the information they had accumulated to date. With an effort to maintain an open mind, he couldn't resist the temptation to speculate about the relevance of the innocuous rock they had just departed, and how the deceased brother of their boat skipper was intrinsically linked to the abduction of eight families in the past six weeks. It seemed to him that, with the commitments and onerous schedule of the owner of the island, it would be entirely feasible for an employee, especially one who had managed to cultivate a privileged position of trust, to undertake extracurricular activities, undetected.

The conundrum of motivation was perplexing to him. With no apparent connection between the victims and no financial demands, they had no profile for the perpetrator. Barry Searle was connected by a tenuous link, comprising a phone record and the ownership of a white van. A white van that had disappeared seemingly around the same time that its owner had disappeared into the Bristol Channel.

He checked his partner in his peripheral vision, noting that she too seemed to be in the midst of executing her own mental review. Jonny remained focussed on the skilful handling of *Orinoco*.

None of them had looked back to notice that the lights from the boat behind them had disappeared.

CHAPTER 21

Emma enjoyed the warmth of the vernal sunshine on her bare, milky shoulders, as she led the way towards the splendid frontage of St Audries Manor. She hadn't disguised her disagreement with Jack's proposal to visit the eminent inhabitant uninvited. However, he managed to convince her that they ought to arrange an official visit to the conservation island as soon as possible. In fact, he was more than confident that she had already arrived at the same conclusion herself.

The fine spring morning served to amplify the magnificence of the estate, and the early season foliage provided a stunning accessory to the Georgian manor. The red and green colours of the ivy that climbed the antique structure shimmered in the sunlight, giving the manor house a majestic quality. The unseasonably warm temperature was responsible for DCI Robson witnessing his partner in a summery dress, which ruffled around her slender thighs in the light breeze as she walked. Her decision to take the initiative had afforded him the opportunity to relax his discretion, but appreciation soon gave way to guilt, arriving typically on cue, as the door to the manor drew inwards.

Robson arrived on the porch to hear the butler explaining that his boss wasn't currently in residence. He noted that even the professional attendant wasn't immune to the effect of the inspector's radiance as he appeared far less formal than their previous meeting.

"I'm awfully sorry," he continued apologetically, "if you had called ahead, I could have saved you a wasted journey."

"No, it's our own fault for arriving unannounced." The message hit the target without her needing to look back at the recipient. "Is Sir Geoffrey at the power station? Perhaps we could visit him there?"

"I'm afraid he's away in London, madam. He is attending a government briefing today and tomorrow. And I believe he intends to stay on beyond that for a military reunion. We're expecting him to be away for quite a few days."

"Ah. Do you think we might trouble you for a few minutes instead?"

"If I can help in any way Inspectors, of course. Do please come in."

"We don't want to put you to any trouble. Perhaps we could have a seat in the garden on such a fine morning?"

"As you wish, madam. Shall I fetch some tea?"

Jack and Emma both shook their heads.

"No that won't be necessary, sir. I'm sorry, we weren't really introduced previously."

"Carl Potter at your service, officers."

Potter led them around the rear of the large house to a large patio area. A parasol was already erected and was swaying in the gentle breeze. They sat on the antique pine furniture lined with comfortable cushions.

DCI Robson had already noted that the butler didn't seem particularly comfortable in their presence as his colleague continued with her amiable inquiry.

"So, Mr Potter, I don't imagine that you must see an awful lot of your boss, given his work commitments?"

"That's very true, madam. Given the nature of Sir Geoffrey's position on the ONR, he pretty much has had a full-time commitment at the power station, with it coming into operation and continuing to expand."

"Yes, we thought the same. So, it seems rather impressive that Sir Geoffrey seems to manage to make time for his other work. How do you think he achieves that?"

"Indeed. I've heard more than one person offer the same observation, that he is almost machine-like in his drive. But I think careful recruitment helps his cause."

"Oh?"

"He has a small core of trusted employees that he has selected, based on their ability to act under their own initiative, with minimal guidance."

"How many employees are we talking about?" asked Jack, judging that Emma wouldn't object to him forming a tag team, now that she had done the ground work and established an ostensibly open dialogue.

"Never greater than four, I would say sir."

"Do they all contribute to his work at the power station?"

"Oh no, sir, I don't believe so. The employees at the power plant are not appointed by Sir Geoffrey. I was referring solely to his private interests."

"Are you referring to the conservation project?"

"That has been his primary focus and passion for the past five years sir, yes."

"But he doesn't oversee the work there in person?"

"Well he certainly directs it, sir. But of course, you understand that he cannot be there to observe every shovel operation, as it were."

"Of course not," Emma took over. "We're trying to piece together the final movements of one of Sir Geoffrey's employees, Barry Searle. You might have learnt about his sad fate recently?"

The eyes lowered momentarily, in a mark of respect, Jack presumed.

"Yes, madam. Sir Geoffrey has been quite upset about it all. We all have. Of the core personnel that I have just referred to, Barry was perhaps the closest and most trusted of them all."

"And has been for some time?"

"Quite."

DCI Robson took advantage of the pause.

"So we understand, Mr Potter. Just going back to what you said a little earlier, we also understand that Barry did work with Sir Geoffrey at the power plant?"

The butler didn't seem impressed at having his own responses queried.

"As I implied, Barry was an exception. Sir Geoffrey no doubt pulled strings to get him appointed as his personal assistant at Hinkley."

Inspector Wilson nodded and gave a gentle smile, quickly regaining the slight figure's cooperation.

"We'd really like to know who these others were, and who Barry worked with. It seems that the employee circle at the power station is, understandably, well regulated. So, we were wondering what kind of company he might have mixed with in connection with his other duties?"

"I see. Well yes, I think your summary is accurate enough. But we don't really get to see anyone here. Barry was different, because he worked on the estate also."

"I understand. Tell me, where do the crew launch from typically, when they travel to the island?"

"Sir Charlesworth has a cargo boat moored at Hinkley point. Just around from the power station. That is used, I believe, as the primary launch port for the island."

"Do you think Sir Geoffrey would allow us to visit the island some time?"

"I have absolutely no doubt that he would be delighted to host you. If you wish to leave it with me, I can see to it that Sir Geoffrey gets your request."

"Thank you."

Emma again took the lead in standing, prompting the butler to adopt the appropriate formalities as he stood with her.

"My pleasure, officers. And once again I'm sorry that you missed Sir Geoffrey."

As they arrived back at the car, the sound of Emma's mobile phone warbling provided a disagreeable interruption to the birdsong. Wilson took the phone from her handbag and inhaled deeply before answering, causing her pale bust to rise slightly so that the very top of her cleavage was displayed. DCI Robson averted his gaze and unlocked the vehicle.

"Hello sir. Yes, he's with me. We're just leaving St Audries house, sir. Is everything all right?"

Robson knew from her furrowed brow that the caller hadn't been asking after his wellbeing.

"We're on our way, sir."

Their eyes locked for several seconds before she spoke again.

"Apparently your phone isn't on?"

Jack extracted his mobile from his pocket.

"Fuck sake. Are there no mobile phone masts in this part of the world?"

Emma remained impassive as he returned his phone to his pocket in disgust.

"What was he after anyway. Or should I say, what have I done?"

"There's been another kidnapping."

As they both opened the car doors, DCI Robson noted that the top of her dress had fallen back to its normal position, forming an arc around the breastbone.

CHAPTER 22

The duty sergeant didn't waste any time on salutations as he looked up and saw them enter the CID headquarters together, simply pointing along the corridor with a contrite expression.

They entered a briefing room, as a red-faced Thorpe was conveying instructions to the small team of detectives. Each one looked back at them before promptly averting their gaze as they entered the room. The briefing was hastily concluded, and the officers vacated the room with awkward nods of acknowledgement, leaving the three of them.

DCI Robson could never stand a silent standoff.

"Sir. Sorry about the communication issues. I think I'll have to look into changing service providers while I'm here."

A grunt was followed by a long pause, and it seemed for a while that the Superintendent wasn't prepared to dignify the statement with a response.

"Perhaps that'd be a good idea, Robson."

"What's the situation, sir?" Inspector Wilson interrupted

the frosty engagement.

"More missing people. Peter and Janet Armitage, a couple of local artists, were expected to attend a convention yesterday in honour of Mr Armitage's work and they didn't show."

Jack felt the examining eyes of the Superintendent as he tried desperately to recall why on earth that name had awakened a degree of recognition. He felt obliged to think of a question.

"Where was the convention, sir?"

"Bristol. They should have been there at 6 p.m. yesterday. By 8 pm the event was abandoned when it was clear that they weren't going to show. Apparently, they stood up a few local dignitaries by all accounts. Their car hasn't moved from their home in Doniford."

"Have we got people there now, sir?"

"Yes, including your colleagues."

"Right. Well if there's nothing else, sir, we ought to join them," Inspector Wilson said.

"Indeed you had. Just before you go – you said on the phone that you were at St Audries Manor?"

DCI Robson understood that he was the target of the challenge, despite the query being ostensibly directed towards his partner, and stepped in to respond.

"We were just trying to piece together the final movements of Barry Searle, sir, but Sir Geoffrey is away, unfortunately."

"I see. Doesn't seem to be getting us anywhere that line of enquiry, does it?"

Raised eyebrows confirmed the fundamental message, adding the silent footnote, *and in the meantime, the kidnappers have fucking well struck again!*

"If that's all, sir?"

Thorpe waved them out of the room.

CHAPTER 23

Inspector Wilson once again used the journey back to the station to evaluate what they had seen. Another apparently abandoned house, without sign of disturbance or struggle. *Another vanishing act.*

Each time she snuck a glance at her partner, he seemed to be doing the same, while driving too quickly along the narrow roads along which they travelled. When the Superintendent had announced that a big shot Chief Inspector from London had been assigned to assist in the case, she had been sceptical of the potential benefits of such a move. But she had to admit that, whatever he sometimes seemed to lack in tactfulness, he made up for with a dogged thoroughness that reminded Emma of her mentor when she first joined the CID.

She meditated on the fact that, for all their growing familiarity, there was a perceptible barrier between them. Perhaps that was down to the fact that they were opposite genders. She knew little of his life, other than the fact that he was a widowed father of one. She had tried to imagine him as a father, that this seemingly stoic, somewhat brusque man could act in a paternal manner to a little girl, but found the idea alien. But she also sensed a tender, vulnerable trait, which he seemed to do his best to conceal. Inspector Wilson was instinctively guarded about getting too close to male colleagues, which perhaps, she had to accept, might have contributed to the distance between them. What was becoming increasingly difficult to ignore was the matter that, for the first time, for some reason, she felt the desire to drop her guard. That frightened her more than anything else.

They had only caught the tail end of the forensic examination, having been caught by a combination of holiday traffic and a jack-knifed lorry which delayed them, despite having the privilege of blue flashing lights on the roof. The meeting at the Armitage's home was a bland affair, which, as usual, left Sergeant Matthews and company with the task of researching and providing any details they could find on the latest apparent kidnapping victims. Despite it being seemingly futile, Jack had insisted on tracking down the forensic investigator when they returned to the station, while the remainder of the team were dispatched to the makeshift incident room at St Audries.

*

"Why do I get the impression that Thorpe thinks we've been completely wasting our time?" Emma murmured, as they entered the half-empty canteen. Bob Jefferies, the grey-haired forensic specialist, was holding court, engaged in apparent light-hearted dialogue with two colleagues, while at the same time tucking into a plate of fried food.

"You can see the pressure he's under," Jack responded thoughtfully and somewhat tactfully by his own standards. "Hello Bob." Jack's voice returned to its normal volume.

"Hey guys, we were wondering where you both got to!"

Inspector Wilson found the accompanying wink to be slightly condescending. DCI Robson politely grinned.

"Could we borrow you for five minutes?"

He cheerfully held his palm out to the vacant chairs around the table.

"Be my guest."

The two plain-clothes officers took their leave.

"So, what did you conclude from your little visit out to Doniford?" Jefferies boomed.

"That was going to be my question actually, Bob. But since you asked, even less than we got out of the last one, to be perfectly honest." Robson answered, as he took the seat next to him.

"Well, you're not the only ones. Quite extraordinary really. I went to brief the Super but he's nowhere to be seen. Probably for the best really."

"What do you mean?"

"Well, anyone can see the guy is at breaking point. Apparently, the Chief Superintendent has demanded his presence, again. I wonder how much longer the poor man can keep his job. We just haven't been able to demonstrate any progress in all this time. It's as though these people disappear of their own free will."

"Well, surely there has been some progress of note, has there not?" Robson said.

"Sure. I hear that we now have a registration number for the van that was caught on the CCTV footage at the O'Hara's. Guess what? It belonged to Barry Searle. A positive ID on a vehicle that has disappeared. And a guy that was taken out the second we found out about him!"

Inspector Wilson, who had remained standing, found the pessimism of many of her experienced colleagues intolerable. Robson was not unfamiliar with this type of attitude, but sat silently, apparently pensive for a moment, before pursuing.

"Bob, don't take this the wrong way, but I just can't fathom why we're not getting any forensic clues. Has any DNA been recovered from this one at all?"

Wilson took the seat next to Robson, bracing herself for the inevitable fiery response from the experienced investigator. But Jefferies remained impassive, giving no indication that the frank question had offended him.

"Nothing. And I think there's probably a good reason for that, don't you?"

"Such as?" Robson probed further.

Wilson shifted in her seat, feeling slightly uncomfortable about the DCI's direct questioning. She also had a reputation for not shirking confrontation, but the bluntness of Robson's approach surprised her. However, Jefferies seemed to remain affably engaged in the conversation.

"Well, it seems to me that our abductor, on this occasion, did not even need to enter his or her victims' property. These latest people, the Armitage's, were due at an art function in

Bristol, as I understand it?"

"Apparently so. Mr Armitage's work was being displayed at the Royal West of England academy. It had been organised by the Royal Society of British Artists, of which he was going to be made an honorary member."

"Yes," Jefferies nodded, "I was in the house when Matthews was interviewing Mrs Armitage's sister, fragile thing."

"We met her briefly too," Robson continued, glancing at his female partner, who had relaxed into her seat, crossing her pale legs. Robson immediately looked away from her slim, right ankle, which had drawn his gaze. "She was already at the function as she was working in Bristol, so was expecting to meet up with them. They spoke yesterday and apparently Mrs Armitage seemed very excited about her husband's work being given its own, dedicated display."

"Mrs Armitage is quite well known around these parts, for her own work." Emma joined the conversation. "She Paints local scenery and wildlife."

"Yes, you often hear about her work in the local press," Jefferies nodded in agreement and continued his reasoning. "So anyway, I heard the sister tell Matthews that the organisers of the exhibition had arranged to pick the Armitages up in a private car. They were putting them up in a swanky city centre hotel too. Hence my theory, that perhaps the Armitages didn't need to be persuaded to leave their home. There was no sign of breaking and entering and no belongings were taken. Unfortunately, there was no CCTV camera this time. Do you know if the official car turned up for them?"

"Sure did," Emma responded, "16:30 as arranged. Matthews

called the hotel – they received no communication directly from the Armitages."

"I rest my case." Jefferies folded his arms, sitting back in the plastic canteen chair.

"What are you saying?" Robson tilted his head slightly to one side as he spoke. "Do you believe that someone else collected them, masquerading as their lift?"

Jefferies shrugged, eyes wide open, as if to confirm his theory. Both he and Inspector Wilson sat in silence as they waited for DCI Robson to continue. After a few more uncomfortable seconds, it became evident that he had completed his questions, albeit somewhat abruptly. The fact of the matter was that Jack was elsewhere at that moment. He stared into his coffee cup following the moment of clarity in which he realised where he'd seen the name Janet Armitage, and considered the implications.

CHAPTER 24

Janet Armitage felt that she had awoken from the most unnatural sleep. Perhaps the excitement around the prospect of the exhibition had got to her. The last thing she could recall was getting into the back of the dark limo with her husband, then chatting to the nice chauffeur before he closed off the partition to give them a little privacy. *Had there been a strange smell?*

Have we arrived? What a time to sleep! Better liven up a little, she thought. Her confusion was exacerbated as she contemplated the reason for her being laid flat out.

She glanced to her left, expecting to see her husband on the comfortable leather car seat next to her, but found a dull wall instead. She instigated a somewhat panicked twist of her neck so that she faced to the right and saw that her husband was lying about six feet away on a narrow mattress like hers. The nice chauffeur was gone, ponytail and all.

CHAPTER 25

The thin veil of mist had begun to give way to a bright and cheerful morning vista, as DCI Robson and Inspector Wilson set sail aboard the impressive, thirty-foot cargo vessel *Albatross*. They were buoyed by the opportunity to meet one of the late Barry Searle's ex-colleagues. Sir Geoffrey Charlesworth had arranged for them to be chauffeured by his very own skipper.

It hadn't been difficult to identify their pilot as they approached the small marina at Hinkley Point earlier. Tall and thin and with a worn, yet healthy outdoor complexion, Mikey had introduced himself to them with earnest pleasure.

Robson noted that the boat captain held control of the vessel with the same effortless skill as Jonny Searle. They both watched his lithe figure at the helm, dressed simply now that the spring weather was setting in and bringing a little more warmth to the Somerset shores, but still, like Jonny Searle, he wore a robust-looking jumper, in preparation for the gusty channel that lay ahead. Inspector Wilson thought that the nautical cap not only completed the look perfectly, but fulfilled the practical purpose of concealing a scruffy mop of hair beneath, evident from the odd group of loose strands that fell from its rear.

For the second time since arriving in Somerset, Jack was both surprised and disappointed in himself to discover that he endured the sea voyage with a notable degree of trepidation. He had buried his anxiety during the previous voyage with Jonny, but suddenly his mind raced with permutations of risk not usually associated with what, before the helicopter accident, he would have considered to be as run-of-the-mill journey as getting in the car. Mikey simply responded with a sympathetic laugh when the DCI enquired as to the requirement to wear life jackets.

The anxiety he now felt was nothing compared to the palpitations he'd experienced when Charlesworth's PA had offered them the chance to travel by helicopter. His hands had perspired in the short period that it took him to steady his voice and decline the offer, under the pretence that he would look forward to a journey across the Channel.

"We'll arrive in less than 'alf-hour. Boodiful day for it!" came the jovial travel update from their skipper, almost as soon as they'd set off from the peninsula.

Mikey had begun to slow the boat down as they neared the south coast of the island. They had all watched the morning blanket of mist lift to allow the island to appear before their very eyes as they approached. They closed in on the jetty that had formerly been dedicated for nature-lovers' tours to the island, which protruded alongside the small pebbled cove. A lone figure could be seen as they drew nearer, forming a perfectly upright silhouette. As they arrived within a few metres of their landing point, it was possible to establish that the tall form was male and wore walking boots and a jumper, and was holding a lightweight weatherproof jacket over one of his lean arms.

DCI Robson and Inspector Wilson both returned Charlesworth's wave, as their skipper expertly brought *Albatross* alongside the jetty before securing her moorings.

"Lovely day for a boat trip, officers, I trust Mikey was gentle with you?"

Robson noted the way their larger-than-life skipper appeared to suddenly become uncharacteristically reticent before his governor, who appeared to assume the role of commanding host.

"Very pleasant indeed. Thank you, Sir Geoffrey, for accommodating us," Wilson beamed.

Jack was impressed. She was clearly a talented detective, but was not ashamed to use feminine advantage to establish a bond with a potentially useful ally. He swallowed the childish emotion that grabbed him by surprise, as he found himself questioning the possible motive behind the coquettishness that seemed to emerge when she was in the aristocrat's company.

"Glad to hear it. Welcome to Steep Holm! I've been excited about having the opportunity to show you around; it may not appear much yet, but just wait until the tour!" With instinctive chivalry, he took the inspector's hand as she disembarked.

"Thank you, Mikey!"

The gratification offered by his boss seemed to give their skipper a lift and his face appeared relaxed again for a moment. The detectives offered their gratitude to the boat captain as their enthusiastic host dragged them from the landing jetty and towards the opening to a sycamore wood. They followed a pathway which cut through ancient trees flanking them on either side.

An incline was detectable from the first steps onto the well-worn path, but became less severe after a climb of about a hundred yards, where it plateaued to a gentle slope, still bordered by brambles and vegetation. Both visitors appreciated the simple beauty of their surroundings as they zig-zagged through the sycamore-lined path, in the shadow of the luscious canopy the trees created.

The path cut to the left one last time and then, as it straightened, the outline of a significant structure came into view, metal perhaps, but mounted on a concrete base. It was almost entirely covered by seagulls. Sir Geoffrey stopped.

"There are, in total, eight of these around the perimeter of the island. Former gun batteries from the Second World War; and cannon posts before that! But of course, what's more interesting to us are those beautiful little things sitting on top – Herring Gulls, no less!"

"Jeez, look at them all! So, this is where they must bring their stash of cold chips!" DCI Robson quipped.

Charlesworth gave an aloof chortle.

"Ah, yes. Anything that gets in the way of the human machine always gets a bad rap, doesn't it?"

Jack offered a non-committal smile, unsure as to whether he had managed to upset their host already.

"Anyway, let us progress. I'd like to begin the tour by showing you something quite magical!"

Their host seemed to have regained his childlike passion after the momentary blip, and after a further five minutes of pursuing the path the dense vegetation gave way quite abruptly as they arrived at the opening of a large expanse of long grass, scattered with millions of tiny white flowers. Robson was puzzled by the grin that Charlesworth wore, and all the more so when he noticed his partner's apparent mutual appreciation. After studying a little harder, he discovered the source of their apparent entertainment. If it hadn't been for the prompt from his two companions, Jack wasn't sure he would have noticed the elegant species of deer grazing at the very edge of the opening, where it met the boundary of large trees beyond, marking the beginning of another dense, wooded area.

"Those deer don't look like your average species?" commented Emma.

"Muntjac deer," Sir Geoffrey whispered. "They are in fact native to Asia and the Himalayas. We introduced them here a couple of years ago and I am rather proud to tell you that they are absolutely thriving!"

The man's eyes seemed to ignite.

"Amazing – can we get any closer?" Emma asked, looking slightly contrite as she felt Jack's gaze. Their host was clearly delighted by her interest.

"We could certainly try."

Charlesworth led them around the perimeter of the opening and they ducked low in the long grass.

"They are incredibly timid, and believe me, sightings are rare. But obviously they are not entirely unfamiliar with homo sapiens, and we are but a small congregation."

They reached a spot some fifty yards from the herd of graceful creatures, the group of three observers remaining crouched beneath the top of the wild grasses. The close-up view served to emphasise the unequivocal enchantment the animals produced as they edged forward.

Sir Geoffrey stopped abruptly and raised a hand to indicate that they had reached their limit. As they settled into their optimum viewing position, Jack felt the branch beneath his left boot too late and the cracking sound was amplified by the tree-lined perimeter. The deer looked up in unison and vanished into the trees, seemingly without running.

Almost too ashamed to apologise, he managed to exhale a futile whispered, "Sorry". The disappointment was plain on the faces of his two fellow viewers.

"Never mind," it seemed to take a degree of resolve for Charlesworth, as he visibly fought to control his frustration. "Let's continue."

Their host now led them to the western perimeter of the opening, where they encountered the beginning of another path. The reduction in density of foliage allowed DCI Robson a glimpse of what almost appeared as a mirage, such was it at odds with their natural surroundings. The grey building rose from nothing, in what appeared to be the centre of the island.

"Is that one of your constructions, sir, an observation point?"

He pointed towards the lump of concrete that had caught his eye.

"No, nothing to do with us," answered Sir Geoffrey. "That's the remains of the old inn that used to cater for the smugglers.

And the remains of an ancient monastery beside it. We're not allowed to touch them."

From the contrastingly lacklustre response, Jack got the impression that he had departed the sphere of importance.

"Wow, sounds interesting. A historical site of interest as well as a nature reserve," said Emma enthusiastically.

"Indeed. However, it is listed by English Heritage and, alas, it's out of bounds even to us currently. That large expanse of crop between us and the buildings constitutes our most protected flora: wild leeks and Geranium molle."

Jack looked out at the purple flowers and wondered at the potential for the perspectives of human beings to differ. Their host was clearly more interested in waxing lyrical about wild weeds than he was in a structure that doubtless retained a fascinating past within its walls.

"Anyway, I have something far more impressive to show you both. May we continue?"

He led them along a new route, which continued in a westerly direction, until they arrived at the edge of a shallow precipice, affording them a view towards the bottom western edge of the island as it met the aggressive tidal channel beneath.

"It's beautiful," Emma beamed transcendentally towards the shore. "I watched the documentary last year. What made you choose the name 'Hibernation' for this project?"

A smile indicated that their host was pleased to have returned to the core of his raison d'etre.

"Our goal is to provide a sustainable environment for the species that we have cultivated here – some of which are indigenous to the region, while some are not. I wondered what

I could do to make this a little different from other conservation schemes. I wanted to attract species that would be able to exist through all seasons, and not simply visit when the climate is right. Clearly, they don't all strictly hibernate, but the term represents a principle."

He seemed to sense Jack's sceptical, albeit silent reaction.

"Well, put it this way: it seemed like a good idea at the time, but it is merely a name, and has little other significance. If we have time, I could take you down there to show some fascinating sea-life in our plethora of rockpools? We have some very rare species of seaweed on this island and quite a population of hermit crabs, if you're interested. We might even get treated to an appearance by the resident seals."

Charlesworth reacted to the momentary silence.

"But I sense that you are pressed for time, officers."

Jack wondered if his boredom had shown that plainly, or if it was simple politeness on the part of their host. On the other hand, Emma didn't seem to be tuned in to her partner's inner thoughts and Jack interrupted before her pause resulted in further indulgence and an extension to their tour.

"Perhaps, Sir Geoffrey. I think we ought to be on our way before too long. If you don't mind, I was just wondering – what construction work has taken place on this island since you took it over?"

"Well, if I take you a little further, we have built some ingenious observation bases, if I may say so. We just passed one actually – did you notice it?"

"No." they answered in unison.

"Good, aren't they? You won't find any concrete

monstrosities here, not built by us, at least." Again, he seemed to sense Jack's thoughts. "Everything is in harmony with the natural landscape."

"Impressive. So, is that the kind of thing that Barry used to assist with here?" Emma asked.

Jack saw that she had finished buttering up their host.

"Yes, indeed." He seemed to adopt a slightly sombre, respectful tone. "The poor fellow was probably involved in all the construction work here, I would say."

"And who else might he have worked alongside here?" Wilson continued.

"Well, that's actually rather more difficult to answer. As a trusted member of staff, or family even, I allowed Barry to recruit his own little workforce. None of his helpers were ever in my employment, I simply provided the funds, in accordance with Barry's requirements. Have you checked his own business banking details?"

"It seems that Barry liked to deal in cash. Most of Barry's banking transactions appear to have been completed at a cashpoint." Emma responded.

"Now, why doesn't that surprise me?" Sir Geoffrey chuckled melancholically to himself.

"I wonder if you could take us to look at some of the construction work? I'd quite like to see it."

Jack sometimes felt frustrated by his own determinedly meticulous principles. Their trip to the island hadn't been as informative as he had hoped, and the chances of making a discovery of significant interest or relevance seemed to be waning by the second.

"Let me show you the one that we passed, not ten minutes ago."

Just before arriving at the opposite end of the path, back at the opening where the deer had been grazing earlier, they veered off to the left and continued along the rugged plain towards the horizon.

Expecting their escort to be leading them to some point in the distance, it took a few seconds before either of them realised that Charlesworth had stopped at a bush, which at first glance appeared as unkempt and wild as the remainder of their surroundings, yet seemed to possess an orderly circular perimeter, perhaps unnaturally, on closer inspection. Charlesworth placed his thumb to the side of a small concealed indentation in the hedge.

A small section of hedge gave way inwards as Sir Geoffrey shoved it purposefully with his slim palm and they followed him into a circular enclosure, which turned out to be composed of a metal cage with vegetation clinging to its perimeter. It seemed to be about twenty feet in diameter, with an apparent viewing section at eye level all the way around.

The ground inside was covered with bark chippings, which provided a soft, dry surface. Sir Geoffrey's boots scraped the floor as he traversed the den, displacing some of the bark, which drew Jack's attention to the faint glimpse of something beneath the superficial surface seemingly not native to their environment. Their host hadn't seemed to notice, being more intent on fetching three pairs of binoculars from a hook in the corner of the cavern.

In a feigned attempt at enthusiasm, Jack attempted to match

Emma's zeal as they accepted the eager invitation to try out the observation post for themselves.

After a couple of minutes admiring the zoomed image of several trees and small birds, Jack continued his enquiries, while all three of them continued gazing through their magnifying devices.

"It's clear that you have made a deliberate effort to keep construction to a minimum sir."

"Indeed, Chief Inspector. The only non-organic material involved in the building of these observation chambers is the metal frame, which we transport flat-packed and assemble on site, along with the anchors to secure it before the vegetation takes hold."

"Has it been quite easy to transport all of the materials to the island?"

"Yes. We kept the cargo to a minimum, partly for that reason, but not only because of that, of course."

"Still, I dare say it must have been quite a job getting all of the materials on site. No doubt we are only seeing a small portion of the project."

Charlesworth's look was not transparent, but seemed to convey confusion, perhaps even naivety, Jack thought, as he continued.

"I certainly wouldn't fancy trying to unload too many of these metal frames at that tiny jetty back there, before then having to lug them all the way up here."

"Honestly, forgive my colleague, Sir Geoffrey. I don't think he's been involved in manual labour too recently. I expect there is another dock for cargo – am I right, sir?"

Charlesworth politely overlooked Emma's jibe at Jack's expense, responding as he accepted their binoculars and replaced them on the hook.

"Well I must admit that I didn't deal with such detail, Inspector. I certainly like to be hands on with my projects, but not to that degree. Barry always made sure he had sufficient resources to handle the job. But, as far as I am aware, all materials were unloaded at the same point that you arrived. As I say, that, in part, influenced our choice of materials. As for unloading, the jetty that you arrived at is not our only landing point. For anything really substantial, we land on the beach that you will have noticed alongside the pier. We have a superb little crane on tracks that we can use to unload, even on the pebbly beach down there. However, we're obviously more at the mercy of the tides if we want to set down on the beach."

Robson exchanged a partially masked look of incredulity with his rosy-cheeked partner as they followed their host from the enclosure. Jack looked at his watch, considering the apparent potential for abusing the gentleman's trust. *You really ought to keep a closer tab on your workforce, sir*, thought Jack. Still looking at his timepiece, DCI Robson intervened before their host could continue his oration.

"Well I think we've taken up enough of your time, Sir Geoffrey. It's been so good of you to invite us out to see your impressive venture."

"It has been my pleasure, officers. But I suppose I ought to be getting to my next appointment also."

"Will you be travelling back with us Sir Geoffrey?" Emma asked.

"I'm afraid not, my dear. Time doesn't allow me such luxuries today. My helicopter awaits. I'd be delighted to drop you both off if you'd prefer a hastier return?"

Jack felt his palms moisten as his head replayed the sound of whirring rotors, feeling mild panic as their host's eyes seemed to him to be peering into his mind. He was disturbed from his anxiety by the surprising sight of their boat skipper, whose decision to join them for the first time since arriving had coincided with their decision to depart. He felt that his fear was somehow transparent as the boat skipper eyed him with apparent interest. *Paranoia, get a grip, Jack.*

He felt a surge of relief as Emma answered.

"I think we're both looking forward to the sea journey. We'll get out of your hair, sir. Thank you again."

"Not at all. Until the next time then! Goodbye both."

Sir Geoffrey exchanged a brief glance with Mikey as he shook both their hands firmly and strode off purposefully.

As the lanky sailor escorted them down towards the shore in silence, the natural beauty of their surroundings took on a more desolate aura, as though the island itself only lived when its caring owner was there to breathe exuberant life into it. DCI Robson considered the apparent change in mood of their skipper to be odd, and wondered what had driven him to maintain an emotional distance, compared with the energetic character who had greeted them that morning. Emma clearly sensed it too and felt a responsibility to include him.

"It's still looking fine for our return journey out there, Mikey?"

"Yep, 'tis looking okay."

The curt response was mumbled without a turn of the head and gave no scope for continuation.

"So, what are your thoughts?" Emma murmured to Jack, since Mikey didn't seem to be in a convivial mood. They allowed their pilot to increase his lead on them. Mikey sensed he was losing his party and gave a slight turn of his head to allow his peripheral vision to detect the position of his passengers. Noting that they were in conversation, he maintained a respectful space between them and continued at the same pace.

"Well he's certainly proud of his project, isn't he?"

"Very passionate," Emma agreed.

As they turned the last corner, *Albatross* reflected the fading, late-afternoon spring sunshine. Jack took a deep gulp to control his new-found travel phobia. Even on a relatively fine day, the channel was an ominous sight this close-up. But it could have been worse. They could have been aboard the helicopter that now peeled away from the island and chugged towards the mainland.

"All aboard!"

Mikey seemed to regain his spirit once he was reunited with the sea and smiled cordially as he took Inspector Wilson's hand to climb aboard. DCI Robson wondered if she would be offended by the second such gesture of the day, but, interestingly, she seemed to be quite tolerant of the chivalry.

Mikey checked that they were both settled in their seats before firing up the engine and gently releasing them from the jetty. As he guided the boat into the Channel, Emma appeared glad that they had taken their skipper up on his suggestion to sit on deck on such a calm evening, seeing that soon after forming earlier, the clouds had parted again to reveal a blue sky.

"So, what do we do now?" Emma asked. "I mean, what did we actually get out of that visit?"

"We return."

"What's the deal with the other entrance we witnessed the other day? Do you think he knows anything about it?"

The calm breeze began to escalate, and grey, thicker clouds suddenly began to move in, overpowering the thinner, wispy cumulus and threatening to obscure the low sun as they left the protection of the island. She removed a few strands of fair hair from the front of her face and deftly tied them back.

"I don't know. But something doesn't feel right about it. You get the impression that there isn't a blade of grass that he doesn't know about on that island."

"Apart from the protected ruins."

"Yeah, perhaps. I think we need an unsupervised inspection of the island. Charlesworth is too fixated on being the tour guide."

"But what more do you expect to find?"

"I don't expect to find anything. But we are supposed to be investigating serious criminal activity, while Charlesworth takes us bird watching. It would be human nature for him to only show off the bits that he finds fascinating. The shiny surface. But in doing so, we're not being granted access to areas that might provide us with vital information, even if it doesn't mean anything to him."

"Agreed. And the late Barry Searle remains our only lead and connection to the kidnappings. We'll need to ask Thorpe to authorise a warrant."

"I know."

"He won't want to upset Sir Geoffrey Charlesworth. He hasn't got many friends left. Sir Geoffrey has really been the chief's only supportive voice in recent weeks."

"How do you mean?"

"As I mentioned previously, he has been quite damning in his opinion as to the lack of progress in this case. However, he has been using his weekly newspaper column to advise the public of the complexities of the investigation. Even declaring that the police need time. His last article was a particularly candid backing of the Super. It more or less stated that if he were removed from this case, then it would lose momentum rather than achieve any expediency. About which, no doubt, he's probably right."

Jack nodded pensively.

"But I'm sure that we can convince him of the significance, and it's not as though it is Charlesworth himself that is under investigation. Still, it would be potentially embarrassing for him if we were to go wading in with a warrant."

Inspector Wilson noticed that the DCI seemed to have stopped listening, his mind apparently elsewhere. She followed his puzzled gaze towards the cockpit. The peninsula ahead of them had grown larger and suddenly the waves in the tidally active channel had picked up. She eyed Robson enquiringly. "What's up?"

"Does he know something we don't?"

"Pardon?"

"Ol' maverick Mikey there. The same guy that laughed at us earlier when we mentioned life jackets."

She looked again, still puzzled. The skipper still wore his hat, but was now also adorned with a sturdy weatherproof jacket.

"Maybe he feels the cold up there?"

"Look at the bottom of the jacket."

Wilson looked again and for the first time took conscious note that the bright orange weatherproof jacket Mikey was wearing was filled more than expected given the slight build of the wearer. The lifejacket straps could be seen protruding beneath the bottom, where the jacket had ridden up slightly above the small of his back.

She looked back at Jack and shrugged.

"Force of habit?"

Robson responded with an incredulous chuckle and settled back in his seat while continuing to shake his head.

The North Somerset coastline glistened, as the dying sun peered through a rare hole in the grey cloud cover. The rocky shore and dramatic rust-coloured cliffs, with their luscious green blanket, all contributed to the breath-taking vista. Not quite a Caribbean shore, Emma thought to herself, but it had an honest and rugged beauty of its own. A beauty that had captivated her since first arriving in the West Country.

Jack was surprised by the speed of their progress on the return voyage.

"Impressive timing Mikey!" he shouted, making himself heard above the cocktail of noise caused by the wind and turbulent sea, along with the engine roar.

Mikey turned his head slightly to give a nod. It was then that Jack noticed the jagged rocks in their path beyond and decided it would be wise to avoid disturbing their captain any further until he had finished negotiating their route around the peninsula.

Both Jack and Emma were oblivious to the expertly concealed operation that was taking place in the cockpit. The skipper elevated his lanky frame from its previous hunched position, as they approached within a hundred yards of the aggressive ridge. Jack had just begun to consider that the peninsula didn't seem familiar as Emma let out a gasp. They both watched with equal disbelief as their skipper leapt from the edge of the boat, not before adjusting the throttle control to maximum.

Emma's reaction was swift. *Albatross* threatened to go out of control as she raced towards the cockpit. The locking device that had been fitted prevented her from altering either the course or velocity that Mikey had set for them. The wall of rocks appeared like giant shark's teeth only forty yards away.

"We'll have to jump!"

The panic in her scream released Jack from his frozen state. She leapt from the boat only a second before it made its initial contact with the rocks. The boat, along with DCI Robson, left the surface of the Channel with an echo of thunder that rebounded off the surrounding cliffs. *Albatross* gained a good twenty metres of air before crashing back to the water surface in utter wreckage.

*

Inspector Wilson tuned her mind into its well drilled ocean survival routine. She felt her body respond and within moments the effects of the freezing water temperature had been isolated and, for the time being, she succeeded in overriding the natural system reaction of panic. As she kept herself afloat, she could feel the tidal current dragging her against her will, towards the nearby serrated rocks. She knew that she would have to overcome a strong undercurrent in order to reach her target. A small area of pebbled shore had come into view each time the swell raised her enough to be able to estimate the distance.

About a hundred yards.

As her head bobbed up again she watched the figure in the orange jacket climb aboard another craft.

Thank god, the lifeguard boat is already in the area!

Pieces of fibreglass debris had risen to the surface around her, but her partner had not shown the same instant buoyancy. She tried to evaluate if Jack had been on board the vessel at the time of impact.

The fierce swell covered her again and she tipped her head back in an effort to consume more air as she bobbed back to the surface again. Her muscles had begun to tighten against the cold water. As she heard the prop engine of the lifeboat roar into action, she waved frantically to draw attention to herself, not knowing how much longer she could keep herself afloat. She came back to the surface after being smashed by another wave, and could no longer hear the boat engine. She listened, desperately trying to tune into the sound of the prop above the roaring sea and wind. Finally, she located the sound again.

Why is it growing fainter?

The swell lifted her so that she momentarily had a view of her immediate surroundings. Fibreglass lay around her, splintered and smashed. Then she caught a glimpse of the boat again, moving. She watched it get smaller and realised the sound of the engine had all but disappeared, as the next wave moved in and swallowed her.

Fuck! Fuck! They've fucking left us!

As the process of rational thought ran its course, she ranked her chances of survival as desperately poor, diminishing every second she remained stationary. She was mindful, that like her, DCI Robson hadn't donned a life jacket. However, her new partner probably wasn't equipped with the same training and experience at dealing with such situations. Few were. Risk versus benefit analysis informed her to save her own skin first, but she told herself she could afford five minutes to search for her partner, who would surely be incapacitated.

In her frantic efforts, she hadn't paid attention to her own growing exhaustion, until it threatened to sap her last ounce of endeavour. After surveying the area for ten minutes; having gone a little deeper with each dive, Inspector Wilson decided to increase the radius of her examination.

It was another five minutes later that she took cognisance of her diminishing strength, forcing her to acknowledge that she had run out of time. Her reserves were empty, but the good news was that the beach was now only fifty yards off, having battled free from the drag that had attempted to bind her to the rocky peninsula.

With both athletic and mental endurance, she dipped her head into the water and used her last reserves to power through the strong current towards the stretch of shore. It would not have been obvious to anyone watching that the athletic form cutting through the water was in any trouble, as each stroke was expertly executed. Neither would it have been evident that the amount of effort used for each movement had been calculated such that she had just the right amount of fuel to make the pebbled cove.

She lay with her head just out of the shallow water, the side of her face resting on crossed arms, unable to move another muscle. After a couple of minutes her chest continued to heave, but she managed to crawl across seaweed, which popped occasionally beneath her light frame.

Inspector Wilson began to shiver, feeling her wet clothing cling to her, as she sat up on the dark wet sand and looked out into the Channel. Her eyes darted across the water surface, in desperate hope of spotting another survivor. The ghostly white remains of *Albatross* could still be seen in the distance, drifting on the swell, while another large shard of fibreglass was still being slammed against the rocky outcrop. However, both the water before her and the small pebbly cove to which she had retreated were apparently devoid of any other human life. The fine spring day had passed, leaving behind an increasingly cool air as evening descended. She pulled her mobile phone from her sodden trouser pocket and she felt her last vapour of hope disintegrate as she gazed at the blank, waterlogged screen.

The only means of gaining assistance would be to leave the shore. She made her way to the cliff face, searching for a way up. She couldn't see a route. Evidently this part of the shoreline had not been accessed by tourists. Shaking with cold and shock, she eyed the fifty-foot cliff face before her, searching desperately for a means of getting to the top.

She then noticed that the face on the eastern extremity of the bay was less severe and the formation of the cliff offered a potential rocky stairway to the higher ground. Inspector Wilson began to climb the steps carved by Mother Nature's deft use of her tidal chisel over the millennia. Her thoughts constantly reverted to her absent partner. She could not accept that he wouldn't make it, but she understood that she was taking her only available course of action.

Close to exhaustion, she halted after every five steps to catch her breath and looked back to survey the shore from her steadily improving vantage point. The thundering from a helicopter somewhere above seemed to be getting closer and almost distracted her from spotting the dark form slumped across the seaweed at the far eastern edge of the bay.

It was as if the voice calling from above had emanated from another dimension. She subconsciously chose to ignore it as she focussed on descending the rocky steps, stumbling breathlessly across the beach again. She stopped briefly, allowing her eyes to confirm that her target was indeed what she had allowed her mind to portray. However, the human form before her appeared lifeless – a blood-soaked head and torso, with a mess of spaghetti-like limbs attached.

There was no reaction as she slapped the figure's face and shouted. She leant across the flaccid man's chest and checked his airway. There was neither a breath nor pulse. She took up position beside the body and began to administer CPR, eyes wild with panic, praying that DCI Robson would respond.

CHAPTER 26

Time seemed a nebulous concept to Inspector Wilson as she sat slumped in the soft, high-backed chair in the stereotypically bland hospital surroundings. A full twelve hours had elapsed since the helicopter had delivered them to the accident and emergency department. However, to her, time had shrunk to nothing. The hospital staff had stopped answering her when she enquired after DCI Robson, and as far as she knew, the miracle that she wished for still eluded the medical team.

The sight of Superintendent Thorpe bursting through the double doors at the end of the long corridor brought her back to the present, whatever that was. After a glance at the white clock on the wall, she re-emerged suddenly from her trance. Her emotional defence system advised her to give up hope, and prepare for the inevitable, tragic news.

Under different circumstances, the sight of the large, overweight frame trundling along towards her in a half running, half skipping gait, may well have seemed comical. He slowed up as he spotted her, alone in the rest bay that was set back from the vinyl-floored thoroughfare. His reddened face displayed intense concern as Emma rose gingerly from her seat in the recovery area in reaction. He paused in front of her long enough to take several panting breaths.

"Wilson … " He seemed to notice the hiss of his own tongue and adjusted his tone. "What in the Lord's name has happened?! Are you okay?"

She knew from her reflection in the lavatory mirror earlier that her appearance went some way to revealing how battered she felt, yet she could only think of one response.

"I'm fine, sir."

"Robson?"

She returned his stare. Inspector Emma Wilson had never shown emotion to anyone other than family members, and the difficulty she felt at that moment in keeping it together compounded the tight throbbing at the pit of her stomach.

Thorpe knew his inspector well enough not to overdo the sensitivity, and opted to ignore the tear that escaped one of her bloodshot eyes, a sign of emotion that had never been shared between them before. Still, he adopted a gentle demeanour as he helped her back into the chair and sat beside her, his hand on her arm.

"You've been through hell and you need to get some rest. Can you just tell me what's happened to you both? Take your time."

She shook her head and fixed her eyes on the tiled floor. The silence of the last few hours had been replaced by the sounds of voices and the clattering of catering trolleys, accompanied by an aroma of toasted bread, indicating that the breakfast routine was underway. Emma considered the sudden eruption of activity to be quite in contrast with the peace of the deserted hospital overnight. Then, only the distant beeping sounds had denied her complete tranquillity, as the nurses carried out their disciplined observation schedule through the night. She had been resolute in her insistence that she didn't want to remain in bed, and she knew that the skeleton staff wouldn't be able to dedicate any further time to imploring that she return to her room. As her emotions whirled uncontrollably, she felt some regret for not heeding their advice.

The sight of his normally resilient inspector in such disarray seemed to dent Thorpe's energy, and he appeared to take stock of the implied seriousness of the situation. He removed his hand from her arm and allowed his head to drop dejectedly. At that moment, the double doors that separated them from the operating theatres and recovery wards swung open, announcing the entrance of a surgeon still in operating attire. The tired-looking specialist's serious countenance was offset by the nurse who accompanied him, presenting a doubtlessly well-rehearsed display of sympathy. Emma recognised the surgeon from some indeterminate time earlier, when he had given discourse on the desperateness of the situation after DCI Robson had just been admitted.

She braced herself for the impending news while Thorpe exchanged introductions with the surgeon. The plain white walls and empty seats offered no solace. She had not struggled to maintain perspective to such a degree since experiencing the sudden death of her mother. Aged sixteen, life had not yet equipped her with the tools to cope. But eventually she did cope, subconsciously vowing to live after the model of her much-adored mother. She looked up from concentrating on her breathing cycle to discover that the surgeon had now turned his attention from the Superintendent.

"How are you feeling Inspector Wilson?"

She gulped deeply, desperately not wanting the conversation to proceed, and so keeping the inevitably sad conclusion at arm's length.

"Physically, okay."

Emma Wilson had experienced this kind of small talk before. She found the approach warm yet futile at the same time. Any tactic designed to reframe the mind's reaction to unwanted messages seemed flawed to her.

"Yes, well your obs are looking good, considering the circumstances," the surgeon continued, as he glanced at the clipboard the nurse had placed in his palms. "Quite an impressive recovery rate. But we'd like to see you taking it easy for a while yet. You seem to have escaped relatively unscathed, physically, as you say, compared with your colleague."

The ability to respond totally eluded her, so instead she sat in silence, awaiting the dark confirmation. She hoped that the surgeon hadn't heard Thorpe's question.

"How's DCI Robson?"

The pause seemed to be unnecessarily long.

"He's not out of the woods yet. But I'm pleased to say that he is now quite stable."

For a moment, Wilson dared not accept that the news had sounded far more positive than she had prepared herself for.

She listened to her own instinctive query.

"What prognosis?"

The surgeon seemed to recognise the pleading eyes which accompanied the query and responded with a subtle nod that informed Emma that the situation hadn't been overcome yet.

"We need to see how the next twenty-four hours go. The fact that he is even still with us at all is a minor miracle. Thanks in no small part to the first aid that was administered to him at the scene."

Emma took no pleasure from the complimentary feedback.

"We don't know how long he had stopped breathing by the time you found him. His external injuries have been dealt with. However, there may have been some internal bleeding, so we have induced a coma as a precaution while we monitor the situation further. Would you like to see him briefly?"

Emma nodded as her mind raced over the potential outcomes. Thorpe responded:

"Thank you, we would."

They walked along a short corridor and stopped outside a door marked *High Dependency Unit*.

Inspector Wilson was reminded of her favourite novel *Frankenstein* as they entered the silent space. The patient, connected to an array of wires, looked at peace and a mask was positioned over the lower part of his face. *Artificial life*, Emma thought to herself. A tear fell onto the patient's unconscious face as she leant across to kiss his cheek. She abandoned any remaining stoicism and did not attempt to stem the flow of emotion now. The release afforded her clarity, as she realised for the first time what had driven such uncharacteristic weakness:

she cared a great deal for the man lying helpless in the bed. She fell into the nearest chair, caught her head in both hands, and sobbed.

CHAPTER 27

Wilson looked up at the clock on the office wall and raised her slim eyebrows in frustration. It had taken an hour out of her day, and still Thorpe insisted on running through the events from three days ago, now for the tenth time. She couldn't remember any other time she had experienced forty-eight hours of doing nothing and she felt glad to be back in the action. However, she had described the scene to Thorpe at the hospital and he had visited her at home twice, to check if her recollection had altered or whether she had remembered any further detail. She felt that the time for procrastination was over, but the sudden knock on the office door prevented her from telling the Superintendent so, although her eyes had already revealed her general feelings.

"Enter," Thorpe boomed.

Inspector Wilson felt her pulse race as she watched the proverbial elephant materialise. The receptionist acknowledged the affirmative nod from her boss and allowed a sorrowful-looking Sir Geoffrey Charlesworth to pass her. He entered the open door and made a beeline for Emma, taking her hand in both of his. She couldn't be sure of the emotion that caused her to tremble slightly as she looked into his eyes. If the feeling was anger, it soon subsided at the sight of tears welling up in his eyes.

"Inspector Wilson, how are you? I cannot tell you how mortified I have felt over this incident – I feel personally responsible. I wanted to see you sooner."

Emma looked back at him, as he continued.

"When Superintendent Thorpe told me what had happened, I couldn't quite believe it. I just had to track that scoundrel down for myself." He had lost a fraction of his normal eloquence and shook slightly. "I just can't believe it."

"Oh … " Emma began to respond.

"Sir Geoffrey," Thorpe rose from behind his desk somewhat intimidatingly as he intervened, "this Mikey guy seems to have disappeared. But with respect, sir, we don't wish for you or any other member of the public to place themselves in danger, nor must we entertain the idea of vigilante investigation."

Charlesworth appeared scalded.

"No, of course Superintendent. But I feel more than a little responsible for this. I arranged the transport for your officers and, from what you have already told me, my skipper has made a deliberate attempt to take their lives. I may not be able to take the law into my own hands, but I can sure as damned do all I can to help."

"That is appreciated, sir. But unless there is any more information that you can give us, then there seems little that you can do."

The usual, naturally authoritative demeanour seemed to have escaped the island owner, as he nodded dejectedly.

"I'm sorry. I find it an incredible embarrassment that I cannot even advise you of the rascal's full name. Be assured, the casual nature of my employment will change. Please tell me that there is better news on DCI Robson?"

Wilson felt a pang of guilt at the discovery that her instincts about the Superintendent's inaction had apparently been unfounded. He had evidently acted to interrogate the owner of the island already regarding his workforce, and the reality appeared to have taken a heavy toll on Charlesworth.

"He's remarkably well, all things considered," remarked Thorpe. "His recovery since being brought out of the coma has impressed the medical team. It looks like our own local hero here got to him in the nick of time."

Sir Geoffrey's eyes flickered and Emma felt a degree of pity at the personal responsibility he seemed to have assumed for the incident. She thought again of her colleague. She had found it difficult to contain her emotion before him during her visit the previous day, and she realised that her demeanour must have come across as rather heartless in her impassive show of phlegmatic concern. But the sight of DCI Robson in a wakened state of consciousness had been something that, at one point, she hadn't dared to hope for, let alone the miraculous prognosis announced by the surgeon that he shouldn't experience any lasting damage.

She noted the peculiarly penetrating look that Thorpe seemed to give Charlesworth as he gave a sigh to indicate his clear relief at the news. It didn't seem necessary to Inspector Wilson to impose further guilt on the man. Noticing her watching, Charlesworth nonchalantly swept the scrutiny aside.

"That's good news at least," he offered gently, as he gave them both a farewell nod. He turned as he reached the doorway.

"Please, please let me know if I can help, won't you officers? Give DCI Robson my best regards."

CHAPTER 28

His uninvited flirtation with mortality on the North Somerset coast seemed an aeon ago, as Jack hobbled through his front door. A break had been forced upon him, even though he had tried to persuade the Superintendent that it would not be beneficial to the momentum of the case. Thorpe and Wilson, however, had presented a united front in ordering him to take a weekend at home before continuing. He was mildly intrigued by the unmistakable affection in his partner's manner, particularly, which had been evident however hard she seemed to have been trying to disguise it.

His doubts evaporated, though, as the little girl raced along the small hallway and leapt into his arms.

"Daddy, have you hurt yourself?"

"Not much, just banged my head. How are you little lady? I've missed you!"

Jasmine giggled, not noticing her father suppressing a wince as she squeezed his neck.

"But what about your arm, Daddy, did you bang that too?"

"Yeah, Daddy's been a bit accident prone, but I'm fine now."

He felt he could read Sarah's mind as they exchanged reserved smiles over the top of Jasmine's shoulder.

"Well, it's a good job that Daddy has come back for a rest, isn't it Jasmine? So that we can look after him for a few days, eh? Shall we start by showing him the cake that we've baked?"

"Come on, Daddy!"

*

Jack and Sarah sat across the living room from one another, for a while listening to Jasmine and her friend re-enacting the mundane lives of the adults that they witnessed daily, using for props the extensive assembly of dolls and soft toys from the child's bedroom.

"So, how has the case been going, dare I ask?"

"Oh, you know, slowly. But I'm hopeful that we're getting somewhere."

"So I see. You're looking well for someone that's taken to freefalling on rocks."

"I think if I'd landed on the rocks, I'd be in a slightly worse state."

"But your boat crashed into some rocks?"

Jack left out certain details, such as the matter of the incident apparently being a deliberate attempt on his life. He fended off the lecture for half an hour, repeatedly assuring Sarah that he had no intention of causing Jasmine any further hurt in her life.

"You were lucky Jack. *We* were lucky. You must take care."

She could tell that the lecture had worn out its recipient for one day. "Superintendent Gibson has been enquiring after you. He left a message saying he wants to see you while you're here."

Jack raised his eyebrows.

"He's left me about five voicemails. I've only just picked up a replacement phone."

"He wanted to know how long you'd be back for."

"I'll call him tomorrow."

"How long *will* you be staying Jack?"

"Just the weekend."

The lack of expression on Sarah's face was enough to convey the message on its own, but she responded anyway.

"Jasmine's missed you. She has nightmares when you're away."

"I don't want to be away any longer than I have to, Sarah. It's the last thing I want."

"I'm worried about you, Jack."

"Don't be."

Neither of them had noticed the child in the doorway.

"Daddy, are you going away again?"

"Hey princess! Why aren't you playing with your friend?"

"She doesn't want to play the same thing as me. Daddy, I want you to stay here now."

"I know." Jasmine snuggled into his lap. "Guess where we're going tomorrow."

"Where?"

"The fair!"

"Yay!" She kissed her father and ran off. "I'm going to tell Chloe!"

CHAPTER 29

The street outside was peaceful, following the bustle of the Friday evening commute. Jack shook his head at the sight of the man parked outside talking on his mobile phone, determined to make that last call before finally surrendering to the weekend and going home to his family. A call so important that it couldn't wait another forty-eight hours. *Why don't people wake up to what's important?* Jack knew that the question was self-interrogative, as much as anything, as he drew the fairy curtains together, extinguishing the remaining burnt orange glow of spring dusk from the sleeping girl's room.

The sound of the boiling kettle offered a welcome disruption to the uncomfortable silence, which had allowed him to be alone with his thoughts again. He pondered on the rapid cycle of life, as he found himself, a lone father, alone on a Friday night with the prospect of a cup of tea and a good book. It seemed a mere blink of an eye away that he could have been engaging in similar preparations to those he guessed Sarah would be making at that very moment. Friday nights on the town were always his preference, with the carefree feeling they brought, knowing that the entire weekend still lay ahead.

He certainly didn't begrudge her the chance to socialise – goodness knows she had earnt it. He admired and indeed relied heavily on her maturity, which seemed to surpass her thirty-two years. Her attractiveness didn't elude him either, and he sometimes pondered what might have been had she not been like a sister to his late wife, and indeed to him.

More than anything, her apparent thirst for life and unwavering enthusiasm reminded him of Isabelle, who used to constantly expound on the importance of a couple having their own space. He firmly believed that he would never be able to love or trust anyone to that level again. He tore off a piece of kitchen roll and dabbed his eyes, before pulling the cord in the window recess to close the venetian blind.

After extinguishing the spotlights in the ceiling, he was midway between the kitchen and living room, when paranoia struck. He had acknowledged to himself many times that his own, personal alarm system was a little too finely tuned these days, but that rarely stopped him from acting on it. He placed the mug of steaming tea back on the kitchen side and returned to the window, without turning the lights back on.

He only needed to part the blind slats an inch to get a view of the black car parked in the street outside, still inhabited by the late finisher he had observed from upstairs earlier. Only, as far as he could tell through the subtly tinted car window, the occupant didn't appear to be engaged in his telephone conversation any longer – unless he had switched to hands-free, perhaps on re-evaluating the likely call duration.

The black hatchback happened to be parked as far away as possible from any of the street lamps. However, the residual lighting still illuminated the car faintly, which enabled Jack to make out that the face inside belonged to someone who suddenly seemed to show a particular interest in his property. *Is he supposed to be picking up one of the neighbours? You're looking up at the wrong house, pal.*

Allowing his suspicion to guide him, he exited the kitchen door to the side of the house and peered through the vertical wooden slats of the six-foot high gate, which was set back from the front of the house by a couple of feet. The bush at the front of the garden obscured his view from the new position, so that he could only see the top of the black car now. The foliage seemed to have flourished in his absence, now dominating and almost disguising the short picket fence at the boundary of the modest, ten-foot lawn. Jack returned inside, having lost the motivation to be community-spirited, and decided that he would let the visitor work things out by himself. But, unable to completely override his paranoia, he returned to the kitchen. What he witnessed next fed his preoccupation like petrol to a flame. The man was on his phone again, but this time was apparently using it to take images of Jack's property.

He quickly hobbled back to the gate and gently pulled it towards him as he held his thumb down on the metal catch. He ignored the pain as he crouched low and crawled forward, wincing at every muscle movement, while managing to remain in the shadows cast by the overgrown foliage. No engine noise could be heard, and the night was almost silent already, except for the odd, fading snatch of bird-song.

He made it to the small fence and, still on his knees, edged up gradually, using his strapped right arm as an anchor before the shooting pain reminded him to swap to the left. With the overgrown bush as cover, he elevated himself until he was able to peer over the worn wooden panel, and stumbled awkwardly at the sound of the male voice coming from above him.

"Hello there, Jack. It's a bit late for gardening?"

The sound of the engine revving nearby distracted Jack from formulating a response, and as he rose, he watched the black hatchback disappear with a slight wheel-spin. The driver did an effective job of concealing his face, and all that could be seen from the side profile as it whizzed past him was dark unkempt hair, bunched into a short ponytail. There were no other occupants visible in the vehicle.

"Good grief! And that's why we need speed bumps in this street!"

The sight of erratic driving evidently set the pulse racing in his bespectacled neighbour, who was, no doubt taking notes for his next meeting as community liaison chair.

"Couldn't agree more, Justin. Nice to see you again, I must get back inside to Jasmine."

"I'll be posting invites tomorrow for the next neighbourhood meeting Jack!" he called after DCI Robson as he disappeared inside.

Jack bolted the side door behind him and after checking on Jasmine, quadruple-checked the security of all doors and windows. His aching body and exhausted mind began to crave sleep, as they had done for the past few days. The medical team had authorised his discharge on the strict understanding that he would rest. He had been surprised at how the mere activity of a four-hour journey home had affected him. He strolled into his bedroom and leant over the soft mattress that called out to him. Falling onto his knees, he reached beneath the bed and yanked at the security box beneath. After sliding the numbers to match the date of Isabelle's birthday, he lifted the lid and removed the object.

As he sat downstairs in the armchair, he reflected on the hornets' nest that he had apparently stirred. He felt no closer now to the perpetrator of the kidnappings than he had at the beginning of his involvement in the case. The perpetrator, however, evidently felt that DCI Robson had already got too close. He shifted the automatic pistol on his lap and gazed out of the open curtains into the dimly lit street, before mentally preparing himself for the night shift.

CHAPTER 30

"This is most disturbing, Jack. I agreed to lend a valued detective to the provinces on the basis that the additional support would help resolve the case before it became any more of an embarrassment to the Home Office. I didn't foresee this."

The Superintendent looked thoughtfully towards Jack, who merely returned his gaze.

"But I really do wish you'd called me last night!"

Robson nodded tiredly at the almost paternal rebuke. He hadn't trusted his paranoia enough to sound the alarm, but it had been sufficient to have kept him up until Sarah arrived in the morning.

"Listen, Jack. If you want out, you know you just have to say the word. I'll just say that I need you back here with immediate effect."

"I haven't given up a job yet, John. Well, apart from … " Jack realised that there was no requirement to finish the sentence.

"You know I care about you and that little girl, Jack."

"I just want to know that she'll be looked after."

"It's already done, Jack. I'm also going to speak to Superintendent Thorpe to make sure you're given more protection. You don't take risks, okay? It seems that we might be dealing with something a little more organised than originally thought."

Superintendent John Gibson and DCI Jack Robson had a long history together in the force. Gibson had been Jack's senior ever since he could remember being in the CID. The bond had been further reinforced the day that Jack saved him from a man harbouring a grievance against Gibson for a previous conviction, and wielding a machete. Ever since Isabelle's passing, Gibson had become visibly paternal towards him, doing his best to wrap him in an invisible protective glove. Until now, Jack had never wanted the protection.

"By the way, Jack, this Charlesworth guy – I don't know how much you know about him. He's one well-connected gent, believe me. I mean, at the very top. So, if someone is using him to conceal a criminal organisation, then they must have some real balls."

"My thoughts exactly."

"Keep Charlesworth on side. You don't need him clamming up. But I can imagine what an embarrassment this all must be for him."

"Do you know him, John?"

"I know of him. We met, once. A dignitary like that gets to move in certain circles, which can easily coincide with events that the commissioner attends. I was the lucky 'plus one' at a function a few years ago, and he was there. He mixed with the very top brass though."

"If I can find something to take to him as tangible evidence that there is something going on behind his back, then I think we'll get the access we need."

"Take a couple of days before you bugger off back to the South West, Jack. We'll keep you under surveillance until you go, and then Jasmine and Sarah will be under our protection until this is wrapped up, okay?"

Jack nodded.

"Can I get you a coffee, Jack?"

"No thanks, John. Sarah's got Jasmine downstairs – we've a date with the fairground."

"Go and enjoy your time with her, mate. Then get some bloody sleep. I'll be keeping in touch, but you've no need to stay awake all night – we'll have you covered."

CHAPTER 31

For the first hour of the journey, DCI Robson had seriously considered turning back. It had been some time since he had last left his daughter in floods of tears and he didn't really have a clear plan about what he was going to do when he arrived.

He spent the latter half of the four-hour drive contemplating the case. It was becoming increasingly apparent that a criminal network had been operating under the nose of the head of the Charlesworth estate while he was otherwise engaged in his role of chief advisor for the ONR. The loss of Barry Searle had almost certainly been a strategic one, from the perspective of the kidnappers. It seemed that, with him out of the way, there was nobody yet involved in their investigations that could provide the information that would come even close to leading them to the perpetrators.

His stomach churned as he thought again about the man who had been watching his home on Friday night – what had he been there to do? He supposed it highly likely that the same person already knew that he was making his return to Somerset. The sleepy lanes that led to his hotel would normally have evoked a feeling of relaxation, but Robson's anxiety only grew as he considered what might lie ahead. There was something else that prevented the tightness in his stomach from subsiding, no matter how laterally he constructed a mental map of the investigation.

A car behind had been getting progressively closer as they wound through the lanes. The headlamps beaming menacingly into his rear-view mirror amplified the irritation caused by a downpour that had begun. DCI Robson's heart thumped when the car screeched around him as they arrived at the beginning of a 200-yard straight and raced along his flank. He had half expected the vehicle to stop before him, but it continued and within twenty seconds was lost out of sight.

*

As he approached the large entrance of the hotel foyer, DCI Robson felt a tingle down his spine as he admired the desirable female form accompanying the stout fellow inside. He approached Superintendent Thorpe, with Inspector Wilson beside him smiling pleasantly.

"Good to see you again, Jack."

Thorpe eyed him as he they shook hands.

"Thanks sir, you too."

He nodded slightly awkwardly to his female colleague. He enjoyed her fragrance close-up, as she moved in and gave him a brief, unexpected hug.

He spoke only to mask his awkwardness.

"I didn't expect a welcome reception."

"Superintendent Gibson has explained the incident outside your home. I understand that we have no positive confirmation as to the man's motives. However, considering the recent events, we've agreed that you should be given some protection."

He nodded to a big man in a suit stood a few yards from them.

"This is DS Wilkins. He's also joined us from the Met for a while, and will be supporting you both, until further notice."

"Fine."

There was a brief silence, as Thorpe seemed to be trying to read his seconded DCI's state of mind.

"Okay, I'll let you get settled in anyway. I just wanted to be here to let you know, and to see for myself how you are. I hope to catch up with you both tomorrow. I'm on my way to a meeting now, and will be doing the same for most of tomorrow."

Robson gave a confident nod during the further silent interlude.

"Just take care, Jack. We need to get our heads together before deciding on the next course."

"See you tomorrow maybe then, sir. And thank you."

They watched Thorpe's broad shoulders depart the foyer, his head towering high above those he passed, as if he were a teacher traversing a school lobby.

Jack switched his attention from his partner at the other end of the bar, and gazed out on to the manicured front lawn of the hotel and rain-soaked greenery, which glistened in the late afternoon sun that had arrived. His mobile phone danced on the glass-topped table, which amplified the vibration sufficiently to distract Inspector Wilson and DS Wilkins, who both looked in his direction. He answered the phone, curtly.

"Robson."

The voice at the other end was familiar, but there was a discernible level of anxiety in its tone, DCI Robson maintained his cool.

"Where are you now? Right – we'll come along in the morning then, if that suits you?"

Robson noticed the pace of his heart had increased a notch, as he replaced the phone on the table top and considered the implications of the message. He drew in a deep breath and parked the call in the back of his mind, as he observed Wilson greeting the man and woman who had entered the bar at that moment. As they approached, he returned their smiles and stood to accept the outstretched hand of DS James Matthews and his research assistant, DC Trudy Sanders.

The laptop was on the table before the waiter had finished taking their drinks orders, and for the next two hours, Matthews and Sanders described their findings from the last forty-eight hours of research.

Following a second large Americano, Jack felt what was becoming the familiar onset of a thumping head, which had begun to block any further receptiveness to the sheer volume of data being expounded. From time to time, Matthews would peer over the top of his laptop screen to indicate that he awaited some input from his DCI into their concerted elimination process.

After three hours of ruthless data rationalisation, they had managed to discount several names. No doubt it had been a worthwhile exercise, but Jack thought he saw the same sign of relief in Emma that he felt himself, as they watched their two eager colleagues depart.

Noticing the emerging signs of fatigue in the DCI as he clearly relished the taste of fresh air from the front steps of the hotel, Inspector Wilson made her excuses. The onset of weariness continued to take Robson by surprise. His mind had just about shut down for the evening, but then he recalled the phone call from three hours earlier, and briefed his partner accordingly. After their afternoon of dogged analysis, she appeared invigorated by the unexpected development. They had eliminated more Mike's and Michael's from the North Somerset region than they had remaining on the list, especially when they applied a filter that eliminated all those without a sailing licence. But the list was still built on probability and assumption. Suddenly, their immediate hopes were focussed on their appointment in the morning.

CHAPTER 32

Inspector Wilson rapped the front door for the tenth time, but the outcome remained the same. Shouting through the letterbox hadn't borne fruit either, and they both turned reluctantly and began to descend the steps, in what was becoming a familiar routine. It seemed the appointment wasn't going to go ahead as planned. The detectives exchanged ironic grins, both wondering if there would ever be a time they would find the owner of number 2 Wier View at home. This time they had been invited, yet the owner still wasn't around to receive them.

The sound of the door opening behind caused them both to stop in their tracks and turn in unison. The door that had taken a beating from them seconds earlier remained firmly closed, but on the threshold of the house next door stood an elderly man. He carefully placed the bunch of keys in the pocket of his coat, which seemed overly heavy for the time of year, and more than enough to shield his slight frame from the faint breeze, which ruffled the grey wisps that hung out beneath the flat cap. He tucked his shopping bag under one arm and took a firm grip on the aluminium railing as he eased his slightly crooked frame down the steps. Descending one at a time, he stopped every few steps to cast them an inquisitive glance. After pausing for breath at the bottom, he tipped his cap to them.

"You after Jonny then?"

"Yes, sir," responded Wilson. "Have you seen him at all?"

"Not seen 'im around for a couple of days, actually. Doesn't mean 'e hasn't been around though, of course. Hasn't popped in for a cuppa since last week. Not like 'im, really, but course 'e's not 'imself at the moment. Just hope e's lookin' after 'imself."

"Okay. Thank you, sir."

"Only other place 'e can be at this time of day is the harbour. That'd be my bet."

For a further five minutes, they found themselves trapped in a conversation that ranged from the decline of the fishing industry and the loss of character that their ancient little harbour suffered as a result, to the lamentable situation of long-standing families from Porlock moving from the area to seek work in other industries.

Eventually, they managed to progress by providing a taxi for the man – who turned out to be called Ted – down to the harbourside shops. They parked up facing the strip of huge rocks that formed the boundary between land and sea, and made their way towards the weir gates. The mist still hung a blanket over the Channel beyond, which bared its white teeth beneath the grey, overcast sky, demonstrating its awesome power.

The harbour master was the epitome of a man of the sea. He pulled his chair backwards as they entered his office, and removed from beneath the wooden desk his portly stomach, which threatened to burst through his yellow waterproof dungarees at any minute. He squinted as Inspector Wilson presented her badge.

"Hello, sir. We are from the Criminal Investigation Department. We're very sorry to intrude, but would it be possible to have a quick word?"

"Of course you can, my love, come in, come in."

DCI Robson wondered if all men of the sea ended up with rosy cheeks and what seemed an impenetrable joviality.

"Thank you, sir. I'm Inspector Wilson and this is my colleague, DCI Robson."

"Pleased to meet you both, I'm sure. I'm Jacob. Jacob Miller."

"Pleased to meet you too, Jacob. I'll come straight to the point. We're just trying to locate one of the fishermen. Do you happen to have seen Jonny Searle?"

The joviality disappeared without trace and, unexpectedly, he began to stutter his words slightly.

"Oh well, let me see, perhaps not for a day or two. Jonny normally lives down here or on his boat. But since that business with poor Barry, he's spent most of his time in the Ship drowning his sorrows."

"I see," said Emma.

"Would you happen to know if he was out on his boat now, by any chance?" Jack intervened.

"No, sir. His boat's moored up yonder, where 'tas been for the past two or three days. Is everything okay, might I ask?"

They both studied the area that Jacob was continuing to point towards and recognised *Orinoco*.

"Perhaps we'll call at the Inn. If you see Jonny, would you be so kind as to tell him we were looking for him, Jacob?" asked Emma.

"Yes, ma'am. I'll walk across with you, early lunch!"

If he had seemed concerned or alarmed at first to discover that their enquiries related to Jonny, the harbour master's anxiety seemed to have faded as quickly as it had materialised.

*

DCI Robson and Inspector Wilson both ducked as they entered the inn behind Jacob Miller's bulk. Several tables were occupied, and the volume of speech increased as the door closed behind them. The gaggle of people in fishing attire that were huddled at the end of the bar waved towards the harbour master. Cheery banter ensued as Miller made a beeline for them. Robson and Wilson both nodded at the bartender as they followed along the length of the bar.

Jack decided he would cut to the chase, rather than provide any further opportunity for humour for their self-appointed host, but the rotund spirit stole the limelight.

"Phil; I'd like to introduce you to a couple of friends of mine!"

He was clearly used to adopting centre stage in this particular theatre.

"Detective Inspector Emma Wilson and—"

"DCI Robson,"

Jack offered his hand to the landlord, who took it in a firm shake.

"Any of you boys seen Jonny about for a bit?" Jacob continued, in his attempt to lead the enquiry.

The huddle of fishing folk sniggered as they looked at the landlord, seemingly in muted expectation.

"He was in here last night, although he might not remember it!"

The sniggers turned to hearty laughter.

"Until late?" Emma adopted a patient tone.

"You could say that. Those two over there had to practically carry him out of here."

The barman, whose accent indicated that he was not local, pointed towards a couple of burly men who stood amongst the group of locals.

"Was he making trouble?" asked Jack.

"No, no. Jonny never makes trouble. We look after our own here, sir. Jonny's had a bloody rough time, and it was nice to see him allowing himself a bit of a knees-up last night, even if it's short-lived. It got to eleven o' clock and he couldn't really stand on his own. So, Larry and Foxy over there saw him into a cab."

Two men stepped forward as Jack moved closer to the huddle.

"Is that right, fellas?"

The older of the two men answered.

"Sure is. Don't think he were gonna make it up that hill on his own!"

"Reckon he'll still be in his pit now though," added the other man, "nursing a serious hangover I imagine. He were on the spirits, seriously!"

"Oh dear, thank you." Emma offered an understanding smile.

*

For the second time that day, Jack hammered the front door to number 2 Weir View. Only earlier, he and his colleague hadn't noticed the splintering along the edge of the wooden door jamb. His nostrils caught a familiar whiff of delicate perfume as Emma reacted to his apparent distraction and leant across.

"Stand back."

Jack retreated two steps and braced his right shoulder for the impact. The door gave relatively easily after the second attempt.

"Jonny, it's CID, are you in?" Emma shouted from the hallway.

"I'll check upstairs."

He strode two steps at a time while Emma hurried into the living room where they had left a drunken Jonny on their previous admission to the residence. This time the room looked different. The chairs and sofa were out of position and the cushions strewn around the room. The drawers of the TV unit were open, and the contents spilt out onto the worn carpet. Emma walked out into the hall.

"All okay, Jack?"

"Be with you in a bit," Jack shouted, as he surveyed the devastation in the second bedroom, which like the first, had been turned upside down, almost literally. The mattress was no longer lying on the bed and the wardrobe, cupboards and drawers had either been completely emptied or were left in disarray.

Downstairs, he found Emma in the kitchen, which was consistent with the chaos elsewhere. They looked at one another for a moment.

"Somebody was looking for something," Emma stated rhetorically.

"Yeah, but where was Jonny? Where *is* Jonny?"

The bang outside the back door startled them both. The fenced border that ran alongside the right-hand boundary of the garden was only waist high, which allowed them to locate the source of the sound. Peering through the pane into the small, scruffy back garden, it was evident that Ted had already returned from his shopping trip. They watched the elderly man carry a watering can from the shed at the bottom of his garden.

A key lying on the windowsill successfully opened the lock of Jonny's back door, and they walked out into the garden. The door had expanded in the frame and creaked as it was released.

"Hello again, Ted."

Jack tried a friendly smile, as the neighbour stood and watched them suspiciously, still in his thick, heavy coat.

"Hello there, my friend. I see you managed to track him down then, did you?"

"Not quite."

A disconcerted expression appeared on his face. Jack didn't give him enough time for a counter query.

"I don't suppose you recall anyone here looking for him last night or at any point today?"

"Uh no … oh, 'ang on. The electric people came early this mornin'. I were watchin' 'em through the window but they didn't seem to get any answer neither."

Jack's pulse quickened.

"I see. You're quite sure it was the electricity company?"

"According to the writing on their van it was!" The neighbour enjoyed his moment. "North Somerset Electrical Services."

"Could you describe the vehicle for us?" Emma enquired.

"Not much to describe apart from what I've told you. Just a white van. Big one, just like poor Barry used to drive."

Jack swallowed hard, as Emma continued the enquiry.

"Did you see the electrician?"

The man nodded thoughtfully.

"Yep. Two of them. I reckon Jonny must've given them a key, knowing that he wouldn't be in."

"Oh? Did you watch them enter the property, then?"

"Er, not quite. The flamin' phone rang so I left the window. It were me sister. She wanted me to pick her up some shopping. Anyway, when I returned, the van were still outside but the men weren't. That's all I can tell 'e."

"Ok. Thanks again, sir."

"No problem. Is Jonny okay, then?"

"Yes, he's fine."

It wasn't a lie, but Jack doubted that it was an accurate statement. He locked the kitchen door behind him and they both darted back to the car without speaking.

CHAPTER 33

The wind had picked up by the time they arrived, causing a light swell in the water. *Orinoco* could still be seen floating within the constraint of her tight moorings. They approached the harbour master's office and saw that the door was shut this time.

"Still in the pub?" suggested Jack from behind Emma's back.

Emma shook her head and gestured inside the window. As Jack peered over her shoulder, he could see a pair of size ten boots resting on the desk at the end of two plump legs crossed at the ankles. The chair was fully reclined, and the sleeping figure's head had fallen open-mouthed, in submission to gravity. Emma felt a degree of pity for Jacob Miller's wife as they passed the door, which seemed to vibrate to the pneumatic drill-like sound of snoring coming from within.

She led the way down the narrow stone steps to the water's edge. They sidestepped carefully along the uneven dockside until they reached *Orinoco*. There was only one other vessel in dock now, the other fishermen having started their afternoon shift.

Emma tried to peer through the nearest window, but the view was obscured by fully drawn net curtains. She jumped as the boat began to rock, and glanced to her right to see Jack climbing aboard. He tried in vain to open the door to the cabin. He stumbled as the boat jolted and held onto the handle for balance, as Emma threw a lean but shapely leg over the last step and arrived on deck.

Jack braced his shoulder for use as a battering ram once again. The door bounced under his charge.

"Hmm, sturdier than you might think."

With his shoulder still feeling the full impact of its previous use, he knew he hadn't used his full force. As he adjusted his position to swap shoulders, he saw Emma pass as a flash across his vision. Inspector Wilson flew into the door with a kung fu-like manoeuvre, connecting in a huge impact with the base of her left foot. The door crashed open.

The cabin appeared to be in pristine condition, with nothing appearing to be out of place. Emma ventured towards the open hatchway to the port side of the control room and ducked inside. Jack was examining the collection of maps and the sound of Emma's muffled voice confused him until he turned and saw the opening from where the it had originated.

"Jack, quickly!"

The galley kitchen led to a modest living area. The scene of devastation was reminiscent of the condition of the house they had recently departed. It seemed that no pot, pan or item of crockery remained in the cupboards. Beneath the jumble of broken and bent objects lay the body of a man, face down in a red liquid that appeared to have congealed and dried onto the hard linoleum floor.

Emma was kneeling beside the casualty, holding one if his wrists.

"Jack, he's got a pulse. Call an ambulance!"

Jack was still listening to the emergency services operator confirm the circumstances back to him, as Emma deftly moved the dead weight into the recovery position. The side of the man's forehead came into view to reveal the source of the red liquid. It seemed that there had been some fortune in the prone position adopted by the unconscious man which had evidently applied sufficient pressure between head and floor to eventually stop the flow of blood. With the phone still held to his ear, Jack noted the bruises that indicated there had been a beating. Once the air ambulance had lifted the casualty, they remained on the boat to survey the scene in greater detail. It was not the first time that Emma had ever received praise from a medic for carrying out routine duties.

*

When they finally arrived at Taunton A&E, Jonny Searle was still in the medical assessment unit. Once the new arrival had been allocated a ward, the detectives ventured to pay him a visit. The staff nurse had worn an immovable, professional smile as she gave her instructions that they would be given no more than ten minutes with the patient, who was still under review.

It had just passed 8 p.m. when they walked into the almost silent ward of four bays. Two of the beds were unoccupied, with the third in the far corner next to a window being taken up by an elderly gentleman who seemed to be out for the count. They found Jonny Searle tucked in the first bay on their left as they entered. A loose-fitting hospital gown revealed a suggestion of the scale of his wounds, as he laid back in a slightly reclined position holding a mug of warm Horlicks in his unbandaged hand. Emma offered a doleful greeting.

"Hello, Jonny."

"Officers."

"How are you feeling, Jonny?"

"Like I've been hit hard."

Jack gave a conciliatory smile as he took the armchair to the left of Jonny's bed.

"Shall I get my own chair, Jack?"

Emma didn't wait for a response as she slid a chair across from the unoccupied bay next door. The exchange seemed to lift the patient's spirits momentarily.

"So," Emma continued, "do you remember anything about what happened to you, Jonny?"

"Up to a point. I spent the night on *Orinoco*, after, well, having a drink or two down at the Ship … "

"Oh? We heard that you had been taken home in a taxi. Did you change your mind?" Emma enquired, in a deliberately nonchalant tone.

Jonny looked sheepishly between the two detectives, seemingly swallowing a dose of pride before continuing.

"Unfortunately, I threw up all over the back seat. The driver weren't happy. He kicked me out, not before giving me a bloody bill for a valet."

Jack and Emma both nodded impassively. Seemingly satisfied that there was no judgement in the response, Jonny continued.

"So I locked myself in and got cosy. Next thing I remember is waking up freezing cold as day was breaking. The boat were rockin'. Me head were absolutely thumping, but I managed to get up and take a peek out, expecting to see some of the lads setting off. But there was no one about, nothing. The harbour master's office was still shut, so I knew it must've been early."

His hand trembled slightly as he took a noisy sip from the mug.

"Next thing, I hear footsteps on the deck, like someone's come aboard. I remember lookin' at the clock then and it were just before seven. The door knocked loudly, impatient, like. I shouted out to 'em to hang on to their bloody 'orses. All I remember is opening the door for some bloody great bloke to storm in, knocking me off me bloody feet."

Another loud slurp.

"I stumbled back up and he were bearing down on me. There were another guy right behind him. A tall, thin bloke – at least, compared to the huge fella."

Jack was pleased to see Emma had taken responsibility for note taking as Jonny continued.

"The big guy asked me something. For some information. Then the thin guy said it'd be easier if I just told 'em, then I wouldn't get hurt. I said I couldn't help and the big guy walloped me one. I think I smacked the back of my head on something as I went down."

Emma looked up from her notepad as Jack continued the questioning.

"What were they after, Jonny? Has this got anything to do with why you wanted to see us today?"

At that moment, a large, cheery looking man wheeled the drinks trolley past the ward, stopping at the entrance as he observed that the man in the first bay was entertaining visitors. He walked in with a confident smile, and leant forward.

"Can I get Jonny's visitors a nice hot drink?"

His accent seemed to be eastern European.

"Coffee please, thank you," said Jack.

"Same here, please," added Emma.

The man placed the two drinks on the side table together with a huge, vice-like hand.

"No telling matron now!" he murmured playfully, before swiftly exiting the ward again, whistling an unrecognisable tune to himself.

Emma and Jack returned their gaze towards Jonny, still waiting for his response. Jonny drank the remainder of his lukewarm beverage in one final gulp and continued, as he nodded in answer to DCI Robson's query.

"Some guy came up to me at Baz's funeral. He said he were a colleague of Baz. He were asking some fairly strange things, like who was taking over his house and things like that."

"Did you know the person?"

"No. Never knew the guy. But I kept bumping into him after that. Then never saw him again. Well, not until he arrived on my boat this morning."

"You're sure it was the same guy, the large man?" Emma queried.

"No, the other one. The thin chap. I'm not sure if I could pick out the big guy again in a crowd. Apart from his size, of course. But the thin chap had quite a memorable face. Like I've seen him around somewhere. Oh, 'an 'e 'ad a ponytail."

Emma exchanged a brief glance with Jack before returning to the notepad on which she scribbled. Jack remained silent, allowing the patient to continue.

"I explained to the guy that I was Barry's only remaining family and that I lived in the house with him. Then the questions got even stranger. The guy asked about his mobile phone – Baz's that is. He said he worked for Barry's boss and needed to get it back, because it contained some sensitive information that Barry were supposed to be delivering to him in relation to a client – I think he said."

Jack and Emma looked at one another again, before Jack asked:

"So, do you think that is what someone might have been looking for in your house?"

Jonny gave a semi-startled look, then relaxed his shoulders, as if accepting that it had been inevitable.

"They've been to the house, then?"

"Seems so," replied Jack. "Did the guy tell you his name when he introduced himself?"

"He did. But I can't remember. And I wasn't interested in asking him again for it. Think it were something like, maybe Mark?"

"So, do you actually know anything about this phone,

Jonny?"

Emma was looking directly at him. Jonny nodded as he made eye contact with her.

"It's hidden."

"Why didn't you just give it to them?"

Jonny suddenly transformed and hissed back.

"Because, Inspector, my brother was found lying on a beach with a fuckin' bullet lodged in 'is back! We may not have seen much of one another, despite supposedly sharing a house—" The break in his voice compelled him to pause. "I've had my best pal taken away. I've got nothing to lose. I'm not letting the bastards get away with it!"

"Why didn't you tell us about it before?"

One muscular shoulder escaped from the thin blue gown as he shrugged, slightly sheepishly.

"I don't really know. Trust? But I'm telling you now."

"Where is the phone, Jonny?" Jack gave no impression that he was irritated by the last comment.

"On the boat."

Despairing cringes appeared in unison on both the detectives' faces. Emma shook her head.

"You mean it was."

Jack placed his hands on his hips as he stood, in mild desperation.

"They turned *Orinoco* upside down after knocking you out, Jonny."

The patient appeared unmoved.

"They won't have the phone."

They both returned him hopeful, yet confused glances.

"How can you be sure?" asked Emma.

"Because it's in a place that those ignorant bastards wouldn't even know exists!"

His lower lip trembled as he lost his cool again.

"Will you tell us where we can find the phone, Jonny?" asked Emma tenderly, with a hand on his shoulder. Jonny wiped the tears from his eyes and nodded.

CHAPTER 34

Dr O'Hara fought to prevent his expression from betraying his horror, as he surveyed the scene before him. They had been led to the 'Town Hall' fifteen minutes earlier and he had counted another twenty-three people in the room, in addition to his own family. The others appeared to be in a relaxed state of fulfilment and excited anticipation. He had only been able to smuggle one of the masks from the surgery and was therefore alone in his immunity to the effects of the vapour that had been excreted from the vents into their rooms.

It had become a well-rehearsed routine. The gas didn't have a strong smell, but he had come to understand what it meant when the clunk sounded from inside the vent. It was a technique that allowed their captors full control of the crowd, apparently without the need for force. Dr O'Hara had observed the way the other residents, including his own family, acted under the influence of the drug that emanated from the walls and did his best to replicate the intoxicating effects.

He would lie on the bed and turn his face towards the wall, out of sight of the surveillance cameras, until the valve could be heard closing again. After another minute, the room would be clear of the pollution, which seemingly allowed their captors to enter without being exposed to the drug.

As they all sat around on the floor, cross-legged with vacant stares, he tried to gauge if there might be any unexpected allies among them. However, the rest of the crowd sat in their meditative state, in preparation for the long-awaited visit. The visit that would represent the completion of the planning stage, and therefore signal the commencement of the final phase. The crowd looked towards the door in wonder as the voice from the speaker announced the arrival of 'Noah'.

As the door opened and Noah entered, the crowd gasped in wonder at the messianic soul before them. Dr O'Hara wiped his perspiring palms on his knees as he studied the ceremonious entrance of the person that he had known by a different name, then focussed on the control of his breathing, as his racing heart threatened to initiate hyper-ventilation.

CHAPTER 35

Despite the dock being full of vessels, they were barely visible through the teeming rain. Inspector Wilson pulled up alongside the harbour wall and they stepped out into the uninviting conditions and put on weatherproof coats. She threw on a sou'wester that provided coverage to below the knees. DCI Robson noticed from the corner of his eye that she was eyeing his lightweight anorak mockingly.

"I didn't think to prepare for a fishing trip like you seem to have done."

"Course you didn't, city boy. Shall we?"

They had arrived early and the harbour was deserted, as was typical for a Saturday. If the weather improved later, as predicted, the area would attract a modest throng of tourists.

Wilson pulled herself up onto the deck as the rain continued to bounce off the glistening fibreglass at a relentless frequency. Robson followed cautiously, maintaining his strong grip on the rail of the steps. He climbed aboard the deck to find his partner following the instructions that Jonny had given them.

He proceeded to gingerly traverse the deck, head down in a brace against the incessant downpour, and took hold of the rigging from the port side. They pulled the sodden material towards them in unison, which, as Jonny had promised, revealed a row of four valves that ran along the edge of the deck, beneath the gunwale. The scupper valves were a mirror image of those that were already exposed on the starboard side of the boat. Emma leant in towards the valve that was second in from the left of those that had been covered, then slid a slender outstretched hand inside. The hard rain bounced off the deck into their faces as she removed the sealed plastic bag.

*

The car windows were obscured by the steam that had been generated by their sodden attire. Droplets streamed from Inspector Wilson's hair, running down her face as she pulled apart the top of the plastic bag, and then carefully emptied the contents onto the towel that DCI Robson had placed ready on his lap. Jack held his thumb on the button that was located on the right-hand side of the device for a couple of seconds. The screen suddenly became illuminated and displayed the manufacturers logo, before stating its instruction: *Please enter your PIN.* He felt strands of wet hair strands touch the side of his neck as Emma leant across him slightly.

"Damn," she said, not noticing her partner's discomfort. "We'll have to get it to the techies."

"Hmm, yeah maybe," said Jack, as he turned to face her,

highlighting their proximity. Emma straightened in her seat abruptly.

"What do you mean, maybe?"

"Breaking into phones isn't always a quick process, is it?"

"No, but the alternative?" she raised her eyebrows at him, emphasising her comely deep-blue eyes.

"Simply entering the right code."

"Jonny?"

"Why not?"

She nodded slowly, and they agreed on returning to Jonny Searle.

Jack began to feel claustrophobic as the car vents continued to blast warm air up against the windscreen, and lowered the passenger window to release the oppressiveness. With the window down, he noticed the portly yellow form approaching, from which a booming, jovial voice now emanated.

"Hello there, officers! Looking a bit steamed up there!" chuckled the rosy cheeked harbour master."

Jack opened his mouth to respond but Emma had started to reverse out of the parking space. Jacob Miller gave them a mischievous wink.

"What's he doing here on a Saturday?" Jack speculated, more to change the subject than out of genuine interest.

The plump figure retreated as quickly as he had arrived. As they left the harbour with the wipers scraping rapidly across the front screen, they watched him trundle in the direction of the Ship Inn. He raised a plump hand above his left shoulder as they passed, without turning back to look at them, no doubt more focussed on the breakfast ingredients advertised on the blackboard that he plodded past.

CHAPTER 36

Robson could still taste the fast food in his gullet, despite having consumed it over two hours ago. It had seemed somewhat surprising to him that his partner had decided on that particular brunch option, given the opportunities to take in some local and slightly healthier fare. It had even necessitated a slight detour in order to locate the only such establishment for miles around, which explained why it was so heavily populated with teenagers, desperate to escape the shackles of the stubbornly bygone area. The rain had finally ceased after dropping a good six hours of water on the ground, leaving flooded roads and fields.

"That's the first time I've spotted him today," Wilson noted aloud, as she watched their newly appointed personal guard in the wing mirror. Jack observed the car in the passenger side mirror.

"He seems very clandestine, considering that we know he's supposed to be accompanying us."

He nodded a cheeky greeting towards the bodyguard, as Emma dialled the number displayed in front of her at the hospital car park. The athletically built man reciprocated unenthusiastically and Emma grinned as she witnessed the scene.

"Wouldn't you be pissed off? It's a pretty shit assignment for anyone, really."

"Yeah. I wonder what he's done to deserve this?" Jack pondered.

The ward was quiet as they departed the elevator on the second floor. Visiting hours were over until the evening and the hospital lunch time was complete. Jack looked twice when he recognised the friendly drinks attendant from the previous evening, at the end of the long corridor, heading in the direction of ward 2D.

"Looks like we might be in time for coffee." he said, watching the back of the man's colossal frame disappear around the corner.

"Another?" said Emma.

They rounded the corner of the corridor and headed for the empty ward desk. Jack peered into the office door expecting to find a nurse. In the silence, Emma watched the unattended drinks trolley just outside the entrance of 2D. It was the muffled sound of gurgling that seemed to escape from the ward that drew her forwards, eventually forcing her into a run as her instinct alerted her. As she passed the trolley and burst into the ward entrance, the giant turned his tree trunk neck to see who had joined them, while enormous hands remained wrapped around the throat of the occupant of the first bay. The sight of the blue face slumped on the pillow in the background stayed with her for some time after the event. She also remembered the colossus approaching her at unexpected speed, before it went dark.

*

DCI Robson returned the salutation of the unusually large man, as he rattled past with the drinks. His pace seemed at odds with the general atmosphere permeating the ward that afternoon. Not being certain that Inspector Wilson had ventured off to see if she could get more luck locating a nurse, he elected to chance entering 2D uninvited. Turning the corner into the ward, he noted that the elderly gentleman in the far corner was sleeping off his lunch. He decided at first to retreat when he saw the curtain had been closed around the first bay, evidently indicating the location of the nurse. He nearly didn't spot the shapely foot wearing the simple, familiar-looking pump protruding from beneath the curtain.

Dragging the curtain aside, he paused for a second to take in the scene before him. He took the felled young woman beneath the armpits and gently pulled her towards the high-backed chair. Her chin remained resting on her chest, with signs of a heavy impact to her left temple area. He became aware of a retching sound and adjusted his gaze to see that Jonny held one hand on his chest, the other holding his throat, while he gasped desperately. Jonny accepted the plastic cup containing the remnants of tepid water, and after a couple of sips he responded to DCI Robson's interrogative gaze, managing to rasp, "the drinks guy … " Judging that his partner had begun to regain consciousness, he pulled the red cord above the bed and bolted from the ward.

He passed the abandoned drinks trolley outside the lifts and continued onto the stairwell. The large frame that was their own security guard appeared alarmed, as he realised that the second maniac sprinting through reception in the last few minutes was one of the detectives he was supposed to be minding. Robson was about to tell DS Wilkins to lock down the hospital, but realised it was too late as, over the broad-shouldered sergeant, he watched the familiar-looking black hatchback speed away from the hospital drop-off area. The hulking drinks man was still in the process of closing the passenger door, as the front wheels screeched and the car lurched forward.

*

The swelling on the side of her face glowed beneath the lighting in the hospital cafe, as Emma sipped her tea. Despite her obvious frailty at that moment, Jack was struck by her resilience, as he watched her vitality return with each mouthful of cookie washed down with another slurp.

The fact was that it wasn't in Emma Wilson's nature to dwell on setbacks or hardship. Her father had instilled that in her from the day he became her sole guardian when she was five years old. The degree by which she missed her mother could not be understated, although she found it more upsetting that her memories faded with the passing years. She had never felt robbed of parental love. It seemed to be her intrinsic ability to get back up after any fall both physically and emotionally, which had already impressed her instructors and superiors during the course of her short career. Along with a standout, sharp mind.

"So, you didn't chase after the car?" asked Emma.

"It was too late, but I sent Wilkins out after them."

He slid the plastic chair back against the small square table, and looked around the room apologetically as the metal legs screeched against the hard floor. They walked abreast at a slow pace, both nodding to the lady at the till as they departed.

"So, are you saying it was the same car that you saw outside your house?"

She reacted to the twinge somewhere inside her head and held her fingertips to the source of the pain. Her left temple burnt beneath her cool fingers.

"Just possibly," said Jack introspectively.

The bell sounded, and the elevator doors jolted slightly before parting. The huddle of staff stepped aside to allow them to exit. Jack felt the mobile device inside his jacket, as he followed Emma on to the second floor.

While his elderly ward companion sat studying a puzzle in his crossword book, Jonny was undergoing another examination. The nurse gave them a more hospitable look compared to the commanding glare they had received from the ward sister upon arrival.

Emma smiled at Jonny, and watched the nurse remove the clip from his forefinger. As the armband around his bicep deflated, the portable machine to which it was connected played a short tune.

"It seems that everything is pretty stable now Jonny," informed the nurse. "Just pull that cord if you need anything, okay?"

"Thanks."

The nurse turned and wheeled her trolley of gadgets across to the sink.

Jonny fixed a gaze at Emma's left temple and took a short, sharp intake of breath through pouted lips.

"How are you feeling Inspector?" he enquired hoarsely.

Emma smiled, but Jack thought her expression betrayed her true feelings.

"Just a little headache. What about you?"

He shrugged.

"They say I should still be discharged tomorrow, so it can't be too bad, can it?"

Jonny tipped his head forward slightly revealing a receding patch on his crown, and asked in a quiet rasp:

"Did you find it?"

Jack felt quiet admiration for the way Searle had dealt with the recent attempt on his life as though it had been merely an accidental fall. He withdrew the mobile phone from his inside coat pocket and handed it to the patient. Jack and Emma both turned abruptly in reaction to the frozen look of fear on the patient's face, as he looked over their shoulders at the hulk standing just inside the ward.

"Oh, don't panic Jonny, he's with us."

Emma gestured for their burly security guard to join them at the bedside and proceeded with brief introductions, explaining that he had been appointed to protect their witness until further notice. The large man exchanged handshakes, displaying a muscular forearm, then plodded from the ward.

The nurse, who had just completed her examination of the elderly gentleman, Jonny's only other ward companion, washed her hands and followed DS Wilkins from the ward. Jonny had returned his attention to the phone in his lap.

"Can you turn it on? It's got a passcode," asked Jack.

A grin began to form on Jonny's face for a couple of seconds, perhaps slightly cocky, then disappeared, as if remembering the circumstances by which the device had ended up in his possession in a hospital bed. He held the button at the top of the phone and waited for a couple of seconds. The thin, bloodied tube emanating from the cannula dropped alongside his thumb, as he raised his hand slightly. Extending his forefinger, he pressed the lower half of the screen, entering four separate digits. He returned the phone to DCI Robson, without any indication of satisfaction.

Inspector Wilson rose from the chair to look over Robson's shoulder to see that the phone was now displaying its home screen.

"Only ever one code that brother of mine would have used. He wasn't very imaginative, God rest him," said Jonny.

They both looked at Jonny in silence, allowing him to continue.

"Typical ex-military. Barry's life were totally defined by his army career, even though he left it behind several years ago. 1981 – the year he was awarded his maroon beret, the proudest moment of his entire life."

Jack's instinct told him to examine the obvious first. There were five numbers dialled on the most recent day of use, 25 March: Stevie Johnson; Jonny; Noah; Dick; Mikey. He held his thumb under the last name on the list, making sure that Emma noted the same. A message flashed in the centre of the screen: *Battery Critical.*

Jack cursed under his breath.

"Don't suppose you've brought a charger Jonny?"

"Not for that kind of phone, I'm afraid. Plenty at home, assuming they haven't been taken."

"Well we don't really think it's wise for you to go home at present, my friend. I think we'll leave you to enjoy your last twenty-four hours of recuperation. We'll be here tomorrow to collect you. Don't be tempted to leave here without us, okay? We have some alternative accommodation arranged for you, in a hotel nearby."

DCI Robson nodded apologetically to the staff nurse as they departed the quiet ward. The aroma from the approaching dinner trolleys competed with surgical detergent to occupy his senses, as he puzzled internally about the nature of his new nemesis. He felt a shiver proceed along his spine as he wondered at the audacity and apparent breadth of the mystery perpetrators' reach.

CHAPTER 37

They both felt the same pang of relief to find Jonny looking alert, as he sat in the bedside chair awaiting their arrival when they strolled into ward 2D. They also both noticed the peculiar look of determination on his face, as though he had set his mind to proceeding with a long overdue task.

Robson and Wilson had spent the previous evening in the company of their younger colleague, Sergeant Matthews, who proved that his talent wasn't limited to dogged research, but also included technology expertise. They had methodically rooted through the records of Barry Searle's phone, which, for them both, had served to reinforce their belief that the death of Barry Searle was in some way connected to the kidnappings. Matthews had the bright idea of examining the phone's map application records, and soon uncovered its history, listing all recently visited locations.

The reconciliation of the phone history with the addresses of every one of the kidnapped persons had felt like a eureka moment at the time. DCI Robson knew only too well that the crux of detective work was often a simple matter of chipping away at the simple facts before you, and allowing the story to unfold. But there were also times when you needed a breakthrough. However, in the cold light of day, the latest development didn't quite seem to have the significance they had previously allowed themselves to believe.

There had been one piece of information on the mobile device that wouldn't escape Jack's mind, however he attempted to broaden his thought process. The stored note on the phone seemed innocuous enough, and not dissimilar to the sort of thing one might expect to find on nearly every phone memo. But considering the circumstances attributed to the former owner of that particular phone, and perhaps guided by instinct, he found the relevance of the data highly compelling. It might somehow provide a vital key, and he was determined to find out how. Jonny Searle was their closest link to the person that apparently owned the incriminating data, and he wanted him to help them use it.

CHAPTER 38

Jonny had settled into the hotel room as far as could be expected. The furnishings were perfectly comfortable, and he had as much food and drink on tap that his heart desired, but it didn't have the appearance or smell of home and he privately resented the somewhat abstract reason for his refuge. At first, it also felt slightly awkward being next door to DCI Robson. Overall, though, he was pleased to be away from the hospital and in his new, albeit simple surroundings. He took another sip of tea.

"So what do we do now?"

"We?" Inspector Wilson's forehead wrinkled slightly, and her eyes narrowed.

"Well, as I seem to be under twenty-four hour guard, what am I supposed to do?"

"Funny you should ask," DCI Robson interjected. Jack decided to come straight to the point, since Jonny Searle had inadvertently paved the way for the conversation he had anticipated spending most of the day working on.

"You can say no, but … "

Searle raised an eyebrow. Ever since he was a kid he had found it difficult to turn down the opportunity for adventure – although he never quite had the ability to face danger the way his older brother had, for whom taking risks had always seemed to be a necessary part of life. But Jonny would not shy from risk either. That was the case when he left a perfectly good job in the city to move back to his home town to look after his elderly parents. Many told him he was throwing his life away, but Jonny never saw it that way. He had bought himself a boat and happily eased himself into the simple life of a fisherman, back to his childhood memories and following in the steps of his forebears.

He had grown even closer to his brother when his parents died, and, without being told directly, he understood how much his older brother loved him for his devotion to them in their final years. That they had died within six months of one another had been hard to bear, and it was the younger sibling who had held them together at the time, inviting Barry to move in with him. Barry had struggled, as some ex-military personnel do, to fit into Civvy Street when he was discharged from the parachute regiment. The only thing that kept him going was maintaining contact with his ex-colleagues, the only people, apart from Jonny, who could ever hope to really understand him. His younger brother was his constant, and all the more so after they lost their mother and father.

Losing Barry was a more massive deal to Jonny than he had let on – he would go to the ends of the earth to find the person responsible. The police were keen to find the person responsible, but they had other priorities too, Jonny knew that. He was going to do his utmost to assist them. But he also knew that if they didn't bring the perpetrator to account, then he would. He absolutely would. Jonny wasn't going to decline the opportunity to play a part in achieving that aim in some way. DCI Robson seemed to be hinting that he might be invited to assist, which as far as Jonny Searle was concerned, was a most welcome development.

"How do you fancy taking us on another boat trip, Jonny?"

It wasn't what he had expected, but he thought of only one possibility.

"The island?"

DCI Robson nodded.

"When?"

"Soon. Maybe today?"

Searle noticed that the DCI's attractive colleague had been decidedly quiet so far. She had taken a severe blow from the giant yesterday, but he got the impression that she wasn't the type to be overly affected by that. He suspected that Inspector Wilson wasn't particularly comfortable with her colleague's proposal to involve a member of the public, indeed a victim, in an active investigation.

He was accurate in his appraisal of the circumstances. Emma Wilson was fast becoming a very good detective, but she played things by the rules. And it certainly wasn't correct procedure to take the victim of a crime with you on an investigation, especially without the knowledge of superiors. She had somehow allowed DCI Robson to convince her that they needed to do this in absolute secrecy, expecting that the Superintendent would have serious reservations. She regretted her acquiescence; indeed, it annoyed her. Jack Robson seemed to have a knack for persuasion that she didn't understand, and it made her anxious.

She was freed from punishing her mind by the sound of her mobile ringing. The two men in the room waited for her to speak to the caller but she only listened, for about a minute. They knew from the look that grew across her pale soft cheeks that it wasn't expected news. She finally spoke to the caller.

"We're on our way now".

She returned the phone to the pocket of the dark jeans that clung tightly to her slim, curved hips and peered gravely into DCI Robson's eyes.

"Our little excursion is going to have to wait. We're needed at St Audries, immediately."

CHAPTER 39

The speed at which Inspector Wilson drove the car down the winding approach road seemed to contribute to the destruction of the serenity which had encapsulated their previous visit to the magnificent St Audries manor. It had now been replaced by an abstractly sinister atmosphere that seemed to hang over the estate. A total of three squad cars and another four unmarked vehicles were stationed around the front of the house, which was itself a hive of activity.

They offered their IDs to the officer positioned in the doorway and entered to see that the grand entrance hall, illuminated by its fine chandelier, had also been taken over by a swarm of detectives. Superintendent Thorpe could be seen through a doorway at the far end of the hall, deep in conversation with the head of the forensics team. He seemed to sense their entrances, and terminating his dialogue with Bob Jefferies, approached them. With a sideways nod of his broad head, he indicated for them to join him in the adjacent room.

They followed, and Thorpe pulled the large door into its solid frame to close them inside the stately reception room where they had met the homeowner on their first visit.

Robson instinctively began to study the artwork that adorned the walls nearest them while the Superintendent still had his back to them, apparently composing himself. Inspector Wilson was the first to spot the significance of the area in which Thorpe had decided to stand, and subtly cleared her throat to divert Jack's attention from the walls.

Thorpe remained with his back to them as he spoke. His eyes were fixed on the white outline of a human form before him, marked on the luxurious dark-green carpet, and now ominously darker around the outline of the head.

"The situation has now reached another level. As soon as this becomes public, I am as good as finished."

Both Robson and Wilson fought for the right words, but with the latest circumstances laid bare before their eyes, it seemed a foolish notion to attempt any encouragement at that moment. The apparent fall of what seemed to be the Superintendent's most influential ally would surely signal the end of Thorpe's involvement in the case, and perhaps his career. His key supporter in the case had apparently fallen victim to the very crime that he had longed for Superintendent Thorpe to put an end to.

Thorpe already seemed to have reached a level of acceptance, Jack thought, but he wouldn't be able to stop caring about the case, that much was obvious. The intensity that had defined Thorpe's eyes from the moment Jack had met him, now seemed to elude him. Robson and Wilson were both tuned into the probability that it had now gone too far for his position to be tenable; such was the political circus. His intensity seemed to have been superseded by a state of surrender such as one attains when arriving at the point of no return. When the course of the universe is plainly unchangeable. Jack broke the silence.

"When was Sir Geoffrey last seen, sir?"

"Forty-eight hours ago, we currently believe. He attended a local fundraising event and returned home in a taxi."

"What about the butler?"

The silence lasted too long to have felt comfortable. Emma shifted her feet while Jack continued to hold the Super's stare, until he finally responded.

"Dead!"

Thorpe's inflection emphasised his incredulity, which was enhanced further by the condescending frown as he indicated the white shape on the floor with his eyes.

"Bloody hell, sorry; I ... think I got the wrong end of the stick, sir."

Wilson, though equally flabbergasted, remained silent.

Superintendent Thorpe continued.

"Sir Geoffrey didn't show for a meeting at Hinkley Point this morning. His receptionist grew concerned when she couldn't contact either Sir Geoffrey or the butler. The local bobbies forced their way in this morning and found the poor butler in here, with his head caved in."

At that moment, a junior detective knocked and poked his head around the door.

"Superintendent? Sorry – it's the Chief Superintendent. He refuses to be deferred sir."

Without another word, Thorpe left the two of them alone, closing the door behind him.

DCI Robson could not remember a case in which he had felt so helplessly short of time. It didn't make sense how someone with such bold ambitions could remain anonymous, having now added the single most influential person in the area to their growing list of victims, and assuming that the same perpetrator was responsible.

Kidnappings almost always had clear motives, but none had transpired yet in this case. He ran through the events again in his mind. A dead man who was almost certainly related to the abductions before his demise. And now it appeared that his former employer had become a victim in some way. If indeed the events were related.

As they departed the room together, Robson couldn't understand why his subconscious placed such a degree of interest in the apparent alterations to the artwork in the room from their last visit. He forced himself back to relevant matter.

Inspector Wilson had made her position clear during the drive to St Audries, but eventually she agreed that there was a place they had to visit again. As they exited, she asked Jefferies to notify them if there was any footage available from the security camera.

*

The man in the woods was entirely invisible to the officers swarming around the estate beneath him. The men and women in blue had completed what they had considered to be an extensive search of the surroundings, but hadn't come within fifty yards of him. Even if they had, they wouldn't have seen him.

He locked his binoculars on the two senior detectives who now left the property and walked to their car. He allowed himself a brief smile of satisfaction as he observed the furrowed brow of the DCI, which served to illustrate his frustration.

He quickly dropped his self-absorbed gratification and returned his focus to the DCI's attractive partner. He took a deep breath to suppress the adrenalin surge, feeling the blood burning in his veins as he considered what lay ahead for Inspector Wilson. But she would have to wait a little while longer. Noah needed another matter to be addressed first.

CHAPTER 40

Sergeant Matthews' research had uncovered an inordinate amount of data, predominantly dominated by the subject's distinguished military record, and his career working for the government.

"If I were to ask you for a list of associates, James, I suspect that we could end up with data overload?" asked Jack.

"I think that's a safe assumption, sir. This guy has mixed in some fairly large and diverse circles."

"So, we need to apply a filter, don't we?" Wilson contributed, as the remainder of the personnel in the small room sat in silence.

"Any suggestions?" DCI Robson raised an eyebrow slightly, before rising from his chair. He stood at the window looking out into the dark evening and the ominous dark forms created by the Quantock hills in the distance. He felt perplexed by both the audacity and apparent lack of motivation for this latest development in the case.

"There can be only one way to approach it can't there? Work backwards, starting with the most recent," Wilson offered.

Matthews nodded at the inspector's terse analysis, as the DCI remained with his back to them all, thumbs rotating as his fingers intertwined at the base of his spine.

"Yes," Matthews adjusted the thick rimmed specs in an excited gesture as he responded to his inspector's suggestion, "it seems a local analysis is warranted, given the relatively close radius of the crime scenes."

"What do you think, Jack?"

Robson turned to the room and looked around the tired faces, all desperate to pack up for the evening. Only Matthews and Inspector Wilson remained engaged in the conversation.

"It's a start. I'm not so sure that we have sufficient evidence to suggest that this is anything to do with an associate of Charlesworth's at all, let alone a local one. But we have to start somewhere. Okay, James, we'll call in for an update tomorrow."

When we return from our boat trip, thought Jack.

CHAPTER 41

Porlock Bay had become a postcard image of itself, basking in the remarkable sunset. As they looked out towards the Severn Sea from the deck of *Orinoco*, there were parts of the Channel that still happily glistened beneath the dying rays of the giant red orb, as it steadily descended nearer the horizon. Jack looked back at the stillness in the bay as they floated away from the weir. The car park was now almost empty, and the only sign of human inhabitants came from the few remaining occupied wooden tables in front of the Ship Inn. Most of the customers had begun to file away for their evening meals, or were opting for the comfortable warm interior.

The boats moored against the small weir dock bobbed beneath the ripple caused by their departure, as Jonny Searle confidently negotiated a path through the weir gates and into the Channel, a manoeuvre he had executed on many occasions. Despite the recent turmoil in his life, the skipper was a picture of calm focus at the helm of his boat, completely absorbed in the one activity his soul had been designed to fulfil.

They felt the current grip the hull as they left the calm water of the bay. Robson and Wilson both sat back in their seats on the rear deck, each unavoidably recalling their last sea voyage under a different skipper, as they watched Searle take *Orinoco* in an easterly direction with the fading sun at their backs. They sat close to one another and both pulled their coats up to their chins in a brace against the breeze that greeted their arrival into the Channel, a climate quite in contrast with the modest warmth of the pleasant spring day that had just passed. The detectives were both focussed, desperately hoping that their destination held a link that had to date eluded them. They took one final glance back towards the smoke rising from the Inn's chimney, both silently yearning to be alongside the source of burning logs.

There was very little conversation for the next half an hour until the distant rock became the island of Steep Holm and DCI Robson asked the skipper to navigate a course around to the north of the island.

Jonny handled the boat expertly as they closed in on the rocky needles. The illusion of the impenetrable wall gave way to reveal the concealed entrance. As before, Searle timed their manoeuvre to perfection, and they cruised inside the deep, high cavern, gently gliding alongside the wooden platform that ran the length of the cave. The more Jack studied the apparently natural opening, the more obvious it became that human engineering was evident. The robust platforms on either side of the cave had been crafted from huge planks of wood that must have been six inches thick. These seemed to be supported by a metal framework beneath, attached to the platforms by huge iron bolts. The scale of the construction surprised him. The platform seemed to have been built to handle a considerable load. Extraordinarily, the structures appeared to have been designed to tolerate tidal activity, assisted by the sheer height of the opening.

The containers that were evident during their brief previous visit were no longer visible. The docking platforms on both sides were entirely bare, apart from the mooring posts that rose up through the platforms from the metal substructure beneath. DCI Robson smirked ironically to himself, as he pondered that the fabrication before them was not a particularly shining example of eco-friendly resource usage, which the owner of the island was so passionate for.

Jack and Emma disembarked easily at the end of the sturdy dock, leaving Jonny on board *Orinoco*, in accordance with the pre-journey briefing. They were pushing boundaries involving Jonny Searle, and had to limit his exposure to the investigation.

Searle reclined inside the cabin and unscrewed the top of his flask, watching through the front window, as the wooden platform knocked to the rhythm of the detectives' feet while they marched towards the vast metal doors ahead. From his vantage point aboard *Orinoco*, it seemed the officers had run out of ideas for a moment.

Wilson and Robson exchanged glances, then looked up at the doors, each feeling instinctively uneasy at the level of engineering on display.

They both took up position in front of the small metal enclosure attached to the wall of the cave, immediately to the right of the entrance. Robson pulled the phone from his pocket and keyed the PIN 1981. He opened the memo application, titled 'Holm Codes'. There were two number sequences: a six-digit number labelled 'Entry' and another six-digit number labelled 'Arm'.

They had discussed the possible use for the codes in the incident room earlier and agreed that the 'Entry' code was an obvious contender. The 'Arm' code would be necessary when they left, to avoid leaving any trace of their visit. DCI Robson read out the six-digit code to Wilson at a speed that allowed her to operate the corresponding keys on the pad.

The thunder of the breakers crashing against the rocks outside the cave was interrupted by the sound of a small metal object crashing. They both turned in the direction of the sound to see Jonny cursing, apparently having knocked his coffee onto the deck of the boat. The entrance doors remained tightly closed. Emma extended a forefinger and touched the pad once more. Immediately they heard an electronic beep followed by mechanical clicking, and then whirring.

Robson hastily glanced to his right and hissed:

"What did you press?"

"Hash. Obviously."

Searle watched intently from the cabin, still sipping the remnants of the hot liquid from his flask lid, after a quick refill. The CID officers had unnecessarily stood well back to allow for the doors opening towards them, but moved in closer now as they watched the huge steel panels part gradually, before disappearing entirely into the rock face.

Fluorescent strips flickered into action to illuminate a

contrasting scene as they walked through the high portal on to the hard, level floor inside. Their eyes were naturally drawn upwards, initially surprised at the height and scale of the enclosure. A few small foklifts were stabled on the right, which contributed to lending the place a factory-like feel.

They glanced at each other briefly before continuing to take in their surroundings. Apart from the vehicles in the alcove on their right there was nothing of interest in the immediate area. Directly opposite them, about fifty yards away, the entrance hall tapered to an apparent passageway, which was still impressively wide at about ten feet across. The ceiling sloped down so that the height of the passage appeared to be approximately the same as the width, giving a box-like effect.

They both started at the loud clunk behind, and turned to see the doors glide across the opening, seconds later leaving them enclosed inside the rock.

DCI Robson swallowed the lump in his throat and buried the reservations that swam around his head. Had he looked to his left, he would have noticed similar anxiety on the face of his partner, whom he had convinced to proceed with their investigation of the island, somewhat recklessly and without authorisation.

They continued in the only direction possible. The lighting in the passageway was subtler than that of the opening that they had left behind – the LED strips on either side of the floor evoked thoughts of aeroplane aisles, although wider. The illuminated path was visible for another fifty yards ahead of them. Side by side, they strode along the middle of the lit route, passing an elevator on their right, followed by a recess that housed an iron staircase that spiralled into an opening above. Jack finally averted his gaze from the opening to indicate to Emma that he was going to undertake a closer inspection. He felt panic growing in his throat as he stared into the empty hallway. The only trace of his partner ever being there was her lingering scent.

He paced towards the end of the lit passage and realised as he got further that the light didn't terminate at that point, but continued around a left-hand curve in the walkway. As he rounded the corner, he saw that the passageway glowed for another hundred yards beyond and then terminated once again. *Perhaps another corner? There is only one direction.*

Emma was already halfway along the hundred-yard stretch. He caught up with her as she reached the end of the ground-level lighting section and stood by her side. They both peered silently into the darkness before them, allowing their pupils to dilate before proceeding.

Shuffling cautiously forward, both officers instinctively reached out to detect any obstacles before them. The burst of light was sudden and stunning. Still blinking as his optics adjusted to the significance of the change in luminescence, Jack spotted the little sensors on either side of them. Emma stared into the large space that the automatic lighting had revealed.

The passage had given way to what seemed to be a perfectly circular chamber, some fifty feet in diameter. The circle was fully enclosed, but the surrounding wall was interspersed with seven doors, comprising three on each side and a single doorway in the centre, directly opposite them.

They ambled towards the centre of the room and could see

that there was a small sign above every door except for the one at the tangent of the circle, still directly ahead of them.

Jack followed Emma in the direction of the first door on their left until they could make out the text. They both processed the potential meaning of the sign in silence, considering the context of their surroundings and what they knew existed above their heads.

"Supplies for the winter?" Emma ventured.

Jack nodded pensively, still staring at the sign above the door. He walked around the room until he had confirmed that the labels on the other five doors were identical to the first, except for numerical suffixes, which increased in numerical order around the circumference of the circle. He returned to join Emma who had remained at the first door and looked at the label again.

"That seems to be a lot of storage."

He stepped past Emma and attempted to open the handle-less entrance to 'Silo 1' by pushing. The door was secure and without evidence of an entry keypad.

"Here," said Emma, as she pointed to a small circular shape in the centre of the door. "What's that?"

Jack placed his finger on the shape and took a second to determine the cold material. Glass. His hand recoiled at the beep and they both watched as digital text appeared on the shape before them, scrolling left to right to enable it to be read fully. *Invalid user - Align retina with centre of cross-hairs for one second.*

"Retinal recognition?!"

Emma's breathless reaction was in keeping with the

thudding inside Jack's chest.

"The door at the end isn't labelled."

Jack was halfway to the unsigned entrance when they heard the electronic beeping sound echo through the passage behind. He stopped and they both stared at one another as the groan of the entrance doors echoed through the passage towards them.

"Jonny?" suggested Emma.

"I didn't tell him the code, did you?"

Jack's initial instinct was to investigate the cause of the sound, but after a few seconds, it was evident that it was coming towards them. He turned and paced the remaining few steps to the door he had been originally heading for and pushed against it. The stiff hinge mechanism began to give under the slight force, which he then increased so that the door opened enough for him to enter. He gestured to his colleague with a nod of the head as he walked in sideways. Emma swiftly followed.

They allowed the door to slowly swing shut behind them. They were left in darkness, pierced only by the sharp lighting from the circular room outside, which filtered through the narrow oblong window running vertically in the upper half of the door. They stood abreast, a foot inside the room and peered into the circular enclosure outside.

"They'll notice the lights are on. Why exactly are we hiding anyway?"

Emma looked at Jack, who wasn't sure of the answer himself, but realised there was little chance of remaining incognito.

"They might not be coming this way," suggested Jack.

Another groaning sound began to emerge from the passage, resounding in the acoustic dome. As it grew in volume, the high-pitched noise sounded like an electric motor.

A second later, the lighting in the circular hall extinguished automatically, leaving them in total blackness. A slight bang could be heard as a percussive crescendo to the sound of the electric motor, confirming that the doors at the entrance had slid closed again, sealing them from the cave outside.

Up until that moment it had been only mechanical sounds that could be discerned as the source of the commotion. But now the unmistakable frequency of human dialogue echoed, distorted and drowned by the growing noise of the motor.

"They must know we're here." Emma hissed, still on the brink of stepping out into the hall to confront their visitors, as she thought of Jonny moored outside in the entrance cave. But Jack held his position.

"Strange that Jonny didn't alert us. But I've a feeling that whoever this is might not be approaching if they knew we were here. Let's wait."

*

Another minute elapsed with the voices growing in volume, now raised sufficiently to be heard above the cacophony of machine sounds. Eventually, the motor stopped screaming and the baritone voices sounded no more than fifty yards away. Instinctively, DCI Robson and Inspector Wilson both jerked to the side of the window they had been peering through, as the circular hallway became once again flooded with white light.

A strong West Country twang could be determined as one of the men outside tried to iterate the point that he had been making to the other two. He was certain that he had noticed a shadow drop at the end of the passageway as they made their way along it, as though the lights in the hallway had already been on. The eastern European accent that boomed in response sounded familiar. Jack and Emma both edged sideways just enough to be able to peer through the glass with one eye, to see a gigantic man nonchalantly reassuring his tall, thin companion. Both were dressed as though they were about to embark on a mission to Mars, as was a third person in the party, who sat at the helm of a small forklift.

Jack acknowledged Emma's wide-eyed glance towards him, before hearing the electric motor start up again. The two men on foot led the way to the door labelled 'Silo 6' as the forklift followed with its load of one container, which seemed similar to those they had seen on the dock-side during their previous visit.

From their side view, they witnessed the thin man remove his headgear, allowing a short, greasy-looking ponytail to hang at the rear of his neck, as he crouched slightly to align his left eye with the screen in the middle of the door. He rose again and turned to the colossus as his eye-scan was accepted, and the two hidden CID officers watched on as the door glided sideways to allow the trio to enter. The two detectives both held their breath as they witnessed the forklift enter with the bulky man in tow. Their former boat skipper, Mikey, was a few paces behind as he stopped to replace his headwear.

DCI Robson had become aware of Inspector Wilson's chest pressed against him as they both peered through the narrow window. Noticing that he wasn't looking through the window any longer, Emma shuffled awkwardly.

"Shall we get closer?" Emma said, as a slight flush passed across her pale cheeks.

Jack hesitated, considering the possibility that once they were out into the open hallway there would be no chance of maintaining secrecy if anyone returned. The fading sound of the forklift motor indicated that the group had already travelled some distance inside Silo 6.

Wilson took the initiative.

"Let's stay tight against the wall and try to avoid the sensors, so the lighting doesn't remain active."

Robson nodded and followed her formidable form as she prowled along the perimeter. They passed the two doors, marked Silo 4 and Silo 5, before arriving at the entrance identified as Silo 6. The brilliant light disappeared from the circular chamber at the same time they heard the click.

Inspector Wilson reacted to the sound with feline reflex, darting into the silo.

"Fuck!" DCI Robson exclaimed, his face pressed up against the steel door, which now separated him from his partner. The door had taken a mere second to slide back into position. He waited for the door to be reopened by his colleague from the inside. After five minutes, DCI Robson accepted that that wasn't going to happen.

The white lights illuminated the vast circle once more as he pelted across the hallway towards the corridor, having made his decision. He fumbled for the deceased Barry Searle's mobile telephone as he approached the exit, and keyed in the six-digit code. The cavern echoed to the sound of the doors arriving at the end of their travel. The vessel moored immediately outside the entrance was not the fishing boat they had arrived in. It seemed very similar to the boat that the ponytailed man now inside Silo 6 had written off when Jack had recently been his passenger. Further along the jetty, the mooring point that *Orinoco* had been attached to was vacant.

*

Inside Silo 6, Inspector Wilson inched her lithe frame along a corridor that was of a similar width to the main route into the dome, also lit by strips of LED lighting on either side. She had hesitated at the door for a couple of minutes, wondering how she might grant access to her DCI or at least communicate with him.

The only means of operating the sliding door appeared to be another eye scanner. She had briefly considered attempting to communicate through the door, but conceded that it would carry too high a risk of alerting the three men ahead of her. Wilson finally began to proceed in the only direction available.

She stopped to examine the iron staircase on her right about a hundred yards in, which appeared to be like the one they had passed in the main passageway earlier. The sight of the padlocked hatch at the summit of the steps soon discounted it as a viable access point. She would have to continue alone.

The faint sound of voices reached her as she arrived at a gentle curve in the route. The steel wall felt cold on her back as she slid around the bend. Seeing that there was nobody between her and the pair of hinged swing doors ahead, she stepped out into the pathway again. As she arrived at the double doors, she carefully peered through the Perspex window in the left-hand door, and felt her chest tighten. Nothing could have prepared her for the view.

*

DCI Robson raced back to the circular hallway. The entrances to all six silos remained secured. The door swung back on its hinges behind him as he threw himself into the chamber that had been their hiding place earlier. He activated a small pocket torch to reveal that they had been hiding in an archive room, or perhaps a reference library. He examined the shelves, which were stacked with binders. Some contained larger folders that had been laid flat.

A cobweb hung from his fingertips determinedly as he brushed the dust from the surface of a file, having laid it on the otherwise bare desk in the centre of the room. The collection of engineering construction drawings contained inside the folder did not appear to represent any significance to their investigation, nor their current location.

The second file that he examined contained details of a framework-like construction, which immediately brought to mind the televised NASA rocket launches he used to watch so avidly with his father in the 1980s. His hand trembled as he held the next drawing, while he allowed the implications to consume him. He had to get inside Silo 6.

He hoped in vain to find another exit from the room, which might lead him to the same destination as his partner.

Remembering the staircase near the entrance at the far end of the corridor, he burst through the door. His footsteps were amplified in the vast enclosure as he raced into the entrance passage. He grabbed hold of the rail, feeling the cold metal against his hot, sweaty palms, as he paused and indulged in a couple of deep breaths.

A bead of sweat ran into his eye as he reached the top step, releasing a greasy palm from the iron staircase to shove the hatchway. The access gave way and opened on its hinge, outward into the area above his head. He looked towards a solitary doorway as he rose from his knees to stand inside a small enclosure. His nostrils relished the cool evening air as he released the door before him. The star-laden sky and buzz of insects confirmed that evening had descended on the island. The natural environment was interrupted only by the small observation construction some twenty yards away. His concentration became focussed on the light coming from the small fishing boat that appeared to be circling. Consequently, he didn't notice the door gently closing behind him on its hydraulic hinge, until the engagement of the latch in its recess became audible. Instead of a handle, there was only a small keyhole provided on the exterior of the door.

*

It seemed to Inspector Wilson to have taken an age for her to regain control of her breathing. Only the sight of the men inside making preparations to depart, forced her finally to avert her eyes from the terrifying sight that continued to send shockwaves through her. She turned and began racing back towards the dead end.

She had made it as far as the staircase when the sound of the doors swinging open was followed by voices and the whine of the forklift truck, echoing menacingly along the corridor. It felt to Wilson that confrontation would be inevitable. Although she began to mentally prepare herself for the encounter, her instinct told her to evade the situation if possible. But her mind was devoid of solutions, and she could only hope that the large padlock in the hatch above her head was not properly secured.

One sharp tug as she reached up from her position near the top of the ladder abruptly dispelled that wish. She grabbed her baton from its holder and wrenched, but the sturdy security fastening refused to give. The forklift motor screamed louder to announce that it would be shortly appearing around the bend in the hallway, as she inserted the baton into the lock again. She watched the tips of the forks, which were lowered to within a couple of centimetres of the hard floor, as they appeared fifty yards away. A desperate leap from the ladder applied huge, gravitationally assisted leverage. She momentarily swung from the baton with both arms, until the lock's resistance gave, and it cracked open, smashing to the floor.

The sound reverberated through the corridor, and the forklift truck drew to an abrupt halt at the end of the viewable part of the passageway. The silence only remained for a couple of seconds as the three men wearing radiation suits snapped out of their stunned surprise and began to react. A shout of "Halt!" was shortly accompanied by an explosion, as she pulled herself through the opening at the top of the steps. She hadn't viewed the firearm drawn by the ponytailed man, and didn't initially reconcile the echo of the explosion beneath with the searing heat that passed through her lower leg and threatened to send her body into spasms.

The effort necessary to arrive at the next doorway caused her to pant rapidly, while the contrast of her new, moonlit surroundings, compounded her confused state. Wilson's keen mind reacted to the vision before her, as she registered that the dark red trail on the ground led to her left leg. Her body duly responded in accordance with the sight.

As she collapsed in a heap on the rocky gorse, the last thing Inspector Wilson heard was the sound of frantic activity echoing from the metal ladder, somewhere on the other side of the door from which she had just emerged.

CHAPTER 42

A wave of nausea took hold, as Wilson regained a degree of consciousness to find herself thundering down a rocky bank towards the shore. Thrown across a broad and powerful shoulder, she could make out one other sprinting only a few paces ahead of them. She attempted to improve her focus with a shake of the head. Still only one other pair of racing feet could be distinguished in a blurry haze, with no sign of the third, but she thought she could discern the sound of pounding feet behind her. The bright light ahead grew larger and began to dazzle, seemingly moving up and down in a vertical arc, before her eyelids conceded and fell shut once more.

White and black apparitions overwhelmed her mind and the feeling of intense nausea initiated another moment of semi-consciousness, which brought further disorder to her thoughts. The constant cycle between dark and light seemed to embrace the rhythm of the sea, as she attempted to lift her head to record the identity of her captors. Her body convulsed at the motion and she vomited over the edge of the bed that she had been secured to.

The sound of her vomiting alerted the dark figure by her side, who had been applying pressure to her injury. She was surprised to feel a flicker of recognition, as the eyes of her chaperone became illuminated by the moonlight, turning to confusion, as she struggled to comprehend the vision.

"J-Jack?"

"You'll be fine Wilson, just rest. We'll soon be at the hospital."

"H-how?"

"Jonny and I were trying to work out a way of getting back in to find you, when you found us. We heard the shot and came running. You were just about unconscious by the time we arrived. We just got to you before your friends emerged from the hole and began firing in our direction. Jonny managed to get *Orinoco* around the rocks and out of range."

"Thanks Jack. Th-they … "

She fought the wave of nausea, determined to communicate. "It's a miss—"

DCI Robson held her head gently over a bowl as she vomited, before placing her back on the makeshift pillow formed of waterproof clothing.

"I know, just rest. You've lost a lot of blood, but you've got the benefit of my best effort at a tourniquet. Rest now."

CHAPTER 43

Tearing along the deserted A54, Jack glanced at the digital clock, revealing that it was past midnight. He began to reflect on the previous four hours. The implications seemed a little too mind-blowing to be believed. They appeared to have happened upon a secret facility built into the base of the island nature-reserve, when their former boat skipper-come-assassin arrives with two colleagues dressed in radioactive suits, who then turned out to be armed.

Not immediately what you'd associate with building fucking bird-watching huts.

Robson thought of the drawings again and contemplated what his partner might have witnessed inside the silo.

The air ambulance rested on its helipad, as he drew towards the A&E entrance. The chopper had beaten him to the hospital by a good hour, which was doubtless a blessing, considering the condition of the patient on board. He brought the car to a screeched halt behind two squad cars and a silver Mercedes which were located outside the double doors. The news had already travelled. Robson had intended to call Thorpe after his partner had been lifted, but thought twice about disturbing him in the night. He acknowledged to himself that his decision seemed slightly irrational.

The smell of disinfected corridors, which always spoke to him of trauma, greeted him as he passed through the doors. He stood still in the entrance, in his mind watching Isabelle lying, shattered on the hospital bed, while he had fought to retain a degree of fruitless hope. The sight of Superintendent Thorpe freed him from the recollection. The Super approached sedately.

"Jack, let's go somewhere quiet, via the coffee machine I'd suggest. Inspector Wilson is in theatre."

"Sir."

Thorpe inserted a coin into the vending machine slot and they listened to the machine whirr into action, responding to the selection. The Super led them both into an empty consultation room, the steaming plastic cup in each hand seemingly having no impact on his senses. Jack lowered himself into one of the seats usually reserved for patients, as Thorpe took the consultant's swivel chair, placing his coffee on the desk. DCI Robson felt exhaustion take hold.

"I think it would be best, Jack, if you simply gave me your version of tonight's events, from the top."

"Of course, sir."

The words sounded fantastical to Robson, as he recounted the evening to an impassive Superintendent Thorpe, constantly aware that they appeared to have drifted from a kidnapping investigation into a wholly different scenario.

If Superintendent Thorpe had noticed the distressed exhaustion in the DCI's voice, he offered no acknowledgement of it in his manner. He elevated his large frame, walked to the window, and peered outside in the direction of the helicopter pad.

"This is rather worrying. Tell me, what do you make of it, Jack?"

"I don't really know, sir. Somebody is clearly using that island for something other than its ostensible purpose. And I wouldn't mind betting that the landowner is blissfully unaware of the facility that we investigated today."

"Hmm, indeed. Or perhaps, he *was* unaware."

The Superintendent remained fixed at the window.

"Do you know what Wilson witnessed during the time that the two of you were separated?"

Robson had already considered the suggested scenario, which had been implicitly conveyed by Thorpe's words.

After their experience that evening, it seemed wholly feasible that it would not be unlikely that people would be silenced if necessary, even those of the stature of Sir Geoffrey Charlesworth. Jack's deep breath was audible as he fought to suppress his growing vexation. It frustrated him that the purpose of the kidnappings and the connection to what they had just encountered, still totally eluded them all.

"We weren't able to have a detailed conversation, sir."

As the Superintendent finally turned from the window, Jack searched again for the anxiety that Thorpe had seemed to permanently display for the past few weeks, but noticed for the second time how it suddenly seemed to have been replaced by a sombre resignation.

"Your discovery is alarming, Jack. I should be reading you the riot act for undertaking a search without authorisation and consequently endangering the life of a fellow officer."

DCI Robson had been expecting this, and understood that the lecture was inevitable.

"But more pressing are the implications of your discovery. Sir Geoffrey Charlesworth is more than just a dignitary to me, you see. He is a powerful ally and an influential man, connected in high places. The man has served his country with distinction as a military commander. He has served as a weapons inspector and ambassador for peace. In his spare time, he serves his local community and the wider area as a philanthropist and defender of basic human rights."

It was the most impassioned oration that Robson had witnessed from his new superior officer.

"The fact that your discovery coincides with his disappearance concerns me greatly."

DCI Robson could feel the Superintendent's breath on his face now, as he brought his imposing frame at close quarters to ensure maximum emphasis.

"I need you to understand something, Robson. Until further notice, you will not utter a word of this to anybody. And I mean anybody – that's inside or outside of the force. The island of Steep Holm is off limits."

"Sir?"

"If there is a connection, Jack, it will materialise in due course. The matter at Steep Holm is now outside of your jurisdiction. It will soon be outside of mine, once I've officially handed this over to MI5."

Jack reflected and understood the inevitability of his commanding officer's discourse.

"Understood, sir."

"Further investigation in relation to the island will require discretion, resources and connections that we don't possess. I want you to remain focussed on the primary investigation," a degree of regret appeared on Thorpe's face. "I'm sorry to have to say this, but I am compelled to report your actions this evening, Jack."

"I understand."

"We need results on the kidnappings."

The Superintendent leant in even closer. Jack couldn't read his look.

"Do me another favour, Jack."

"Sir?"

"Get some rest. And thank you for your efforts."

After receiving a consolatory pat on the shoulder, DCI Robson was left alone, literally and metaphorically.

CHAPTER 44

The helicopter was landing on a flat, rocky surface, causing the wild long grass to sway aggressively. The sole passenger hopped from the side opening, ducking as he jogged towards the welcome party consisting of an unusually large man and a slimmer, but equally tall man. The chopper took off again by the time its passenger had reached the welcome committee. They all shook hands adjacent to an innocuous-looking rock before disappearing into the covert entrance. Had there been any onlookers in that wild terrain, they might have believed that they had just witnessed a supernatural event. The former helicopter passenger wore a contented smile, knowing that the day of reckoning was fast approaching and feeling satisfied that almost all the arrangements were now in place. The plan was nearly complete and they had reached the point of no return.

CHAPTER 45

The helicopter had completed four 360-degree turns and it was clear now that this wasn't part of the show. As it spun out of control, he leapt. The opening parachute altered the intensity in a moment, such that the remainder of the event was experienced in slow motion. He looked down at the young woman's body beneath him, blood soaking into the grass-covered mountain. He knew the outcome – it was the same in every dream. But the face was different – Isabelle? Inspector Emma Wilson stared back at him with lifeless eyes, just seconds before Jack Robson woke in in a fierce, breathless sweat.

*

DCI Robson looked at his watch – 18:15. The sweat-soaked shirt clung to his toned chest as he rose slowly and wandered from the consultation room. He grabbed the attention of the nurse as she passed through the desolate waiting room, and felt himself flush as his lips still apparently slept, refusing to articulate the words as he had intended. The nurse seemed to recognise the name uttered, however, and committed to bringing him news.

It was twenty minutes later that a different nurse returned and asked him to follow her. The lack of sleep had left him lethargic. Despite Thorpe's instruction to rest, Jack had spent the night of the shooting at the hospital and the following night in the company of the Superintendent himself. DCI Robson had to admit to himself that he was flagging.

Thorpe had handed responsibility for direct investigation of Steep Holm island over to Special Branch, and awaited further instruction regarding what support, if any, they would require from CID. In the meantime, the Chief Superintendent had decreed that Thorpe would assume direct responsibility for the CID investigation, until further notice. The only thing that surprised Jack, was the fact that he was being retained as part of the team in any capacity at all, following his previous conversation with the Super. He suspected that this was probably down to Thorpe's insistence that his DCI should remain on the investigation, despite his recent disregard for procedure.

In Superintendent Thorpe's first directive as the newly reappointed SIO, he had advised Robson that he wanted to work on uncovering any potential link between the activity on the island and the missing people, for which he still was very much responsible, despite the recent involvement of MI5. They hadn't been able to agree on a working theory, with each suggestion seeming more far-fetched than its predecessor. In the end, they agreed to part company for the night, agreeing to reconvene with fresh minds and with the remainder of the team. That had been some eleven hours ago, having worked through the night. Jack had left Thorpe and called on Sergeant Matthews to assist in further research.

When Robson had arrived at the hospital two hours ago, Inspector Wilson was off the ward, having a scan on her damaged leg. By the time the orderly returned to inform DCI Robson that he would be able to see his colleague, he was comatose.

The staff nurse eyed him from above her lowered spectacles with an appraising look as he followed the junior nurse past the desk.

"Need you on B in a second, Judy," came the curt instruction.

"Yes, nurse," replied Robson's escort, without making eye contact.

They arrived at a door to a single room and the nurse knocked before entering. She pulled the door open, despite no apparent response from within.

Jack felt suddenly agitated by the emotion that swept him by surprise as he took in the scene. The young female inside the room was a picture of carefree nonchalance as she sat up in bed scoffing on a piece of brown toast and sipping the steaming drink in front of her. Yet again, he found himself astonished by his partner's apparent powers of recovery.

"You still have your appetite, then?"

The words helped him recover, and he took pleasure from her smile.

"Well, I missed dinner yesterday."

He briefly considered touching her hand but settled for an affectionate smile. He suddenly felt self-conscious, as though her eyes bore into his very soul, sensing every emotion and thought.

"So, what of the developments?" Wilson continued, replacing the mug on the portable table in front of her.

He allowed himself to chuckle at the stamina and sheer bloody-mindedness of the woman. The day before, it had taken a couple of minutes to update her while she lay dazed, recovering from the blood transfusion. He had also briefed her on the conversation that had taken place with Superintendent Thorpe, but suspected that, up until now, his robust partner had not been capable of entirely digesting the data. Robson, noting that her eyes once again sparkled with perception, patiently recapped the previous two days for her. She sat and listened with a relaxed demeanour, her chalky cheeks touched slightly by a fetching pink flush.

Robson explained that there had been no further sighting of the island inhabitants they had encountered forty-eight hours ago, and the responsibility for pursuing them had now shifted. Indeed, from what Thorpe had advised when they spoke on the telephone only a few hours earlier, there would be no one entering or leaving that mound of land for the foreseeable future, a prospect that allowed DCI Robson to dare to hope that some progress would soon be seen, even if it were to eliminate the island incident from CID responsibility. Wilson seemed unmoved by the news that, despite having taken over responsibility as SIO, Thorpe had ensured that DCI Robson would remain an integral part of the team. It was as though the developments had fully aligned with her expectations.

Silence filled the room for a whole minute.

"So how did you get to me in the end, Jack?"

Robson recounted how he had eventually discovered a way on to the surface of the island and found Jonny Searle, who had thankfully possessed the foresight to circle the island, waiting for a signal. Earlier in the evening, Searle had spotted the other boat approaching on the radar, and had the guile to depart the cave before the new visitors arrived, without being noticed.

As they exchanged tales of what each had witnessed inside the facility, the sinister confirmation of the implications ensured that light-hearted enjoyment of the reunion was replaced with an air of seriousness. DCI Robson closed his eyes as he leant back in the visitor's chair and drifted into an unscheduled nap.

*

Sir Geoffrey Charlesworth stretched his aged but elegant frame and rolled over onto his side, instinctively to the left, where he would normally read the time presented to him by the antique clock in his bedroom. The sight of the plain, cool wall an inch from his nose abruptly reminded him of the fact that he now occupied somewhat less salubrious surroundings. He turned onto his back and focussed on the artificial light that was now emanating from the austere ceiling, signifying morning.

CHAPTER 46

Sergeant Matthews had the undivided attention of the small incident room. He tried to stifle his enthusiasm, while dictating his well-prepared notes. He had provided a summary profile of the recently abducted Sir Geoffrey Charlesworth.

James Matthews explained that Charlesworth had, until recently, chaired a local community action group which had been responsible for several impressive contributions to the local area. The most recent comprised a library and a walk-in mental health support centre. The information had been met with the usual mixture of detached interest and frustration at the lack of apparent relevance to their investigation.

It was when Matthews proceeded to read aloud the short list of group members, that the officers in the room became engaged.

"Charlesworth was the chair. The other members on record included: a certain Barry Searle; a local artist, by the name of Mr Armitage; a well-respected musician named Mrs

Adams; a teacher by the name of Miss Jameson; Mr Bertrand, a psychologist; a local GP, Dr O'Hara."

The look of incredulity grew on every face in the room, while Matthews, relishing the attention of the audience, continued until he had stated the name of every kidnapping victim, or someone that was closely connected to one.

Despite no longer being the senior investigating officer, DCI Robson was currently the leading detective in the room, due, typically, to Superintendent Thorpe's presence being demanded by more senior CID officers. It was Jack who broke the meditative silence that had resulted from Matthews' briefing.

"Great work, James, really great, thank you."

The young man gave his best effort at displaying a modest reaction, and sat down. Wilson puffed her youthful cheeks and inhaled.

"So what are we talking about, Jack? Is this a vendetta?"

A voice emanated from further back in the room.

"Against a group of philanthropists?"

DC Sanders' brow furrowed as she spoke. The room nodded and murmured in agreement.

"Unlikely, I grant you, Trudy," continued Wilson, who remained seated, with the bottom of her bandaging visible below the trouser line of her outstretched left leg. "But what other explanation is there? It can't possibly be coincidence."

"Agreed," DCI Robson intervened. "This is not coincidence. A vendetta also seems unlikely, but stranger things have happened. Maybe not everybody agreed with their plans for the area."

Again, the room seemed to nod, in pensive synchronisation.

"James," DCI Robson continued, "I need you to find out about anyone who could conceivably have stood to lose out as a result of any of the recent projects that have been championed by the community group. Focus particularly on anyone likely to take a financial impact."

"Okay. I've also got the list of O'Hara's patients through at last, which we've been waiting on."

"Oh good, at last. Anything of interest?"

"Nothing earth shattering. I think you'll find that most of the names I've just read out were his patients at one time or another."

"Not surprising, as you say."

"But there is just one detail above others that might just be of interest. He was treating one of the members of the group for a long-standing medical issue."

The room looked on in silence once more, as Sergeant Matthews described the symptomatic relief prescribed by O'Hara for one of his patients. One of the patients that they now believed was among those kidnapped by the same perpetrator, for reasons yet to be revealed. The medical disorder of Depersonalisation was not something that any of them had heard of.

CHAPTER 47

The clandestine nature of the telephone call transported Jack back to another case several years earlier. He hoped that the potential implications weren't of the same magnitude as they had been then. It was the sheer persistence of the confidential caller that made him pick up eventually, answering in a somewhat hostile tone. The caller was totally impassive to the initial irritation in DCI Robson's voice, and calmly proceeded with the message. Robson was asked to repeat the instructions given to him, including the number that he was to ring at a precise time. The telephone with which he would need to make the call would be delivered to him by a courier at his hotel at ten o'clock that morning.

Jack returned to his room after breakfast and continued analysing the data on the most recent version of their 'Mike's' shortlist. It was a painstaking process that hadn't yet unveiled anything of significance. The LED clock in his room displayed 09:59 when the call from reception came through. The receptionist apologised for the interruption, but unfortunately there was a particularly obstinate delivery driver at the front desk that insisted on personally handing over his bounty to its intended recipient.

After signing for the small parcel and thanking the pair of eyes beneath the dark helmet worn by the dispatcher, he walked outside, as instructed. To anyone watching, he presented the appearance of someone taking in some fresh air in the picturesque surroundings, despite the cold wind that the spring morning had brought. Within ten minutes, he was deep into the woodland surrounding the hotel and judged that he must be well out of range of any potential listening devices, with no building or vehicle in earshot. As the phone flashed into life, the display stated that it was 10:13. *Two minutes to wait.* There was one single, unnamed contact stored in the phone memory, as promised.

The surrounding greenery rustled as it swayed under the might of the increasingly ferocious wind, largely shielding the lone stroller from its effects. He carried out a final survey of the area and dialled the number. The call was answered immediately. Without greeting, the voice at the other end blandly stated the agreed password. DCI Robson reciprocated with his part of the covert dialogue and the line went silent. Over the course of the next twenty seconds, Jack's pulse intensified as he considered the potential reason for the silence. Finally, a familiar voice came clearly through the receiver.

"Jack; sorry about all this secrecy. Listen carefully. I need to see you. Be in my office by 16:00 today, is that understood?"

The permutations rolled through his mind like those of

an endlessly spinning one-armed bandit, but he realised the timing wasn't right to resolve his current queries.

"Affirmative, sir."

"See you at four, Jack. Leave soon, do not tell anyone."

"Okay, John."

CHAPTER 48

The hotel car park was relatively quiet, with most of the clientele having arrived for the evening. No one noticed the man in the saloon car as he sat observing the window of room 418. Since he had been watching, there had been no movement in the room next door, and its light hadn't been turned on in response to the oncoming dusk. The man wanted to be doubly sure that the inhabitant of room 418 was alone, and that the tiresome DCI hadn't decided to keep the occupant company for a while.

It was mildly disconcerting that the London-based detective chief inspector seemed to have gone off the radar for the past few hours, although there was the undoubted bonus that Sergeant Wilkins had been diverted away from the hotel, which meant that Jonny Searle was alone at last. If he had to deal with Robson as well, he would.

His large torso wobbled slightly as the man sniggered menacingly to himself, reflecting on the fact that the sergeant had been deployed to look after the security of a certain

Inspector Wilson, while she conducted her enquiries to follow up a recent lead. *Enjoy your flimsy security while it lasts. Your time is coming, and the beefy sergeant won't be able to help.*

The man immediately chastised himself for giving way to anger. He had to admit that he had begun to be rattled by the progress that DCI Robson and his team had made of late. But he took solace as he thought of Noah's reaction. The great man had assured him that it was too late for anyone to spoil their work now. But first he had to deal with the man in the room upstairs. The occupant of the room had a choice. *One last chance.*

He answered the phone after only one ring, the voice at the other end stating the message clearly and without salutation.

"The coast is clear – he's alone."

The thick, spatulate fingers then dialled the hotel reception and he asked to be put through to room 418. Within seconds, a genuine smile passed across his face as he listened to the familiar voice of Jonny Searle.

*

The four-hour drive back to London was an unwelcome addition to his schedule. He would have felt greater motivation if he was returning to see his precious daughter, but he couldn't risk that visit currently. The fact that he had spent most of the duration of the journey scrutinising his rear-view mirror had left him feeling jaded. Whoever had orchestrated the kidnappings seemed to have the ability to remain invisible, hidden behind an impenetrable veil. DCI Robson had also spent considerable time contemplating the possible reason for the urgent and unnervingly secretive summons. The address that he had been given for his appointment could not be mistaken, despite it not being his usual place of work.

His superintendent had been clear in his instruction that their rendezvous should not be discussed with anyone, without exception, so he had taken his leave under the pretence of attending to 'family matters' as instructed, and without informing either Thorpe or his partner directly.

After negotiating the typical central London gridlock, Robson had allowed himself forty-five minutes recuperation at one of the trendy riverside cafes. He now headed alongside the northern bank of the Thames, constantly switching his right foot between accelerator and brake, maintaining the customary twelve inches between him and the black cab ahead of him. The clock displayed 15:35. He would be on time to take his space beneath the iconic building he now observed, towering over the city traffic ahead and further emphasising the contrast with his recent work environment.

DCI Robson couldn't quite discern the terse request that he had received from one of the two serious-looking security men at the front entrance. *Am I being refused entry?* One of the guards had made a call that lasted less than five seconds. With his back to Jack and the other guard between them, it was not possible to overhear the conversation, but within a minute of the call, a sober-looking man wearing a well-tailored suit arrived to collect him. Robson obeyed the mild-mannered request and followed his pristinely dressed host into a glass lift. There seemed to be no machinery audible, as they were smoothly elevated above the city skyline. Jack looked out over Millbank and the intense, concentrated blend of industry and leisure below, not attempting to break the silence within the glass cube. He understood that the formal approach was most likely to be a matter of security, rather than a consequence of his escort's personality. *Perhaps he is listening to someone through that earpiece?* Once they were outside the elevator, the same bland sentence that had been spoken prior to taking the elevator was repeated: "Would you follow me please, Chief Inspector?"

He was ushered into a doorway and received a courteous smile, albeit the smart woman behind the desk ensuring that the greeting was impeccably formal. She informed Jack's escort that the Director General was waiting.

Robson felt his palms moisten as the identity of his mystery host had been apparently unveiled. He was suddenly conscious of his comparatively bedraggled attire as he considered the prospect of having an audience with such a high-ranking officer. He tucked the rear of his shirt into the top of his faded chinos, as he was escorted through another door. He took a gulp as the escort gave a slight nod to indicate that he was handing over to the four-person committee inside the room, before leaving and closing the door.

He recognised each one of the committee that sat before him, although, apart from his direct superior officer, he had only ever met two of the remaining three of them. He had once been in the audience at an intelligence briefing delivered by the man that now addressed him in person. The previous briefing had taken place some years ago, shortly after he had been appointed to his new post – Director General.

DCI Robson had only met the other man in the room once, almost exactly twelve months ago. The connotations of that previous encounter occupied his head now, and he tried to control his thoughts, as they unravelled the implications of being summoned by such an extraordinary panel. He had only encountered the fourth member of the group through the medium of television. Jack began to feel claustrophobic, acutely aware of her eyeing him with apparent deep interest.

Robson accepted the invitation from the head of MI5 to take the comfortable chair that had been reserved for him, doing his best to appear composed as he was introduced to the Home Secretary and the Prime Minister of the United Kingdom.

The Director General led the briefing again on this occasion and Jack felt himself relaxing slightly, thanks to the personable approach of the man before him, as he lived up to his reputation. A man, no doubt, who was accustomed to dealing with unimaginable pressure daily. The other three looked on seriously, yet amicably, it seemed, as DCI Robson responded to their request to describe the events of the past few days.

It felt like an interview, as the Director General eyed the other panel members to his left and right, evidently obtaining the required silent looks of approval from all three of his colleagues before proceeding with the next set of instructions, which had doubtless undergone careful consideration and debate prior to Jack's arrival.

The orders were clear and concise.

"We need a positive identification for at least one of the operatives that you encountered on Steep Holm. You may have access to any resources necessary. As far as your colleagues are concerned, you continue to be engaged in the investigation into multiple kidnappings, in accordance with your original brief and fully under the authority of Detective Superintendent Thorpe. Thorpe will be advised of your revised brief, but it shall never be discussed between you. Neither will the discussion inside this building be mentioned to any other person. Any contact with us must be via the communication channel that was used to arrange this meeting. Should you need any support in addition to the routine assistance of the team that you are working with, please seek out Sergeant Wilkins in the first instance. Although appointed by Thorpe, he is reporting directly to us."

The room fell silent, and each member of the four-person committee trained their eyes on him, apparently signifying that the floor was his.

"Do you have any questions, or is there anything you are not totally comfortable with, DCI Robson?"

His head swam with questions. But Robson knew that they would all be outside the boundary of information that he would be entitled access to. The intent of the question from the head of the secret service was undoubtedly his only opportunity to withdraw his involvement.

"No, sir," he heard himself reply, simply.

"As soon as you have any news, please report via the communication channel that has been established. In the event of any breakdown in that communication, please contact Wilkins, who will advise on alternative arrangements. All understood?"

"Understood, sir."

"Your resources are unlimited. Do not place yourself in disproportionate danger, but understand that this is a matter of national security and your mission must be undertaken with maximum urgency and discretion."

"Of course."

He nodded respectfully to the remaining panel members as he stood up from the upholstered chair and took his leave. The faces before him remained stern. Robson noticed for the first time that the seriousness did not seem to be an indication of hostility; they did in fact appear to be even more anxious than him. He left the room and gently closed the door on the mood within. A mood of fear.

DCI Robson ordered a black coffee and a burger from the drive-through on the outskirts of the city, and consumed it without enjoyment before racing back to the South West.

*

Jonny Searle sat on the edge of the hotel bed, contemplating the telephone call. He was being honest when he explained that he no longer had possession of the mobile device, but the caller refused to accept that it was the truth. He hung up again as the phone in room 419, next door, continued to ring, unanswered. He hadn't seen the DCI all day, and the big security guy, Wilkins, had told him to remain in his room, as he had to accompany the attractive inspector and her burly boss on a visit somewhere.

He lay back on the firm mattress and began to turn the

volume up on the television again, as the knock at the door came. So soon after the disturbing phone call, Jonny felt his stomach tighten, before telling himself to exercise some control.

He stopped on his journey between the bed and the pale brown wooden door and cringed as his socked feet caused the floorboards to creak. Then again, he thought to himself, the TV was blasting at the time of the thump on the door, *I can't exactly pretend to not be in.*

The silver coloured spy-hole cover made a faint scraping sound as he slid it across the opening. Searle's chest was thumping as he aligned his left eye with the viewer. The sight caused him to jerk his head back in surprise. He stood for a moment and contemplated the visitor, whom he knew well. *How did he find out I was here?*

He allowed his anxiety to pass before opening the door to his friend. They exchanged pleasantries before Jonny invited the man inside. Pleased to have some familiar company, Searle walked to the side to put the kettle on. Meanwhile, his guest ensured that the door had been properly closed behind them and subtly operated the security lock.

Jonny still had his back to his friend, as he continued to describe the circumstances that had led to him taking refuge in a hotel room. His visitor casually moved across to where his host was standing and raised a plump hand towards his shoulder. Jonny turned abruptly as he felt the hand land. Both men chuckled at the overreaction to the friendly pat on the back.

"Sorry, buddy. All this protection seems to have put me on edge even more!"

"It's okay, Jonny," the portly man laughed as he walked away towards the small seating area by the room's only window.

His cheerful demeanour faded as he read the warning text message displayed on his phone, then observed the vehicle reversing into a vacant space in the car park below the window of room 418. He watched the detectives return, no doubt to drop off Sergeant Wilkins, and knew that he would have to move very fast now.

He took one of the seats and unzipped his coat, before slipping a hand inside to ensure that the weapon was readily accessible. He knew that he would be able to rely on his colleague to buy him five more minutes.

CHAPTER 49

The timepiece on DCI Robson's wrist was in synch with the clock display in the dash: 23:59. *One minute until tomorrow,* he thought.

Since receiving his instructions, Jack had spent twenty-four hours surveying the only area that he could think of that might allow him to get a glimpse of one of the team members from Holm island, without being seen again himself. The truckers' service area, directly opposite the entrance to the power station, provided a convenient vantage point from which he was able to carry out inconspicuous surveillance from his own vehicle. Despite not occupying one of the many heavy goods vehicles which housed most of the heavy-eyed occupants, DCI Robson blended in as one of the several people in smaller vehicles that were compelled by their tachometers to take rest, before continuing their journeys. He had managed to hold his own when one of the lorry drivers had been particularly sociable earlier in the truck stop cafe, but had decided to keep to himself after that. He considered describing the person that he was looking for, but decided that there was a distinct possibility of others being on the payroll of whatever invisible organisation it was that he pursued.

The comprehensive lighting arrangement at the plant's security point made it possible, just about, to make out the faces of the drivers as they departed the plant. He was also particularly interested in one particular style of car, given its recurring appearance. The registration plate hadn't thrown up anything interesting and whoever had arranged the long-term rental had done a very good job of covering their tracks, the vehicle simply being booked to a certain G. Charlesworth of St Audries manor estate. A simple but effective cover – using the company car for any extra work that the user might choose to undertake.

He still kicked himself over his decision to stretch his legs at 01:46 on the previous morning. Taking a stretch to ward off sleep, he had spotted the car that was of interest, departing the entrance at speed.

By the time Robson first touched his accelerator pedal, the black Audi had long since flown past, leaving a trail of smoke in the floodlit, grit-filled air behind him, as the thick tyres whipped up the dusty road surface.

It was just after one o'clock the following morning, nearly 24 hours since the previous sighting, and the urge to sleep had begun to take a firm grip on him again, as he fought hard not to submit to his heavy eyelids. The headlamps of the car at the security gates flickered, blurred by his tired retinas, as the gates slowly opened. The sudden recognition of the driver snapped him from his slumber and he sat upright in the seat. He started the ignition as he watched the ponytailed driver exit the plant in the black Audi, and swiftly followed the car out towards the main road.

DCI Robson allowed a generous separation distance between him and the tail lights up ahead to avoid alerting the driver, which meant that, for many stretches of relentless curvature, he did not have sight of his prey. They continued west along the main artery of North Somerset for three and a half miles, cutting a route between the coast on the right and the imposing Quantock hills on the left. The car in front didn't slow down for the villages they traversed. The inhabitants of the modest stone dwellings would awake none the wiser that a man racing through hadn't respected the behavioural code, displayed by the polite road signs at the entrance to the village. Neither would they know that the man in the black Audi was hell-bent on changing the course of their cosy village existence forever. Their bubble was about to be burst.

Jack had to drive at seventy to maintain the distance between the two cars, which felt inappropriately fast along the narrow route. All four tyres left the surface of the road on reaching the summit of another hill as it immediately dipped down. The half-mile long stretch ahead was devoid of any other vehicle. The Audi's tail lights had disappeared completely, perhaps alerted by the distant headlights present in the rear-view mirror since the beginning of the journey, Robson thought. He only noticed the dim, red glow in his peripheral vision as he passed the right-hand turn, and his tyres let out an almighty screech as he managed to swing the car around, just making the divergence towards Doniford.

DCI Robson knew that he would have to get closer now that they had turned off on to the even narrower, windy coastal road. The stretches between bends were no greater than a couple of hundred yards and the road ahead was thrown into darkness as soon as he extinguished his headlights. The overgrown hedge scraped the left side of the vehicle aggressively as his eyes took their time to adjust to the subtler lighting provided by the solar system above. He was relieved to see the vehicle take a right turn, about four hundred metres ahead. A sign declared that they had arrived at the ancient port of Watchet.

The vehicle continued at a speed far above any level of acceptability for the narrow high street, which was still illuminated by street lamps. Jack applied the brakes hard as the black saloon up ahead took the left-hand hairpin bend, eventually easing around the tight corner thirty seconds behind, and half-expecting the car to be lying in wait for him. He slowed down to a crawl as he observed the vehicle turn into a small cul-de-sac housing estate on the left, halfway along the hill.

Robson eased up to the turning slowly, noting the street name, before performing a U-turn and ambling back along the high street again. The town car park was deserted, lit by street lamps at either end. For ten minutes, his brain whirred with possibilities, but sleep eventually conquered his mind and his body finally closed down for the first time in two days.

*

The phone alarm sang its irritating melody, announcing that it was 04:30. Having dozed in batches of fifteen minutes, Robson now felt worse than he had before his broken sleep. He forced his numb shell out of the car and made a token effort to stretch, before wandering over to the public conveniences. The doors had been locked since 18:00, according to the sign, and wouldn't reopen for another four and a half hours. He moved around to the rear of the building, out of the potential eyeline of the person that occupied a mound of sleeping bags, and relieved himself before returning to the car.

Inside the car, he found a half-full bottle of water in the back footwell he couldn't remember purchasing. He took a swig and threw the rest over his face. The pile of sleeping bags against the building ruffled slightly at the sound of the ignition, and DCI Robson was once again out on to the sleeping streets.

Five minutes later, he had killed the ignition again and let the car idle along the gentle gradient of the silent cul-de-sac, heading towards a cluster of garages. There were cars parked outside several of the garages, Jack presumed belonging to those that had missed out on the typically restricted on-street parking. The sight of the black saloon slapped him from his dreary state.

He allowed the car to freewheel until he reached the rear of the back-to-back garages, eventually stopping out of sight of the houses. The street remained in dark silence, broken only by the intermittent bird song that had begun in the trees that overhung the block of garages. He inhaled the cool air deeply on exiting the car, allowing it to fill his heavy head and re-calibrate his senses. As he emerged from the blind-side of the garages, he bent low, creeping between the garage doors and the small row of parked vehicles. He took advantage of the refuge offered by the white van that was conveniently located adjacent to his target, and straightened to enjoy more bracing spring air.

Another glance around the side of the van confirmed no movement in the neighbourhood. He slipped his hand into his jacket pocket and removed the device he had been issued with in London, almost two days earlier. The device beeped to confirm that it had been successfully activated, and he could feel the cold morning dew on the dark bodywork of the Audi as the strong magnet snapped the device into place, hidden beneath the wheel arch.

He wiped his damp fingertips down his trousers as he returned to his own car, content that he had diligently followed his instructions, and completed the first phase of his assignment. The second objective was to establish the precise address of the vehicle's current user. His baseball cap lurked on the back seat, along with other forgotten paraphernalia, generally more interesting to a child. As he pulled the cap down low, so that the peak nearly obstructed his vision, he remembered the day Isabelle had purchased it for him. The U2 concert at Wembley seemed a million years ago, but he still remembered how it made his wife chuckle mischievously, knowing that he objected to wearing any item of clothing carrying a logo. He caught himself drifting and opened both front windows, letting in a draft of the cool, moist early-morning air.

Robson continued to fight the impulse to shut his eyes until

9 a.m. doing his best to convince his body's nerve centre that sleep was currently unnecessary. He had witnessed most of the little neighbourhood departing for work and school. No. 7 had been the earliest to rise. A young man in his twenties, togged in high-visibility orange overalls, appeared to sleepwalk over to the white van parked outside the garage block. Next to surface was the nurse at No. 3. By 08:45, the school runs seemed to have all departed and the cul-de-sac went back to sleep as swiftly as it had awoken.

His patience was tested until 09:17, when a man wearing a black coat opened the front door of No. 9, the house at the far right-hand end of the row. Jack felt his pulse quicken and senses sharpen as he watched the tall man make his way swiftly towards the garage block.

He had let his car roll back out of sight behind the garage block before the ponytailed man reached the end of his pathway. Jack waited until he heard the sound of the engine start. Hearing the vehicle move, he started the ignition and inched forward just enough to see past the corner of the garages. The black Audi made a speedy exit from the close.

Jack turned off the ignition. Pulling his new mobile device from the glove compartment, he touched the screen to open the app that had been loaded on to the phone. The red dot flashed next to the green dot, then gradually started to move away.

CHAPTER 50

DCI Robson left his car and nonchalantly wandered across the deserted street towards No. 9. After a couple of knocks on the door, he concluded that Mikey lived alone.

He had seen most of the street depart for work that morning, but knew there was a good chance that not all the residents were out. *Discretion isn't easy when you're breaking and entering.* Robson raised his eyebrows at the irony, as he placed himself in the shoes of the person that he typically hunted. The tired wooden door gave at the first attempt. *Must be getting the hang of this again.* Inside, he rubbed his shoulder and closed the front door.

The interior of the house was by no means generously furnished and gave the immediate impression of a temporary squat. Mikey didn't seem to own many belongings. Reacting to a sound outside, Jack rushed to the front window in time to witness a woman at No. 6 struggling out to her MPV, laden with an occupied baby seat and enough provisions to support her intrepid expedition. He hoped that the young mother hadn't seen the man in the baseball cap break into No. 9 minutes earlier.

He instantly recognised the picture leaning against the wall. DCI Robson had always had an affinity with art, and paintings particularly, but not to the extent that he would ever have claimed to be an expert. Nevertheless, he was quite sure that actually hanging the piece on a wall might have helped to optimise the artistic statement. However, the reason it grabbed his attention more than the other items randomly strewn about, was the fact that he had recently seen it displayed in a far grander abode before it had disappeared, along with its owner.

The other furnishings in the front room were limited to the flat-screen television and a large bean bag, along with a folding camping table and chair.

The kitchen was accessible at the end of the short hallway outside the lounge. DCI Robson walked gingerly into the tired, retro wood-effect kitchen, still half-expecting an attacker to be lurking behind each doorway. He paced across the faded laminated wooden floor towards a door that led outside to a narrow back garden, containing a small shed at the end of a lawn, overgrown with knee-high grass and weeds. The garden was fenced on the left-hand side, with a wall to the rear that ran around the perimeter to form the rear and right-hand boundaries.

He checked his phone again. The red dot had moved a considerable distance from his green one. *You've got time, Jack.* He began to methodically open each of the cupboard doors. The first one at eye-level revealed a scarce supply of crockery, and the remainder were bare. The tall larder cupboard housed tins of food and a single loaf of bread, along with a bottle of cheap bourbon and what appeared to be around a month's supply of dried noodles. *Not a chef then.*

The dented fridge-freezer looked to have seen better days, but remained quite capable of fulfilling its role. One lonely carton of milk sat in the door, with two shelves containing a tub of butter and a few bottles of beer.

The drawers didn't reveal a great deal more: cutlery in the top drawer, a single kitchen knife in the middle drawer, while the bottom one contained paperwork. He momentarily stopped rummaging to examine the name on the utility bill that he held between thumb and forefinger. He quickly photographed the top of the bill, before replacing his phone to continue searching.

The passport sat at the bottom of the pile of paperwork. The photograph inside was that of a slightly younger version of Mikey. He took another photo, before replacing the document to consider the name, which differed to that on the bills. *Mr Michael Andrew Knight.*

Upstairs, he swiftly completed a search of the two bedrooms, followed by a token examination of the tiny bathroom. The first bedroom he inspected was a typical modern-day box room, containing several cardboard boxes and a couple of large sports holdalls. A brief search revealed that the boxes held personal items, including photos, books, and professional qualifications. Robson unzipped both holdalls to reveal that they were loaded with clothing. *Is this guy still moving in, or in the process of moving out?*

A double mattress lay on the floor of the main bedroom.

The absence of a bed frame meant that the flimsy plastic bedside drawer unit was the only item in the room that constituted furniture. If the kitchen drawer had provided him with a prize a few minutes earlier, then the bedside drawers surely represented the jackpot. DCI Robson realised that he was trembling slightly and focussed on taking a deep breath.

The list of names that had been scribbled on the notepad were instantly recognisable. Each name had a postcode alongside and, somewhat curiously, a tick. He speedily scanned down the list, then began to frown when he noticed the title at the top of the page.

He looked again at the names that had become embedded in his subconscious. He felt frustrated as he stared hard at the bottom name, waiting for his memory to catch up. He removed his own notepad from his inside jacket pocket, and began to correlate the new list of names with his own records. Eleven names, compared with his own list of ten. *What was the relevance of the eleventh?*

The idea struck him like a lightning bolt. He had momentarily stopped trying to recall the last name on the list. The realisation caused the trembling to return with a vengeance. He quickly punched the postcode associated with the name 'Adams' into the map application on his phone, and bolted from the bedroom.

*

From inside his vehicle, the rotund figure eyed the DCI steadily as he flew out of the front door of No. 9. He sniggered to himself as, from his spot in front of the garages, he watched the intruder fastening the front door, so as not to reveal his earlier break-in. The chubby spectator calmly gripped the knife in his left hand as the chief inspector approached.

Robson was too preoccupied to notice the newly arrived vehicle, and was unable to see the occupant behind the darkened window in the side of the white van. The DCI darted out of sight of the onlooker, returning to his car that he had concealed behind the garages earlier.

With the engine running, DCI Robson placed his mobile, displaying the desired route, into the car's phone holder, then hit the button on the other phone which he held in his palm, to access the secure line. He went through the security protocol swiftly and stated three words before hanging up.

The man inside the van had his own phone to his ear as he watched the DCI screech out of the cul-de-sac, and muttered four words. *We have a problem.* The voice at the other end was clear as to the required course of action.

CHAPTER 51

The pleasant female voice contained a delicate antipodean inflection, as it softly instructed DCI Robson to take the first exit off the roundabout. He put his right foot to the floor and sped past the caravan in the wrong lane, not bothering to converse with the gesturing driver of the pick-up that rattled by in the opposite direction. His attention was diverted by the red flashing dot displayed on his phone, which was just heading towards Minehead, about ten miles ahead of him.

It hadn't escaped Robson that he was engaged in pursuit of a man of whom he possessed little knowledge. Apart from now having a name to put to the face, and knowing that the man currently at the helm of the black saloon was prepared to adopt ruthless measures, he knew nothing of the profile of this man, nor his intended destination. His priorities had been set for him, by a highly secret mandate, but his instinct told him to exercise caution, especially while operating solo. He needed to use the recently discovered information to his advantage. He had fulfilled his obligation and given them a name. Now they wanted him to find out more. He was supposed to discuss his objective with no one except the peculiar sergeant who had been assigned to support him. The problem was, there was something about Wilkins that Jack distrusted. In fact, at that moment, there was only one person he felt he could trust.

The strong, warm female voice came through the car speakers and immediately DCI Robson felt his spirit lift, compounding his regret about having to lie to her about his current task.

"Jack?!"

He felt confused at the change of tone, as she had seemingly determined that her recently elusive partner was in fact in an adequate state of health, despite her concerns.

"Sorry, Wilson. I've—"

"Where in fuck's name have you been? We've been trying to contact you for two fucking days!"

"I'm sorry, Emma. I need to fill you in on a few things, but first I need you to help me with a background check, and fast."

"Never mind filling me in. It's you that needs to fucking well catch up."

"What do you mean?"

"It's Jonny."

Her voice immediately softened, almost returning to its default state, but Robson thought he detected a sombre note.

"What about him?"

"He's dead."

The tyres screeched as DCI Robson braked hard, almost too late, as he noticed the car in front had stopped. The elderly driver of the car eyed Jack in his rear-view mirror and shook his head.

"How? Where the fuck was Wilkins?!"

"He was with us Jack, with Thorpe and me. Someone went to his hotel room the day before yesterday. We found him when we returned from door to door enquiries. He had his throat slit."

It was Inspector Wilson that interrupted the silence, as Robson tried to regain control of his thoughts.

"What's going on, Jack?"

"I wish I knew," came the absent response. "Do you think you could run that check for me now?"

After the frustratingly cryptic exchange, Inspector Wilson agreed to undertake a check on the name *Michael Andrew Knight*, along with a particular address in the port village of Watchet.

*

The map display on the dash indicated that DCI Robson was two miles from his destination. Fifty yards ahead the sign read, *Welcome to Minehead – The Gateway to Exmoor,* with a hopeful illustration beneath of a sunny, quintessentially English beach scene. His phone display indicated that the green and red dots were now approximately one mile apart. Jack felt vindicated that he had acted on his instincts.

As he pulled into Merlin Close, he eyed the small collection of executive, detached houses, each incorporating at least six bedrooms. Inside each of the gated, private driveways sat a collection of high spec vehicles. A pocket of affluence in an otherwise ordinary area, Robson thought to himself. He pulled up at No. 2, expecting to find a black Audi nearby, but there were no other cars on the street. He glanced at the phone display again. Until that moment, he hadn't noticed that the red dot had taken a different route and was now about five miles away, heading in a south westerly direction.

He became aware of his slovenly appearance for the second time in as many days, as he ventured through the wrought-iron, gated entrance and admired the grand facade of the contemporary, mock Tudor mini-mansion. He hadn't slept properly for over two days, let alone shaved, washed or even had a meal to speak of. He nearly turned back to take up pursuit of the Audi again, but resolved to cover the existing line of enquiry first.

With both hands, he attempted to flatten his unkempt hair and took a deep breath, standing at the solid wooden door before operating the well-polished brass knocker.

There was no vehicle in view on the gravel-lined frontage to the property, and as he stood, dishevelled, at the grand entrance, he realised that at midday on a Friday, the working day was still underway, despite the amount of time he had been active already that day. Thirty seconds had elapsed as he glanced across at the double garage off to the right, and he prepared to leave, before turning back to face the door as the sound of jingling keys became discernible on the other side.

The door handle began to lower and gave a slight clunk. As the door opened, he stood face to face with a chic, dark-haired woman, around five feet eight by Jack's reckoning, with olive skin and a lissom figure. Jack forced his eyes away from the shapely thighs revealed beneath a high-cut day dress, and managed to offer his best, official-looking smile. The lady of the house broke the ice.

"Can I help you?"

Her voice was breathy and confident.

DCI Robson cleared his throat, now more conscious than ever about his appearance.

"Madam," he presented his identification simultaneously in a well-rehearsed routine.

"Detective Chief Inspector Robson, CID. I'm terribly sorry to trouble you, would you happen to be Mrs Adams?"

Her cheeks paled slightly as her confident expression morphed towards concern.

"Why yes, Chief Inspector. Is everything okay?"

Mrs Adams' voice seemed to go up an octave as her mind no doubt whirred through the potential reasons for the call.

"Please, madam, don't be alarmed – there's nothing to worry about," Robson lied, "but I wonder if I might take a moment of your time to ask a few questions? We're investigating a series of incidents in this area."

Her demeanour returned to its default state of assuredness.

"Of course, please come in."

"Thank you, Mrs Adams."

"Please, call me Jodie."

"Thank you, Jodie, I'm Jack."

He shook her slender hand and walked inside as she closed the front door behind them.

"Would you like a coffee, Chief Inspector, sorry – Jack?"

DCI Robson couldn't remember how long it had been since his last dose of caffeine.

"Sounds lovely, Jodie, thank you."

He watched her figure beneath the rippling dress, as she turned and glided with an informal grace through the wide entrance hall. He followed her through a pair of open, glazed doors, into an impressively large kitchen with a long central island.

Jodie had her back to him while filling the kettle from the polished chrome tap.

"Tell me, Jack, isn't it normal for you detectives to interview in pairs?"

DCI Robson realised that his badge might have got him through the door, but his appearance was obviously slightly atypical of what one might expect from an officer of the law on official business.

He rolled an answer off that seemed feasible enough as it left his dried lips.

"Indeed Jodie. I'm afraid we're spread a little thin this afternoon. It's just my partner and me. She's calling on the next street along."

"Oh, no need for your apologies Jack, I'm glad of the company."

Her grin seemed slightly flirtatious to Robson. "So, what do you need from me?"

Jack's senses whirred in appreciation of the divine smell that filled the room, as she poured the hot water from the kettle and released the aroma from the freshly ground beans.

He pulled his phone from his pocket and zoomed into the

photo of Michael Knight that he had snapped from the passport earlier.

"Quite simply, we're looking for someone."

Jodie moved closer to place the tantalising mug of coffee in front of her visitor. He fought to suppress his instinctive craving as the top of her soft white breasts formed the centre of his vision for a moment. The feeling was quickly followed by the all-to-familiar transition from natural desire to irrepressible guilt. It was the same routine whenever he allowed his feelings to seep through his normally rigid guard as he pictured his wife, Isabelle, standing before him, observing her betrayal.

He took a small sip of coffee before continuing, holding the phone in front of her.

"Do you recognise this man, by any chance?"

She studied the picture and began shaking her head while displaying a pout that seemed to make her lips appear even more voluptuous.

"I don't believe so, no. Why, what is he supposed to have done?"

"Oh, petty theft."

"And they've sent a Chief Inspector?!"

"Well, he keeps getting away with it. Tell me, is there anyone else at home, Jodie?"

"I'm afraid not. My husband, Reuben, is at work and won't be back until tomorrow. And our little girl, Rebecca, is still at school. So, it's just the two of us I'm afraid."

The smile was there again. Robson felt the coffee warming his veins and tuning his circuits again.

"What does Mr Adams do, Jodie?"

"He's a musician. A pianist, mainly. He's playing at a concert in London tonight. We're a musical family, really. Rube's on the piano and me on the clarinet."

DCI Robson smiled.

"I see. And what about Rebecca?"

"Oh, she plays both, and extremely well at that."

"How old is she?"

"Only just seven. We have high hopes for her musical talents."

Robson switched back to business.

"Jodie, some of these crimes have been quite close by. I don't want to make you unnecessarily alarmed about small-time theft, but we are telling everyone to make sure that they are vigilant and to secure their properties sensibly. And we'd like people to report suspicious behaviour to us immediately."

He passed her a card with his name, rank and mobile number.

"Have you seen anything in the last few weeks or months that you would describe as suspicious?"

"No, I don't think so, Jack."

"Okay. I won't take up any more of your time. You may notice officers around the neighbourhood for a while, but it's just a precaution, and nothing to worry about."

"Understood, Jack."

She saw him to the door and they shook hands once more before DCI Robson turned to leave. He turned and admired Jodie Adams one last time as he stood on the front step, while she flashed another coquettish smile.

"Thank you for your time, Jodie. Lock the house properly."

*

DCI Robson glanced at the car clock as he operated his newly acquired mobile phone. 13:05. The map display had zoomed out considerably, to cover enough area to accommodate both dots on the screen. He placed his forefinger on the red dot to zoom in to the location. The dot was now stationary; the address undefinable.

The nearest marked road to the dot was several miles away. The general area was identified on the map as Exmoor. The sound of his own phone warbling disturbed him from his thoughts. The Bluetooth connection kicked in and he accepted the incoming call to allow Inspector Wilson's voice into the car again. She sounded enthused.

"Hi, Jack. Got some info for you. Where are you, by the way?"

"Hi – I'll explain in a bit. What have you got?"

"It's not comprehensive, but we're still working. I just wanted to give you what we've found, in case it's anything relevant".

Emma proceeded to brief him on the team's research.

"Michael Andrew Knight was born in Somerset, 5 September 1971. Grew up in an orphanage but excelled at school. A bit of a sad, yet uplifting story all at the same time, really."

Robson remained silent.

"After an unhappy start in life, it seems he managed to gain sponsorship to go to university, no doubt assisted by his highly impressive A level grades, to study mathematics, physics and chemistry. He graduated with first class honours and got a job at Rosyth Dockyard working on nuclear submarines, which led to him becoming one of the country's leading nuclear engineers. He has spent the last decade working for the private sector but on military contracts. Are you still there, Jack?"

"Still here. I thought you said you didn't have much?"

"He applied for a job at the power station about a year ago."

"Why?"

"Who knows. We haven't actually spoken to anyone that knows him. This is all straight from the records that we've been able to access so far."

"So, no personal information?"

"He's never been married, and no kids on record. We've sent a couple of detectives out to dig for some local info. Are you okay, Jack?"

"Yes, yes. I was just thinking about your research. It doesn't really add up, does it? Why would an ostensibly successful and presumably well-paid engineer be squatting in an unfurnished terraced house in Watchet?"

"That's the billion-dollar question, Jack. Jack, this Michael guy wouldn't go by the nickname of 'Mikey' by any chance, would he?"

He suddenly felt a foreboding danger. He couldn't explain why, but something told him that they had only uncovered a strand of a much more complex web, which was yet to reveal itself.

"Are you at home?"

"Yes."

"Doors locked?"

"Yes – and I've got that lump outside, sat in his bloody car. He's been worse since what happened to Searle."

"Don't open the door to anyone until I get there."

"When are you coming?"

"Later. How long is his contract at the power station?"

A frustrated intake of breath was audible over the phone, before Emma answered.

"We don't have that information. But considering that the work on the new reactor is ongoing, I wouldn't have thought it would be due to end any time soon."

"Well, if he's been living in his house for a year, and his contract is due to keep rolling, then why would his house be unfurnished and why is he living out of bags?"

"Jack, are you saying the address you gave me is related to the name?"

"It seems so. Why?"

"Because the house you gave me isn't being rented by Knight. It's been leased to Sir Geoffrey Charlesworth for the past eighteen months."

Jack took a deep breath as he tried to evaluate the connections.

"I kind of gathered that, actually. It seems his staff are well looked after. Not only company cars, but housing too."

"Well, as we keep being reminded, he's a jolly nice chap."

"Yes, and look how he's been repaid for it."

"Jack, I'm not sure I understand what this is all about. But if it turns out, when you decide to share the rest of your information with me, that the guy we're talking about is the one and only 'Mikey', then the first question on my mind wouldn't be related to accommodation – what I'd like to know is, when did he decide to become a sailor, and in what capacity did he acquire and learn how to use a firearm?"

Jack ignored the question.

"Could you help me with another name, please?"

"Jack, why don't you communicate with the station directly? Thorpe insisted that I take sufficient rest, otherwise he'll get me signed off sick. If he finds out I've initiated a request for data, he'll shut it down."

"I'm in the field and it's just a lot easier. Thorpe is in London at the moment."

"He is?"

"Yeah. This could be important. I'm interested in Reuben and Jodie Adams of 2 Merlin Close, Minehead."

"Okay, Jack. I'll call you back. But this information sharing needs to be a two-way street you know."

"I'll tell you all about it soon enough. More importantly, can you get a presence at the address I've just quoted, just to keep an eye out until further notice?"

"What's going on?"

"They might be at risk."

"I'll get someone there right away."

*

The sound of a large fist rapping the window woke DCI Robson abruptly from his dream-filled sleep. Wearily, he lowered the window to address the smirking detective constable who stood on the pavement at the end of Merlin Close. Collins, who had been dispatched earlier by Inspector Wilson to survey the Adams's house, detected that DCI Robson was in no mood for frivolity.

"Anything to report, sir?"

Robson's response was curt.

"Nothing, Collins. The daughter is still at school. It's Park Primary School at the end of the main road – you will have passed it on the way in. Keep an eye on the school until they kick out and see that she gets back safely. I need to contact the Super to get authorisation to extend the watch while our suspect is on the loose."

"Will do sir. And sir, if you don't mind me saying … "

"What is it, Collins?"

"Sir, you look like you could do with a proper rest."

"Just keep your guard up, Dave, okay?"

"Sir."

CHAPTER 52

Detective Superintendent Christian Thorpe departed the MI5 building at just after 5 p.m. He was satisfied that he had dealt with the situation wisely, especially considering the information he received in return. When he arrived back at his Somerset headquarters, he would implement the measures requested of him. That would have to wait until the morning, though, as he planned to stay overnight in the capital, to attend another meeting later that evening.

*

Jodie Adams had been close to calling the handsome Chief Inspector who had paid her an unexpected visit earlier that day. But the time had flown, having prepared the customary post-school snack for Rebecca and then spending an hour trying to locate the cause of the power cut. She had eventually made a phone call to the electricity company to report the fault.

The initial response had impressed her. Within ten minutes of making the call, the company had got back to her to state that the engineers were on their way. It was 4:15 by the time she finally held the phone in her hand with the intention of making the call to DCI Robson. But the man who had been outside in the van for the past couple of hours had disappeared. *Probably just another block paving salesperson. Although he looked more like a stereotypical fisherman to me, with his flushed plump cheeks and rotund frame.* It seemed a strange coincidence to Jodie that the stranger had arrived on the street soon after the DCI had departed in his vehicle. He had then disappeared when the DCI's colleague had returned at around 3:30, presumably under his boss's instruction. *They make you paranoid, these cops. Better bloody chase the electricity company.*

It was approaching six thirty, and the onset of early spring dusk had set in when she stood from the comfy sofa and sent Rebecca for her nightly wash. As she began to dial the number for the electricity company again, ready to complain that the promised engineers hadn't shown and that it wasn't acceptable to expect a lone woman and her young daughter to experience a night without electricity, she breathed a sigh of relief, as she spotted the white van pull up on to the drive. *At last.* In her relief, she hadn't noticed that the van was the very same vehicle she had spotted hanging around earlier.

CHAPTER 53

DCI Robson nodded to Wilkins in a friendlier manner, acknowledging the apparent silent understanding that existed between them. The well-built detective cut a not too inconspicuous figure, occupying the only car parked on the uneven, bumpy street, just fifty yards from Summerfield cottage.

It was Jack's first visit to the private residence of Inspector Emma Wilson and for some reason he felt peculiarly nervous about meeting her in that environment. He had toyed with the idea of bringing flowers or chocolates, in recognition of the fact that she was supposedly still recuperating, despite that recuperation somehow including an element of active service. But having stopped twice on the way and abandoning the idea on both occasions, he had eventually settled for the option of purchasing a home-made cake from the local village store. *Less risky.*

With the pristine lawn, tidy flower beds and skilfully

trimmed hedgerows, he was impressed with the way this single career woman had managed to maintain the property to such a high standard. Somehow, he felt intuitively that it would have been the fruit of her own efforts. Emma Wilson didn't seem to be the sort of person to pay others to do the work for her.

As he waited for a response to his knock at the door, he also wondered at how a young woman came to have such an apparently mature soul, to prefer this simple existence and reject the alternative draw of the city lifestyle that had been offered to her on a plate, almost from the moment she graduated from her training programme with distinction.

Detective Inspector Wilson answered the door wearing jogging bottoms and a white crop top, revealing a trim waistline and a pierced navel, adorned subtly with a small diamond stud. The effortless look was completed with hair roughly tied back in a ponytail, the odd strand hanging either side framing the elegant cheekbones and a blemish-free, pale complexion, which, as usual, had not been touched with makeup. Her smile indicated that she was genuinely pleased to see her colleague at her doorstep and, for a moment, he witnessed a new side to her personality, as he was greeted by a coy schoolgirl mannerism that showed itself only briefly. He gave her a peck on the cheek as he entered.

"Good to see you, Wilson, you're looking well."

He meant it. The only evidence that she had been involved in a scrape was the bandage that showed beneath the left leg of her jogging bottoms, which had been pulled up above the top of the dressing.

"Thanks, Jack. Um, I wish I could say the same for you."

He followed her through to the kitchen and once inside the cosy cottage, he started to feel every bit that he hadn't slept for two days.

"It's been an intense few days. I haven't really slept since … since the island."

"I don't know whether to offer you a coffee, or a sofa to sleep on?"

"Well, let's start with the coffee, shall we? I don't want my baking efforts to go to waste."

He smiled proudly as he held the lemon drizzle cake out for her.

"Wow, what a coincidence!"

"Sorry?"

"You use the exact same wrapping as the village store. Must be a baking thing."

He looked sheepishly at her.

"So, did you get anywhere with the latest enquiry?"

"Yes. Why don't you go through and take a seat and I'll come through with some coffee and your lovely cake."

Robson chose the cosy-looking armchair and had to fight the desire to close his eyes as the low ceiling beams, sash windows and smell of the dormant fireplace all lulled his senses into a state of relaxation. The method that he used to maintain consciousness was not entirely chivalrous, but worked nonetheless. The thought began as inquisitiveness as to how many times his partner had entertained a companion in that room – perhaps on the sofa or even the armchair that he was now sitting in. Inspector Wilson limped graciously into the room carrying a tray, just as his mind had started to wander salaciously. He rubbed his face and stood to help her with the tray, feeling embarrassed, as though his thoughts were visible.

He placed the tray down on the coffee table and Emma sat in the small two-seater sofa to his right.

"So, Mr and Mrs Adams."

She was keen to begin the dialogue, understanding that her partner had more information of interest to offer her than she had to reciprocate.

Jack poured the coffee while she continued.

"Nothing exciting to report there, I'm afraid. Married, obviously. The wedding was ten years ago. Reuben is in his forties and Jodie is mid-thirties. They have a young daughter, Rebecca, who is seven years old. They have lived at No. 2 Merlin Close since getting married."

"And?"

"Like I said, nothing exciting. Now, who is this Michael Knight? Our boat skipper–come-sniper?"

Robson nodded.

"I followed him home, broke in when he left. And found this."

He handed his phone to her, which displayed the image of the torn sheet of paper. She studied it for a moment, pausing as her eyes reached the bottom name, before handing it back.

"And where is Knight now?"

"I thought he was on his way there, to the Minehead address."

"What made you think that?"

Jack felt that it was too soon to have to explain the full magnitude of the situation, and judged it wiser to omit the detail of the tracking device for now.

"I followed him."

"Oh? Not very well, by the sound of it."

"When it was clear that he wasn't headed for the address, I wanted to get there as soon as I could."

Jack avoided his colleague's piercing eyes.

He carried on, avoiding any period of silence that would allow his new partner to scrutinise his thoughts any further, and described the list he had found at the residence in Watchet. Emma examined the list entitled 'Arcam' again.

"Did you advise Mrs Adams of your suspicions?"

Her voice seemed slightly disconnected as her gaze remained on the phone display.

"I didn't want to alarm her before her husband returned. We have the house being watched."

"Twenty-four-hour surveillance?"

"No, just routine patrols."

The longer she sat in silence, eyes thoughtfully locked on the phone display, the closer Jack finally came to conceding his ongoing battle against sleep. But he was unable to disguise a startled reaction, despite the softness of the voice that sounded to his right. Emma continued, without acknowledging his embarrassment.

"Jack – there is one other anomaly with this list, of course."

Robson pulled himself out of his slouch, straightening his back against the soft but firm chair.

"Such as?"

"Well, if this list is what it appears to be, then isn't there a name missing?"

Jack realised what she was getting at, having contemplated the point himself.

"Yes, it seems there is."

"Was Sir Geoffrey a late addition to the plans, do you think?"

"Possibly. Or perhaps he discovered something that he wasn't supposed to."

"Possible. But judging by previous form, wouldn't they have opted for a more final solution than kidnapping?"

"Indeed, it's perplexing. We're missing something. Perhaps they need him for some reason, or perhaps his standing is simply too high for them to take such a risk."

"And there's been no ransom demand, despite his apparent wealth. I had expected us to have flooded that island and turned it upside down by now, but apparently Thorpe says he's been instructed to hand that side of the investigation over to MI5."

"I know. They seem to be playing it cagey for some reason."

As am I.

"I'm surprised you accept it, Jack. Do you no longer believe in the connection?"

"I'm really not sure. In all honesty, I'm just absolutely fucking knackered."

Wilson's eyes pierced his again, partly revealing concern and partly indicating that she wasn't convinced that DCI Robson had shared everything with her.

"Don't drive again. Put your feet up for a bit and I'll prepare us some dinner."

She shoved a foot cushion towards him with her good leg, which Jack accepted in full submission.

"If you insist."

CHAPTER 54

The sound grew louder inside DCI Robson's head. *Was that the third or fourth time?* One eye opened just enough to register the appearance of Inspector Wilson in her dressing gown, and he began to return from his lengthy slumber.

He had slept for most of the past eighteen hours, interrupted only briefly the previous evening by his partner bringing him a quite stunning chicken stew. He checked his watch for the second time and then looked at the phone for confirmation. It had stopped ringing but it confirmed that he had slept through the night. The phone display flicked on by another minute to read 09:31, before changing again to flash 'Unknown number', as it began to vibrate alongside him and the beginning of AC/DC's *Thunderstruck* sounded again.

"Whoever it is, really wants to speak to you."

Wilson smiled, revealing attractive white teeth, as she placed a steaming mug on the table in front of him.

Robson hesitated, wondering what excuse he could use to

take the call in private. It took a few seconds for him to register the fact that it was his own phone and not the secure line. His voice croaked slightly as he answered.

"Jack Robson."

The voice coming through was male and so obviously full of anxiety that Jack could almost picture the hand of the panicked man, shaking at the other end.

"Who is this please?"

The DCI was in an upright position now, with Inspector Wilson looking on inquisitively.

"Chief Inspector, this is Reuben Adams." The voice still trembled. Robson threw the blanket off his legs and stood, attempting to awaken his senses. "Sir, I believe you paid a visit to my wife yesterday morning?"

"Yes, yes sir, how can I help? You sound troubled."

"You could say that. Jodie told me about your visit. Last night over the telephone, just as I was preparing to go on. You had her properly freaked out. She started telling me she thought she had seen some guy hanging around."

"Where, Reuben?"

"She told me that a man kept driving past in a white van – seemed to be looking for an address. She convinced herself in the end that it was related to your earlier visit. On top of that, the electricity had gone, so she was properly stressed."

Wilson watched the colour drain from Robson's cheeks. The DCI gulped before continuing.

"I wish she'd called me. Have you spoken to her since? When will you be home?"

"I am home, DCI Robson. That's why I'm calling. Jodie and

Rebecca are missing. Our performance last night didn't finish until gone midnight, so I didn't try calling until this morning. She sent me a run-of-the-mill text at just before half six, yesterday evening, which indicated that everything was okay, and saying that the electricity people had finally arrived. I've been trying on the car phone all the way here. I've already called the police, but when I found your card next to our bed—"

"I'm on my way. Please stay there, Mr Adams."

Robson was breathless now, and Wilson watched him wide-eyed, trying to imagine what had occurred.

"Jack?"

"They've got them!"

"Who?"

"Jodie and Rebecca Adams'"

"Shit – how?! While they were being watched?"

"They weren't being watched overnight. Fuck, he hasn't moved. Or at least, his car hasn't."

"Who?"

Emma looked perplexed as she watched Jack studying a second phone that he had pulled from his pocket. Robson realised what he had revealed and abruptly dressed in his jacket. His confused host followed him to the front door, both ducking beneath the eaves as they entered the small hallway.

"I'm coming with you, Jack."

He looked back to protest, but her face informed him the statement was non-negotiable.

Wilkins watched them with deep interest as they both flew from the house, acknowledging DCI Robson's indication that something had gone very wrong. As Inspector Wilson slammed the door to the cottage behind her, Robson cast another look in the direction of Wilkins that told him 'Follow'. Within seconds the car was spinning out of the sleepy street, bringing the local cottage dwellers to their windows just in time to see the second car leave in a whirl of dust.

Emma watched Jack briefly scrutinise the mobile satnav display.

"Twenty-four minutes – do you think that'll be long enough for you to fill me in on all the details that you've been leaving out?"

Robson swallowed, as his eyes remained fixed on the road ahead. Briefly, he contemplated attempting to hoodwink his partner. He inhaled deeply and began detailing the events of the last few days.

*

Dr O'Hara didn't have to work at looking bewildered any longer. The latest daily briefing delivered by Noah had been the most remarkable yet, at least to him. Those ahead of him skipped back to their individual accommodation, their optimism evidently embedded by the implied utopia that had been promised to them over a succession of visits to the 'Town Hall', and somewhat aided by the mind-bending chemicals which poured out of the little vents in their rooms, marking the arrival of another briefing.

He had seen his own family transformed over the past few days, becoming more acquiescent in general, even when not under the direct influence of the drugs. The doors to their rooms were no longer locked and people were now free to mingle around the complex that was, essentially, their prison. The doctor had decided that he was going to join them tonight. He didn't know that, soon enough, the drugs would no longer be necessary.

The psychological stress of being the only unaffected person among the group was becoming too much to bear. He had a decision to make: submit to the indoctrination programme or act, thereby revealing his immunity.

The latest briefing had left him concerned about what action these people were planning, and why. Noah's language was ostensibly metaphorical, promising, among other things, that the 'Age of Aquarius' was upon them. O'Hara's instinct told him that these guys were simply crazy, but he found the serene manner of his captors disturbing. Regardless of the literal meaning of their rhetoric, it seemed to the doctor that if he was going to act, it would need to be soon.

He thought that they had stopped bringing new 'guests' into the complex, but last night, for the first time in a while, it was 'requested' that they all remained in their rooms with the doors secured. With his ear to the door almost constantly throughout the evening, all had seemed quiet, until he was certain that he had heard a sobbing female. *And, possibly a child?* All the original guests were present and correct that morning, but he noticed on the way to their briefing that the door to the previously empty Room 12 was secured for the first time.

Dr O'Hara was needed in surgery in an hour's time. He would begin his investigation after the shift.

CHAPTER 55

The man's portly fingers reddened a little deeper, as he pressed his phone to his ear. The gratitude that came from his leader was all the reward he needed, and he couldn't disguise his pride. He certainly had reason to be proud, he felt. For, despite the growing intrusion from the tiresome DCI, he had successfully completed what was asked of him. Noah didn't wish to deviate from the plan unless it was essential, but he knew it was likely that they would have to deal with Robson properly. But first things first. It was now time to execute their plans for the DCI's charming partner.

Their objective was almost complete, and Jacob Miller had completed his last shift as the general of Porlock harbour.

*

When Jack and Emma arrived at Merlin Close, it had been difficult to locate a parking space, the street being lined with police vehicles. Their interview with the broken Reuben Adams didn't provide them with any additional information of value. Mr Adams had typically decided to blame himself. Right up until Friday morning, he and his family had been due to spend the weekend together at home. Then he got the call – a last-minute request to fill in for a sick musician, as part of the orchestra for a well-known West End production. Rehearsal wasn't necessary, he could have played the pieces in his sleep. He agreed to do one night for them, to the disappointment of Jodie, and had he been there to witness it, the disappointment of his daughter, as she arrived home from school to find that he wasn't going to be home that night.

Inspector Wilson wanted to take a look around, but her DCI seemed in a great hurry over something. She was going to insist on giving the place a thorough going over until she realised the source of his apparent distraction. Robson was still scrutinising the handheld device as they walked out through the elegant front door that Jack had admired not twenty-four hours earlier, leaving the uniformed officers and forensics team at the house with Mr Adams.

Even Bob Jefferies seemed to notice Robson's distraction and suspended his examination of the entrance hall to peer curiously towards the DCI, as he left the residence seemingly remote from his surroundings.

"He's back at home again."

"Knight?"

Jack nodded thoughtfully.

"Or, at least, his car is."

He placed the phone back into his jacket pocket and revved

the engine, as Emma buckled herself in.

"Are you going to bring him in?"

"No. We can't."

"What do you mean?"

Robson hesitated momentarily.

"There's something else I think we should check."

He pointed to the destination that he had just set on the map displayed on his mobile screen and they sped off.

They were heading south-west out of Minehead within ten minutes. Jack silenced the siren and switched off the flashing blues as they left the Saturday congestion behind and swung off the A39. The scenery quickly became more rugged as they cut along the moor, passing grazing sheep and the eponymous Exmoor ponies. Another twenty minutes gave Wilson the opportunity to coax her partner into elaborating further on the purpose of their latest escapade. The picnic areas and parking spots seemed to have all but terminated, signifying that they were deep into Exmoor.

DCI Robson slowed the car to a crawl, the display on the dash now indicating that they were within a mile of the last recorded grid reference for the red dot before it had departed again on a route back to Watchet. He switched to four-wheel drive and chose the least severe change of gradient to ease off the road and on to the gorse terrain. They continued for another ten minutes, on their new off-road course, heading a constant south. Jack brought the car to a standstill – the satnav indicated that they were at the spot.

"This is it?"

They both remained silent and took in the wild panorama

of uncultivated lowland heath, spread out as far as the eye could see. Gorse bushes grew out of the ground at random intervals. Robson silently began to question the accuracy of his newly acquired piece of technology as he surveyed the remote landscape, seemingly beyond even the boundaries of where the wildlife roamed. Wilson broke the silence.

"What are we looking for, exactly?"

"I haven't got the foggiest idea," came the somewhat distant response.

"I can't imagine there's anything of interest here. Unless you're on another nature trail. Is this definitely the spot?"

"Apparently so. But we don't know how far he went beyond this point. The journey history is broken, but he left the moor further east than the tracker showed him arriving."

"Shall we cover that ground now? If a vehicle has been out this far, then the ground should reveal it. Surely there would be tracks?"

Jack was nodding.

"Just what I was thinking."

He touched the accelerator gently and the vehicle began to crawl eastwards.

*

Superintendent Thorpe was arriving back at Somerset CID headquarters, following his trip to the capital. The previous day's meetings had been productive, and his objectives were clear. The first thing he needed to do was to get DCI Robson and Inspector Wilson both on board, to enable the plan to be fully executed. He felt more confident than ever that, between them, they had the capacity to bring this mystery to a conclusion. In the mean-time, MI5 had formed an impenetrable, yet, discreet circle around the island, ready to pounce. It had only been made possible by the excellent, if somewhat cavalier work by his two senior detectives. The link between the strange facility in the middle of the Channel and the kidnappings was still missing, however. And Thorpe would now put in place the necessary plans to ensure that remained the case, at least until it would be too late for anyone to stop them. For as long as everyone remained focussed on that island, they would be distracted from the epicentre of their operations.

He noticed his hand trembling slightly as he held the phone to his ear, not so much from nerves, but more in anticipation that they were now so close. The same automated message was delivered by each of the two numbers he tried. *Both out of service?* He wondered if they had decided to make another trip together to the island. But the security barrier would have prevented them from getting through.

The next call he made was answered almost immediately.

"Hi Christian."

"How are things your end?"

"Same as ever, no new forensic evidence, or signs of disturbance."

"Are they with you?"

"No, they both left about half an hour ago."

"Did they say where they were going?"

"Afraid not, but Robson seemed fairly distracted, like he was on to something."

"Okay, thanks Bob. I think it's time to get that situation sorted out. I'll see you very soon."

"Take care, Chris. See you soon."

Thorpe felt concern deep in his gut for a split second, before dismissing the annoying negative thought. *They couldn't possibly know about the location of Arcam.*

CHAPTER 56

They both noticed the trail they had hoped for in unison. The vehicle tracks stretched away towards the north east from the summit of a steep incline, proceeding along a slightly reduced gradient as the terrain began to level. They had abandoned the vehicle, not only because DCI Robson hadn't tested it in such extreme topography before, but it seemed wise to adopt a discreet approach. In truth, neither of them had really expected to encounter anything other than a lost sheep in the remote landscape.

The relentless wind that circled them reduced the effectiveness of their senses such that they hadn't heard the other vehicle approach until almost reaching the brow of the hill. Wilson was the first to react, pulling Robson to the ground. They both laid flat, panting, their exertion from the climb intensified by the surprise arrival of the vehicle. Still breathless, they crawled the last metre to the grassy precipice and risked peering over the top. The van had parked some fifty yards ahead of them in an area of already worn grass, and they now watched Michael Knight exit the driver's side door.

Inspector Wilson looked at her partner and rasped.

"Meeting place?"

DCI Robson's thoughtful nod turned to wonder as he watched the huge and familiar frame of a second man appear on the scene, seemingly having approached from inside a rocky mound beyond. The two detectives watched in mute awe as the comrades offered one another friendly pats on their respective shoulders.

"Looks like it," panted Jack, "but where the fuck did he just appear from?"

"He must have been there all along? Perhaps we were busy focussing on the car?"

Her theory evaporated as they both witnessed the men walk towards the rocky outcrop, about sixty to seventy yards away, and disappear before their eyes.

Jack knew Emma had been gazing at him for the last minute while he formulated the next move. She looked mildly bewildered as he left his cover.

"I'm going for a closer look."

"Jack, you do recall that these people are armed. We should do nothing, except for requesting backup."

He nodded impatiently.

"I don't know about you, but I lost my phone signal about three miles back – here, take this."

Wilson knew he was correct about the mobile reception, but her look of incredulity grew as she looked up from the firearm that Jack offered her with his outstretched arm and studied his eyes, as though searching for signs of insanity.

"Where did you get this?"

"It was issued to me at the MI5 briefing the other day. Cover me. I won't do anything stupid, I just want a closer look."

She noted the unexpectedly muscular tone of his left arm as she reached out and grabbed him, finally taking hold of his sleeve.

"Jack, what were your orders? Surely they didn't include this?"

"I told you, my priority was to establish the identity of the man we now know to be Michael Knight."

"So, haven't you fulfilled that?"

"We can't walk away." He noticed her continued exasperation and pulled his arm away from her gently, yet assertively. "Listen Emma, I told you about the briefing. I didn't mention to you that it wasn't only attended by senior Met and MI5 brass."

"What are you talking about? Who else was there?"

"The fucking Home Secretary and Prime Minister, that's who." His effort to maintain a low volume resulted in an unintentional aggressiveness as he hissed at her. "All I know is that the people in that room would not have been there unless it was a matter of utmost significance – presumably affecting national security."

Inspector Wilson's head swam, as her DCI's had during that meeting.

"Presumably you're comfortable with a firearm?" asked Robson.

Her face completed a cycle of confusion followed by insult, signifying that she didn't wish to dignify the comment with a spoken response. She gave a curt nod, while accepting the small firearm.

"Thought so. Use it if you need to."

DCI Robson gulped at the implications of his own words. Had he looked behind him, he would have noticed Wilson experiencing a similar reaction. But he was focussed only on his target as he prowled on all fours, using the gorse and long, wild grass as natural cover.

Emma felt a surge of confidence as she settled into her role. She watched her partner advance slowly towards the rocky summit ahead, feeling comfortable with the firearm under her control. She had been an excellent marksman in her training days and had always continued to keep her eye in.

*

Dr O'Hara had completed his routine check-ups of all the familiar residents and had also seen the two newcomers. The mother and daughter came together at the end of surgery. Every fibre of his body wanted to offer them some reassurance, especially on seeing how obviously petrified they both seemed. It served as a vivid reminder of their first days there, just a few weeks ago. The mother had been heavily sedated to enable them to transport her easily and she became both angry and hysterical as she began to come round in the consultation room. She only calmed when O'Hara had whispered briefly in her ear, after sending the nurse around the corner to the store for medication. He knew he would have around three minutes, based on previous experience. He allowed Jodie thirty seconds of silence in which to process his message, before going on to explain that she would find a mask had been placed inside her pocket while she had been laid on the bed. Her eyes were wide with a mixture of terror and hope as he described the drill that she would need to follow if she was going to remain immune to the indoctrinating toxins. They couldn't risk a mask for Rebecca, for fear of her immunity being too obvious.

After his final consultation, he went back to an empty room and eventually found his family, evidently in good spirits, mingling with the other residents in the square. He did his best to blend in with their behaviour for a few minutes, before slipping away unnoticed to carry out a little exploration he had been planning.

*

The foreboding sense in the pit of her stomach had remained with Inspector Wilson since first losing sight of her partner. She had been tempted to break cover a couple of times during the long five-minute spell during which she had lost visual contact. She exhaled long and hard as she watched him rise against the upright, grass-covered rock where the other two men had performed their physics-defying act some twenty minutes earlier. She wiped a loose strand of hair from her face and stood, disbelieving, braced against the wind, and blinking in an effort to recalibrate her vision. Her eyes saw Jack Robson performing the same disappearing act as the two men before him.

By the time he had reappeared and signalled her to join

him, she had already covered half the distance to the rock.

Neither of them had any sensible theories to offer as to what they now saw inside the ingeniously, and, surely, unnaturally positioned rock formation. Wilson thought it was alarmingly similar in its effect to the approach to the hidden cave entrance at the northern side of Steep Holm island. DCI Robson glanced at the three different phones he had just extracted from his pocket, before promptly replacing two, to leave him holding the only one that might be able to assist him.

He examined the three numerical codes. The 'Holm Code' had been used, and events had dictated that they never got the chance to use the 'Arm Code'. That left just one. Robson took a deep breath before punching the 'Ark Code' into the keypad adjacent to the unique entrance before them. An entrance that seemed to lead in an unusual direction – downwards, into the Earth.

CHAPTER 57

Dr O'Hara maintained a sufficiently anodyne smile to enable him to avoid any interest, doing his best to portray just another aimless wanderer, enjoying the freedom and camaraderie of his new homeland. Ten minutes later, he was out of the area of familiarity and heard men approaching him from somewhere just ahead. His pulse raced and he froze to the spot, knowing he would be unable to give a plausible explanation as to why he had deviated so far from the common areas.

As the voices grew alarmingly close he noticed the doorway and dived to his left. A split second later, the door at the end of the passage swung open. The doctor risked a stealthy look through the window in the door he now stood behind from an acute angle, and instantly recognised the two men. He watched Mikey and Ben pass, seemingly engaged in light-hearted conversation. He now had an idea which direction was out, he thought to himself, as he watched them disappear around the corner carrying their supplies, each with a firearm visible on his belt. They would no doubt remember to conceal their weapons before returning to the community.

The doctor waited a few minutes before quietly moving back out into the main passageway and proceeding through the exit that the other two men had just emerged from. He followed the passage, as it continued in a tangible incline in the only direction possible from that point, until he arrived at a security door, similar in structure, it seemed, to that of an aircraft, or perhaps even a spacecraft.

The doctor operated the huge lever mechanism to one side of the door and heaved the opening outward into the small chamber. A dead end. He may not have spotted the entry hatch directly above his head, had he not heard the voices.

CHAPTER 58

The green LED flickered synchronistically with the beep coming from the bland looking keypad. The mechanical sound of bolts disengaging inside the robust entrance hatch confirmed to them that the code had worked, and that, according to the evidence still displayed by the phone in his left hand, they had found the facility known as 'The Ark'.

They had both spent time researching the evidence acquired to date, but it hadn't taken a great deal of digging to reveal the translation of 'Arcam'. Considering the connotations, they both suppressed shudders as they now stood on what could well be its threshold.

DCI Robson imagined himself about to embark on a submarine as he pulled the heavy, circular hatch outwards. He wondered at his ability to do so as he examined the thick structure of solid metal that he held, before realising he had been assisted. Two hydraulic actuators, fully extended within the hinge system, held the entrance in the open position as he removed his hand from the cold steel. They both leaned over to peer into the pit beneath, which provided no indication of the extraordinary construction that lay beyond, deeper underground.

In a flash, Inspector Wilson drew her gun and pointed towards the dark figure below as soon as she caught the movement in the shadows.

"I have you in my sights – show yourself or I will fire!"

Robson squinted to see the form his partner had been so quick to identify, but it was only when a figure stepped out into the centre of the chamber beneath them that he was able to make out the spectacled, sober-looking man.

"P-please, I was merely exploring. I realise I've probably ventured too far, I'll return now."

"This is the police. Do exactly as I tell you, and you will not be hurt. What's down there?" Emma demanded, while pointing the firearm in the direction of the visibly frightened man below, as he tried to protect his dilated pupils from the burst of daylight.

Dr O'Hara processed the possibilities as he squinted up at the two silhouetted forms. Was this some sort of test, or had they really been discovered? As his eyes adjusted gradually to the change in lighting, he realised that neither of them appeared to be wearing uniforms, but somehow, they seemed different to their captors. He was sure he had heard them discussing backup before the door had opened. He decided to take a chance.

"I don't know how to explain it – it's like a kind of underground village I suppose. We're being held against our will … "

The desperation in the voice beneath was tangible. But the accent was cultured and oozed intelligence, indicating to Inspector Wilson that she didn't require the firearm. She handed it back to Robson, who replaced it inside his jacket.

"How do we get down there?" Wilson enquired with a steady voice, casting aside the aggressive edge.

The man shrugged his tense shoulders as he remained glued to the spot.

"I haven't been here before, at least not consciously."

Robson judged that it must have been at least a fifteen-foot drop, perhaps twenty. He frowned at his partner, wondering what she found so interesting in the hatchway construction. His eyes widened when he saw the source of her interest. She grabbed the lip of what appeared to be another layer between the ground level surface on which they were crouched and the top of the chamber beneath. It jerked a couple of inches as she gave it an initial tug, then slid across the opening as her fingers located the convenient recess. Robson leant across her chest and helped her to pull the thin metal sheet across as far as it would traverse, before they both felt it engage into a sub-mechanism at the opposite end of the opening. He pointed to the toggle switch that was now evident on the right-hand side.

"Seriously? A bloody elevator?"

They stood facing one another, millimetres separating their faces. It was apparent that the construction was more than capable of supporting them, so Wilson operated the toggle. The platform reacted with a sudden jerk, causing her to grab onto DCI Robson's torso, letting go again as they slowly descended into the pit beneath. As they were lowered towards the man below, Wilson grabbed DCI Robson's arm with her free hand, noting that he had reached inside his pocket for support. With a subtle expression, he silently conceded that the firearm wouldn't be necessary and relaxed, just a little.

The pulleys on the underside of the chamber's ceiling squeaked as the steel ropes unwound and they approached the end of their short journey. The man at the bottom seemed keen-eyed, if a little bewildered, having moved aside to avoid the descending platform. Inspector Wilson felt a tinge of recognition, as she followed Robson and moved off the simple elevator to greet their new acquaintance.

"I'm Detective Chief Inspector Jack Robson, and my colleague is Inspector Wilson."

Jack's hand twitched, ready to grab the six inches of cold steel from his jacket pocket at the first sign of a bluff.

"I-I am Doctor Darryl O'Hara."

Of course you are! Wilson resolved the uncertain familiarity, while Robson was confirming to himself that he was apparently face to face with one of the listed abductees. The DCI presented his identification to the doctor, sensing his growing anxiety.

"Can you tell us how many are being held here?"

He kept his voice low, now noticing a huge door ajar to their left, which appeared to provide an exit from the small chamber.

"There are now twenty-seven of us, including myself."

"Now?"

"Another two were brought in last night. A young lady and her daughter."

The detectives both felt close to screaming 'eureka!'. After weeks of being led a merry dance and chasing down blind alleys, they had now stumbled across the prison, which potentially held all the kidnapping victims and surely led to the elusive perpetrator. But it still made no sense. No ransom demands, and on the evidence of the good doctor before them, no apparent mistreatment either.

"We need to be quick, before anyone notices you're missing. How well are you guarded in there?"

"They've been employing hypnotic drugs, so everyone is fairly amicable now, and the security has relaxed somewhat, in comparison to what it was like at the beginning."

The detectives both suppressed their inner thoughts and DCI Robson continued probing the doctor, at pace.

"So, are you saying that people are free to roam around as they please?"

"Not indefinitely, no, but at certain periods. Hence my ability to venture out here, albeit in secret."

His eyes seemed to flicker with a vital recollection. "But they are armed."

"What can you tell us about the drugs?"

"It's in gaseous form. It is blown through the air vents in the rooms, before everyone gets marched to what they call the Town Hall, for another briefing. It's generally a kind of rhetoric about how we are 'the chosen few', who together will rescue mankind from its failings. It really is extraordinary stuff."

"What seems to be their objective?"

"It's not clear. It's all a little abstract, really, cajoling people by metaphor and inference – there's nothing literal in the pep talks. But all I would say is that it seems they are planning to keep this little community together for the long term. There have been discussions about generations after us living in peace and harmony, while the earth is restored to its former glory. 'The new beginning is nigh'. Pretty fanatical stuff."

DCI Robson felt his heart thumping as he inhaled, thinking of the level of seniority at which this case had generated interest, and forced himself to stop processing the permutations.

"Is it apparent who might be running this ... this, institution? I mean, is it clear who the boss is?"

"Yes, I know exactly who the boss is. He's known as 'Noah' down here. But I also know him by his real identity. I've treated his family for years."

The detectives watched the doctor intently, and both were poleaxed when O'Hara spoke the name. The reason for the high-level briefing in London suddenly made perfect sense. In silence, they both separately connected the pieces of evidence and all the experiences of the past few weeks. They were currently holding a meeting with a press-ganged inmate of a high security nuclear bunker. The name of the principal had eliminated any doubt that the organisation would have the connections and ability to duck under the most sophisticated surveillance.

As they stared fixedly into one another's eyes, they both understood that they were contemplating the same thing, and the criticality of time now became devastatingly clear. There was a connection between the bunker beneath the rugged terrain of Exmoor and the facility on Steep Holm island, the discovery of which had attracted the interest of the country's secret service. The penny had dropped. It appeared they were hunting more than just a kidnapper. They were on the trail of someone intent on changing the future of the human race.

DCI Robson registered the urgency that flashed across Wilson's face, as she visibly shook off her thoughts and parked the theorising for later.

"Okay, here's what we're going to do, doctor. You need to get back to your quarters, wherever they might be, as quickly and discreetly as possible. Don't speak to anyone about what you know. You will know when we are coming. We need to get support. Within a couple of hours, we'll have you all out of there, I promise. We don't want to arouse suspicion in your captors and consequently place your associates in any danger by removing you from this installation now."

The doctor seemed to have lost his anxiety, and stood in silence for a few moments, holding the DCI's gaze.

"I have no intention of leaving here without my family, Chief Inspector."

Robson realised that he had been wrong to expect a protest, and the doctor's reply served only to remind him further of how high the stakes were. They both watched the doctor's slim back disappear through the only entrance, wondering if they had made the right decision. They both understood it was a decision in the interest of the majority.

*

Back on the surface, Inspector Wilson double-checked that the entrance door had been secured. Beneath their feet, Dr O'Hara had carried out a similar check on the large porthole once again to seal him and his fellow inmates deep underground.

The two men holding their guns at his back were silent. It was the colossus that spoke first after he had turned from securing the door. He felt himself trembling at the flawless English, spoken in deep, eastern European tones.

"So, Doctor, you've arranged for us to entertain some visitors later, how pleasant. Mikey, go out to the entrance and alter the access code as discussed, please. You come with me, Doctor, if you would be so kind."

O'Hara fought to control his trembling, as he obeyed the gesture from the man with the gun and walked ahead of both Ben and Noah, who had joined them following the call over the radio from Mikey. The only thought in the doctor's mind was that of extinguished hope.

*

DCI Robson fell heavily as they both pelted down the hill. Wilson continued in her awkward descent, feeling the pain shoot up through her left leg, and not turning in reaction to the faint sound of expletives behind her. Jack caught up with her at the car, finding it parked as they had left it on the barren moorland. Emma called up the number for Thorpe, but the phone still displayed there was no signal.

Robson was planning a different phone call, one which he would pull over to make as soon as a signal could be found.

CHAPTER 59

Inspector Wilson watched her Superintendent through the blind-laden window. The moment he sensed her presence, he looked up, beckoning her inside while terminating the phone call simultaneously. She had already briefed Thorpe in full on their way back to headquarters and he had been ready to deliver their orders. For a second, she thought he might explode after he was informed that DCI Robson had been given special orders from MI5, which he had left to attend to as they spoke. After several expletives and rhetorically questioning who was heading up the investigation, he recovered his composure to inform Wilson that he had seconded DCI Griffin from his current investigation, who was assembling a team at that very moment, to augment the one that special branch had dispatched to meet them on the moor.

Inspector Wilson travelled in the passenger seat alongside the Superintendent, as the Mercedes cruised back in the direction from which she had just arrived. The SWAT teams were already roaring towards the moor and Thorpe had explained that he expected there to be an impenetrable cordon around the area by the time they arrived.

*

Meanwhile DCI Robson obeyed his summons and returned to the hotel. He hadn't been there for a few days, and not since the murder of his neighbour, Jonny Searle. He was duly escorted to a guarded conference room as soon as he arrived in reception. The head of MI5 stood before him, a stern figure, fully suited and deadly serious. He briefed Robson on the mission that was already underway. Nobody had moved on to or off the island in the past two days and the specialists were poised to move in. They did not wish to alert the men currently holed up on Exmoor, for fear of causing them to expedite their next move, and until they were in a position to disengage the action. Thorpe had been briefed accordingly, and would be standing by at a discreet distance, with his team on the moor. DCI Robson's attendance was required on the island, to assist the specialist unit in locating the critical points of interest he and Inspector Wilson had located previously – almost at the highest cost, Jack recalled.

*

Deep underground, the atmosphere had become less convivial and everyone had been instructed to return to their rooms until further notice. The reason hadn't been clear to the rest, but the doctor had appeared tense for some reason when he returned with Noah, and seemed particularly wary of the bear-like figure at his rear.

Following his short interview, Ben escorted Dr O'Hara to a single room. He had been expecting the sound and it wasn't long before he heard the familiar click from inside the air vent. The captors needed to reinforce their control. O'Hara was no longer immune to the mind-controlling instrument, and was now without his defence. The situation would have been no different had he been allowed to return to his family. The men had discovered his stashed mask during the search of his room and were keen to have the doctor on board. He would be exposed to the drug along with the others.

Just along the corridor, the young woman again felt another pang of guilt as she lay on her bed and turned to face the wall, before adorning the mask. Her little girl would soon be drunk along with the others. She had been surprised, like the doctor, at the way the drug seemed to have an identical effect on the children as it did the adults. Jodie had not missed the furtive glance that the doctor had briefly shown her as he entered the common area with the others. She also suspected that she would soon be the only rational person remaining in the community, as she looked over her shoulder before being closed in her room with Rebecca. The last thing she noticed was O'Hara being escorted towards the Town Hall, under the close attention of the large, normally so affable, man.

CHAPTER 60

DCI Robson let his mind wander to the incident that nearly cost him his life, as he leaned back in the bouncing RIB, wedged between the two marksmen. Their pilot powered through the Channel at such exceptional pace that contact between boat and water was not continuous. Anyone watching the breathtaking approach of the power boats in V formation, with Jack's at the arrow's point, would have surely believed they were witnessing the filming of a spy movie. A ring of dark helicopters awaited the boats, looking menacing as they circled the insignificant little island in the distance. A mist had descended, filtering the moonlight into sinister shadows.

Within a quarter of a mile of their destination, the mission commander gave clear and concise instructions over the radio. The leader oozed confident mastery over all he surveyed from his position at the helm adjacent to the pilot. He surveyed the scene ahead of the protruding rock. After another second, the formation broke, but the speed did not. As the marksmen cocked their rifles, Jack's boat led another four around the northern face of the island, while the remaining five thundered towards the southern coast.

The marksmen leapt from the two moving boats as they entered the cave via the concealed northern entrance, while another ten armed specialists were disembarking at various points around the perimeter, listening to the commander's directions in their earpieces. Along the jetty, the armed men resembled statues as they held aim towards the large steel door ahead of them, while a lone boat remained just inside the entrance and covered their rear.

Two gun-wielding professionals sprinted past in their black wetsuits and placed incendiaries left and right of the door before retreating. DCI Robson had already been told they wouldn't be wasting time with a code that would have been changed as soon as it had become clear that it had been leaked. The sliding doors experienced a new sensation of motion as they flew inwards. The detonation echoed within the cave, but the destruction was impressively focussed. It would be the only controlled explosion that the commander would risk, in the knowledge of the secret arsenal that reportedly lay somewhere inside.

Two marksmen ran in first to secure the entrance for Robson and the others to follow. The small collection of forklifts lay redundant and, after a moment of careful examination, the commander was sufficiently satisfied to instruct his men to proceed in the direction that their mission guest had indicated. The SWAT team proceeded towards the passageway that DCI Robson had previously traversed with his partner.

The surroundings were not new to Jack, yet, appeared different. The lighting that had guided them on their previous, unannounced visit was no longer active. Having pulled on their night vision goggles, they advanced down the passageway until reaching the large circular room. The only lighting now consisted of six LED lights above the entrances to each of the silos.

The commander gave the signal for his team of technicians to take up position at each of the doors and begin their specialist work, which demanded a rather different skillset to those of the emotionless professionals that stood in the centre of the room covering every position with composed precision. Once erected, the mobile lighting transformed the space into an area of familiarity for Jack.

The engineers at each of the entrances began their work. Jack was watching the concentration on the face of the young man at the entrance to Silo 1 and couldn't be sure how long the commander had been signalling to him when he finally caught the gesture in his peripheral vision. He paced across to join him at the central door, feeling slightly surprised that he still retained any purpose to the commander and his crack team.

"The whole island is secure, DCI Robson. Except for the six silos, we are confident that we're the only ones here. I want you to take me to the other points of interest on the island."

Robson couldn't stop himself from looking instinctively upwards.

He led the commander and one of the non-armed team members, who Jack presumed to be another technical expert, given his slight frame, fresh face and wavy hairstyle, as opposed to the stereotypical, severe crop beneath the headgear of the armed personnel. They were met by more armed team members as they stepped out into the dusky evening sky. The air felt cold on their faces, as they proceeded across the raw wilderness. Jack forced his attention away from the breathtaking Jurassic coastline only a few miles in the distance, and surveyed the immediate area. He had only been there twice, but it didn't take him long to get his bearings. The commander's eyes followed the DCI's pointed finger, which indicated the far side of a clearing that was bordered by trees on every side, and where there seemed to be the faintest trace of two flickering lights.

Within minutes, they swept across the clearing under the cover of unseen marksmen who were in constant communication with the commander of the operation. They were greeted by the owners of the two light sources on arrival at the observation shelter, who had taken an interest in the fact that the ostensibly natural object appeared to have an entrance, which they had already taken the liberty of breaching.

Inside the shelter, the commander and his technical assistant stood back and combined their torch-beams to illuminate the area around DCI Robson's right foot, as he dragged the loose ground surface away. Without a word, the commander strode towards the clear outline of a hatch in the floor and was joined by his two marksmen. The three men heaved at the portal and secured it in its upright position using the integrated stop. Jack watched the commander's breath condense into steam as he peered down into the dark hole. It seemed surreal at first to watch him place a foot into the hole, followed by another, before disappearing out of sight. The light that shone up from below revealed the steps that had been cut into the side of the excavation, and the young assistant acted on the prompt to follow. Jack presumed it to be an open invitation and followed them into the earth.

The engineer examined the cutting-edge microwave reception device with nervous fascination, as the commander received another message in his earpiece. The receiver mast they had already uncovered some fifty yards away confirmed the discovery of a highly-sophisticated communications hub. The commander plucked a phone from his inside pocket and called the Director General.

Somewhat surprisingly to Jack, the commander ordered the engineer from the enclosure. His eyes bulged as he watched the size eight walking boots disappear from the last step before turning to Robson, his face displaying anxiety for the first time that evening.

"DCI Robson, can you confirm the last contact that you had with Inspector Wilson?"

Robson gulped as momentarily, he felt a tinge of suspicion in the commander's tone, the same effect, no doubt, experienced by countless interviewees. He took a breath.

"Approximately two hours ago, commander, when I left her at HQ."

"Did you tell her where you were going?"

The colour had drained from Robson's face as he responded. "Yes."

"Have you received any mobile communication from her?"

Jack pulled out his phone, puzzled by where the line of questioning was heading. The phone indicated that there was no signal, as expected, which meant that the unread text displayed on the screen must have been received some time earlier, before arriving on the island. The time confirmed that it was sent whilst Jack was in the boat heading for the island. The implication of the wording was too peculiar for him to comprehend at first, so much so that he couldn't repeat the message, and instead held the phone a foot from the commander's inquiring face. The man seemed more imposing than ever as he accepted the device unceremoniously, before promptly reading the text and silently handing the phone back. The commander's expression remained neutral as he grabbed his own communication device with one large hand, and spoke almost immediately.

"Sir, it seems our advantage of stealth has been compromised. Yes, sir, right away. Will confirm upon arrival."

He replaced his phone again and stared fixedly and somewhat seriously at Jack.

"DCI Robson. It seems the situation has reached a rather critical stage. Our orders are to attend the moor." He pointed a finger towards the opening above them. "I need you to wait up there with my men while I prepare. I expect to leave within fifteen minutes."

Jack considered the implications. It seemed extraordinary that Emma might act in such a maverick fashion, especially given that she was aware of the stakes. "Okay, Commander. Are my colleagues acting alone?"

The commander paused at the bottom step and his broad neck creased as he swivelled to eye Jack.

"Your colleagues, DCI Robson, are acting entirely without

authority, and, consequently, are endangering both themselves and this mission."

"Is it worth putting in a call to Superintendent Thorpe, sir?"

"Already done, Chief Inspector. Thorpe is incommunicado."

Jack shivered as he pulled himself out of the pit and nodded at the remaining two armed men as he walked outside the enclosure. He held the phone in his palm, still displaying the message from his partner, and prayed for it to pick up just a single bar of signal so that he could make contact with her. His shoulders sagged, and he let his head fall back. Above him, millions of galaxies proudly shimmered. He was aware of the irony as he stood on what seemed such an insignificant rock in comparison to the sea of majestic sparkling dots overhead. And yet that insignificant rock could soon have a pivotal role in the order of things.

The serenity of the universe above seemed to help him regain his composure. He pulled the second mobile phone from his other pocket, which he had almost forgotten, having surrendered the other, third device at the MI5 briefing earlier. Feeling energised with hope, he pressed the power button and watched Barry Searle's mobile kick into life. It was receiving a signal. He punched Inspector Wilson's number in, taking care to accurately replicate the number displayed on his own phone. His heart promptly sank again as he listened to the bland, automated message stating that the receiver's phone was temporarily unavailable.

He hesitated for a moment before deciding to attempt a second call. It seemed unlikely that there had been a breakdown in communication, given the professionalism of the team he was currently working alongside. *So, what the hell are they doing? Have they discovered something new?*

He entered Superintendent Thorpe's number from his own phone into Searle's. He was unsurprised but still disappointed by another automated voice at the other end.

It wasn't until he had replaced the phone in his pocket that his consciousness caught up and registered what he had just seen. Breathlessly, he withdrew the phone again and brought up the recently dialled numbers with his trembling thumb. *It can't be. Something is very wrong here.*

He raced towards the commander, who was already returning with a small team. The marksmen stood aside and watched Jack warily, as he appeared to brief the commander on something troubling him.

DCI Robson fought to keep his voice steady as he conveyed the terrifying development to the commander, who remained impassive throughout. The sound of the crickets could still be heard intermittently above the noise of heavy breathing, whispered exchanges and thudding boots, as he ran alongside the commander, his muscular limbs enjoying a break from the tension. They followed the dark silhouettes of their fellow team members across the rough island terrain, seemingly headed for a large, dark object in the distance. His mind jangled with the possibilities implied by the content of the phone that he felt in his trouser pocket. The last number he had dialled had been that of his Superintendent, yet the device already had the number registered in its address book as that of 'Christian Thorpe'.

As Jacob Miller sat in the car and watched the activity of the day dwindle to that of a few remaining detectives, he wondered at how life would change for these people within the coming days and weeks. It wasn't a thought that made him particularly happy, but as their incredible leader had explained many times, *it was the only way*.

He had expected to be the one responsible for bringing the delectable Inspector Wilson in, at long last, but a couple of last minute changes to the plan had been necessary. His interest was focussed on another female, and he watched her now through the open blinds as she prepared to leave for the evening, having completed the objectives that had been set for her. One final check of the office door coincided with a glance at the name above. She paused momentarily, eyes fixed on the sign: 'Superintendent Thorpe'. Her boss had been distracted for the past few hours, after the phone call from the detectives describing their findings on the moor. But he had wasted no time in responding to the call to action, and he and his inspector were making their way to the scene at that very moment.

The harbour master sat up, poised in the driver's seat, as the secretary to the Superintendent strode purposefully from the building and headed in his direction. As their eyes met through the windscreen, Miller moved swiftly, and the vehicle door creaked on its rusty hinge as it flung open. The secretary stopped and watched the rotund man approach and place a hand on top of her arm.

"Evenin', Louise."

"Jacob, how are things?"

"Very well, my love. Your carriage awaits."

She allowed a faint smirk to show at the corners of her mouth.

"Everything is in place?"

"It's about to be."

"Good. Shall we, then?"

Jacob Miller nodded and smiled at how much the lady's enthusiasm seemed to match his own, as she climbed through the passenger door and prepared to embark on their final journey. She turned to look over her right shoulder as she buckled herself in, smiling enthusiastically to the passenger in the rear seat.

"Hi Bob. This is it then!"

Bob Jefferies remained silent, and leant forward to give her a peck on the cheek.

CHAPTER 61

Inspector Wilson had expected to see a larger presence than just the solitary white van that sat on the edge of the moor, feeling that the opportunity for discretion was surely behind them. The right-hand side of the sleek, silver Mercedes rose as the Superintendent unfolded his large frame and confidently approached the van. She wasted no time in following her commanding officer, standing shoulder to shoulder in support.

Initially, the familiarity of the vehicle registration didn't sink in. She caught her breath at the eventual recollection of the combination of characters on the van's plate, and tried to regulate her breathing as she became aware of a pistol close to her temple. The man holding it seemed to be alone.

Inspector Wilson glanced at Thorpe, anticipating the telepathic signal to strike in unison. The man may have been a colossus, even towering above the Superintendent's frame, but he was outnumbered two to one. But the signal never came, and she stood in confused silence as her boss approached her instead, holding another shiny object. Within a couple of seconds, her hands had been fastened behind her back in the cuffs. Wilson was dumbstruck as she watched Thorpe instruct the other man to lock her in the back.

She held her commanding officer's eyes for only a second, and noticed for the first time how devoid they seemed to be of emotion.

The big man pushed her up into the back of the van unceremoniously, after removing her phone and baton during a rough search. She fell on to a mattress but then the space was plunged into darkness as the doors closed. The last thing she witnessed was Superintendent Christian Thorpe getting back into the silver car. For the next few minutes, in a state of shock, she imagined all the kidnapping victims sat on the same mattress that she now occupied. She continued to gaze wide-eyed into the black space, until the van jerked suddenly and threw her backwards on to the bed.

*

Jack's knees threatened to buckle at any moment as he fixed a horrified gaze upon the large, dark machine, feeling the gust on his face caused by its spinning rotors. He remained paralysed as the authoritative voice of the commander reminded him of the urgency of their voyage. He thought of Emma as he dutifully climbed aboard, as panic threatened to overwhelm him.

DCI Robson weakly buckled himself into his seat, hoping that the machine would fail, and that they would have to revert to alternative transport. He reminded himself of the critical requirement to undertake the journey, but remained unable to break free of the chains of anxiety as they increased their grip around his chest, causing his breathing to become progressively shallower.

The chopper began to lift, while the commander was still discharging instructions. Unpleasant memories flashed through Jack's head like a damaged film reel, cruelly tormenting him.

The marksmen were too focussed on their duties to notice the DCI's panic-stricken symptoms, as the chopper soared swiftly away to the mainland, still climbing in a seemingly effortless display of power. As they were propelled forward, the vision in his mind's eye intensified until he gasped audibly. An unexpected hand of consolation appeared on his shoulder as one of the shooters noticed his discomfort, but it did not allay his suffering. His eyes still unable to focus, he dared to allow his gaze to drift below them and saw they were now well above the dark cliffs, as they thundered across the night sky, high above the lighting that could be seen emanating from the towns and holiday camps beneath. Within minutes the landscape changed again and appeared just as barren and uninhabited as the territory they had left behind. DCI Robson's pulse still threatened to overpower him, when within ten minutes of departure, the pilot eased them down on to the wild terrain of Exmoor.

As Jack wiped his sweat-laden brow with a sleeve, the machine cast a powerful beam, illuminating a battalion of dark vans streaming on to the moor. Within seconds, a large company of armed personnel swept into formation.

Robson was swept along by the commander and his team towards the entrance to the underground dwelling. The engineers had already established that the access had now been permanently sealed. The vision of the commander in passive thought seemed an unnatural sight. His eyes moved thoughtfully between the secured bunker entrance and his army, which surrounded it. The strong wind ruffled his flak jacket slightly as he came to terms with the fact that their hopes remained elsewhere. He thought of the team of six hackers left on the island, still frantically working at gaining entry to the silos. Those agents situated on the island understood the risk to their lives, but they also understood that their lives would be at risk even if they were now tucked up in bed. The world was about to change.

CHAPTER 62

Inspector Wilson had followed Superintendent Thorpe into the underground route in silence, persuaded to do so by the gun pointing at her back. She felt perplexed that the entrance was not the same one that she and Jack had discovered earlier. She proceeded in growing disbelief as she took in the underground settlement, noting the cafe, surgery, shops and even town hall that all served to alter her preconception that these people had been holed up inside a crammed prison. But all these sights and smells could not disguise the fact that they were deep underground, even though great lengths had been taken to disguise the fact visually.

She had not expected to encounter a subterranean town.

Her veins pulsed as she watched Thorpe greeting the man he referred to as Noah with a hug. They both appeared content as she was escorted into a room without another word. She recognised some of the furniture from St Audries manor, now relocated to the somewhat less palatial room she now found

335

herself in, and at least one of the pieces of art that adorned the walls looked familiar, as she sat and waited for the reality of the situation to be validated.

It was the familiar, deep agrarian tone of Thorpe that broke the silence, although his voice was now the only recognisable characteristic left. It was a stranger that occupied the former shell of someone she once knew.

"I can see this has been something of a shock for you, Wilson. We would have rather done this another way if we could have." His voice sounded sincere and authoritative, as though he were delivering just another routine briefing at the station. "But your new partner started to cause us a few headaches, so we couldn't risk bringing you here too early."

Emma understood that the pause was an invitation for her to contribute to the conversation, but her jaw was like the rest of her body – paralysed. Thorpe displayed a paternal smile.

"But now that you are here, we can explain Noah's plan." He glanced with deference towards the other man. "And in time we are both confident that you will be grateful, indeed, honoured, to have been selected."

"Selected?"

Her voice, if it was hers, wobbled.

"Sir, I don't know what the *plan* is, but if you are confirming what has become evident in the past few moments, which is that you are party to this little establishment, then you are also an aid to kidnapping. And murder?"

She noticed again how Thorpe seemed to look to the other man in awe, then back at her with a patronising grin, as though waiting for the sage to reveal the principle of the universe – that which was out of reach to mere mortals. Noah obliged, on cue.

"Certain lamentable actions have been necessary, Miss Wilson, to pave the way for us to reach the promised land, as it were."

Noah's voice was also familiar; still sounding cultured, which seemed somewhat paradoxical given the dialogue.

"The people that have been selected to form a new community down here will all have a part to play in our future."

"What future? Underground?"

She could feel herself scowling.

"Your little hiding place has been discovered. How long do you think you have? MI5 will be swarming all over the moor by now!"

Sir Geoffrey Charlesworth gave a condescending chuckle as Thorpe looked on in apparent glee.

"Let me assure you, there is no longer any way into, or out, of this complex. We have now entered our self-sustaining phase and those of us in the first generation have seen the outside world for the final time, madam. Sad it may sound, it is also a most exciting time."

Wilson nearly screamed.

"Are you downright mad? How can you possibly expect to sustain this existence? Regardless of how well you believe we are sealed underground, I think you will find that it won't take too long for them to get access."

"In a very short while, Miss Wilson, this fallen race will have too many other issues to focus on than concerning themselves about a group of people situated beneath their feet. Moreover, they will be responding to the instinctive reaction and priority of self-preservation."

Her heart was in her mouth as she paused and allowed Charlesworth's abstract monologue to sink in, evoking a vision of the arsenal she had witnessed on the little island in the Channel.

"Steep Holm? You're planning to detonate nuclear weapons?!" She was gasping as she spoke. "What exactly are you aiming at?!"

The calm manner of the self-named Noah gave her all the confirmation she needed that the military hero stood before her had indeed become a radical fanatic. She had seen the infrastructure with her own eyes, providing a frightening confirmation that this was no ordinary zealot. This man had the knowledge and power to carry out his vision with devastating impact.

"Let's not get into gory details, Miss Wilson. But the ICBMs that I know you have caught a glimpse of are strategically programmed to have maximum impact at the heart of power on every continent on the globe. Once they have been dispatched, and with a little help from some falsified, coded messages sent 'on behalf' of the world leaders, the Superpowers will each receive scrambled messages indicating the source of the attack, to ensure that retaliation will be forthcoming across the planet and between all nuclear nations and beyond."

Inspector Wilson was breathless, barely able to remain on her tired legs.

"And then what?!"

"Armageddon, I believe it has been labelled."

Emma knew that her part in the conversation was

superfluous, however, she felt compelled to understand the mind of the man standing so nonchalantly before her. A man who apparently saw justification in creating a holocaust on an immeasurable scale.

"What the hell do you hope to achieve?"

"We are saving humanity from itself, Emma. Are you immune to the corruption and savagery that now surrounds us? The world is on the brink of the most fierce and irreversible conflict that humankind has ever experienced. Human rights are being blatantly disregarded while nations manoeuvre to secure power and influence at the cost of all non-indigenous people. The people themselves – we, humans of the western world – have been persuaded that the only future for us is a nationalist, insular one."

He may have been crazy, but he spoke with an eloquence that matched his passion, Emma thought.

"Tolerance for our neighbours is depleting at a rapid rate. This disease has set in and will spread, and we are powerless to stop it. So, we inside this community are going to accelerate the process for them, and while we and our descendants sit out the nuclear winter above our heads, we will re-educate ourselves in the skills of basic human interaction and kindness."

Charlesworth had become animated now, the veins running through his aged cheeks beginning to glow slightly as he delivered his oration with passion.

"Simple communities where everyone has a part to play and those that are too sick or too old to contribute will be supported. Capitalism and consumerism will become a distant memory of a flawed past. And when our beautiful Earth, which has suffered such abuse, has finally recovered and reset itself from human devastation, our people will once again venture to the surface as an emotionally and socially evolved species. And as we spread, the respect and empathy between us will have become embedded in our psyche."

"Sir Geoffrey, you seem to have failed to realise that if your fanatical plan succeeds, on the scale that you're suggesting, it would not be safe for humans outside of this bunker in your lifetime."

"Miss Wilson, do give me some credit. You think we are simply saving ourselves? It is our great- great-grandchildren who will benefit from the selfless actions we now undertake, with great responsibility. In the meantime, we will live in peace and humility down here."

"And the system that you are running away from? Do you not see that you are simply recreating it, albeit on an even more sinister scale, with you as the most monstrous dictator? And judging by your population demographic here, it would even appear that you could stand accused of practising eugenics!"

For a moment, the tall man's frame appeared to vibrate, his eyes piercing hers, before visibly forcing himself to indulge in a couple of deep breaths.

"Come, come. We are running short of time. But suffice to say, the facility that you are now a part of here, is but a fraction of the overall picture. Our brothers and sisters across the globe join us hand in hand, as we speak. However, great things require sacrifice. We recognise that we have been forced to carry out actions that are contrary to the principles that have led us to this solution. But please believe me – they have always been seen only as a means to an end. Oh, and I have decided to adopt my codename permanently from now on, Miss Wilson. No pretence or class system will exist down here, or at any of the other communities we have set up around the world."

Emma didn't want to submit to sneering but felt her restraint weakening.

"Of course, 'Noah'. You also realise that you will have no way of activating your weapons of mass destruction. MI5 has secured the island and will be disarming as we speak. You cannot detonate them."

As Sir Geoffrey smiled silently, totally relaxed, Inspector Wilson felt a shudder through her body.

Thorpe took over.

"The infrastructure that you saw only a small part of on the island, is the most highly advanced weapons activation system currently on the planet, Wilson. We estimate that even the greatest expertise available would require days to discover a means of disarming. And as for detonation – you don't really think that such an elaborate plan would require us to be at the site of detonation, do you?"

Emma fell into silence as she was nudged out of the room.

"We will talk again later, Miss Wilson. Right now, we have our final task to complete."

Charlesworth bowed gallantly as she was escorted out. As they walked towards the square, a gathering of people could be seen gaily obeying the gentle requests given to them by a nurse and the kind-looking man who several weeks earlier had blown a hole in Inspector Wilson's leg. She was too busy trying to evaluate the almost bacchanalian elation of the crowd to notice the ponytailed man's face crack just a little, as he became aware of a presence that understood him for what he was – at least she did for the time being.

Just as the door was closed on Jodie Adams and her daughter, Wilson noticed the surreptitious glance that was determinedly offered to her, indicating that she potentially had an ally.

*

Deep inside the windswept island, the team of technical specialists worked at gaining access to the six silos. They had already judged that the security doors sealing the destructive contents within would not be susceptible to any form of brute force readily available to them on the island. Detonation would only be used as a last resort. The captain couldn't hide his shock at the formidable construction, which had defied repeated abuse from their battering rams. Following the last call from his commander, he had judged that a controlled detonation was now a risk that might need to be taken and ordered the necessary materials. He was aware of questioning eyes on him, as the device was brought by his loyal adjutants.

They would never know how relieved he felt when, within moments, the sweaty young operative at Silo 2 exclaimed, almost euphorically, "We're in!" The elite force all looked towards the slim figure that slouched, holding his hands on his knees while displaying a look of satisfaction. The door to his left had slid open, confirming that the CPU had been overridden.

The engineers gathered in a huddle, before retreating to the remaining five doors to apply the newly discovered access sequence. As the last door slid open, the elite company reacted instantly to the captain's barked commands. The technical experts stood aside and watched six separate teams in black clothing bolt into each of the six silos, before each followed into the silo they had been responsible for opening. Minutes later, the captain requested radio silence as each team tried to come to terms with the sensational sights confronting them. The captain felt his jaw open and then corrected his reaction. Within moments, it became apparent to the technical specialists that cracking the code to disarm the devices would prove to be a far greater task – and one that would likely exceed the time available.

CHAPTER 63

The battle-hardened commander remained in contemplative silence, oblivious to the biting wind that swept across the desolate moor. The noise of shuffling feet could occasionally be heard, with all other sounds suppressed by the whirling gale. He was unaccustomed to events not proceeding in accordance with his design.

He had been advised that the excavation machinery he had ordered half an hour ago would take about another hour to arrive – another detail that hadn't gone as planned. The estimated time to provide a suitable access for his team to enter, without being trapped underground, was another two to four hours. However, the construction expert who had been ordered from his bed in the middle of a cold night had not yet arrived on site to give a more refined estimate. The commander knew they didn't have that time and hadn't required the rather explicit reminder given to him by the Director General over the telephone.

DCI Robson accurately judged that the commander might be open to a second opinion at that stage. He patted his sides and rubbed his hands together to fight off the shivering that was beginning to set in, as the wind howled in constant reminder of its existence. He approached the commander as he stood alone gazing at the sealed entrance.

"Commander, could I have a word?"

His words seemed to have been carried away elsewhere by the wind at first, as the black clad, hard-looking man remained in position, unflinching. After several seconds he turned his head towards the DCI. The normally phlegmatic look in his eyes now betrayed his discomfort at finding himself in a situation that he wasn't in control of.

"Go ahead, Chief Inspector … "

"I was thinking – the fact that they've sealed that bunker indicates that they are prepared to be self-sufficient for some time … "

"That would appear to be so."

"But given the apparent sophisticated engineering that has been employed, it seems incredible to me that they wouldn't incorporate some means of escape in an emergency."

The commander's entire face screwed up into a frown.

"You think there might be another way in?"

"I don't know, but I do think it's worthy of investigation."

The commander seemed to stiffen, as though his drive had been temporarily restored.

"Okay. I agree, it's worth a try. Considering the time constraints we appear to be up against, it may prove to be our remaining hope. But there's a lot of ground to cover and we have both limited lighting and personnel for such an activity. Under normal circumstances, we would undertake the investigation with a larger force in daylight, but we do not have such luxuries."

Jack merely nodded in agreement, not wishing to dent the man's esteem any further and resisted the urge to shout at the commander to give the order forthwith. The plan was finally announced as the goal-driven commander clicked back into gear.

"We need to retain cover here also. I will allocate four teams of two to cover a quarter of a mile radius around this spot for now. Will you be in one of those parties?"

"Yes."

"You will have a marksman with you. Do you possess a firearm?"

Robson nodded, and after receiving the short briefing and completing their radio tests, he was trudging across the gorse-covered landscape, as gusts continued to swirl around them. He carried a powerful flashlight, while his colleague held an automatic rifle, choosing to rely on the powerful torch strapped to his head for the time being.

*

Inspector Wilson stood with her ear pressed against the door of the modest twin bedroom that she had been allocated, listening to the commotion outside. After a short while, she convinced herself that what she heard were scenes of celebration and not, perhaps, the sounds of suffering that she initially imagined when she first heard the crowd.

She retreated to sit on the bed and stared at the framed art on the wall, wondering what had happened to the people here to make them such an acquiescent population. Hadn't they been forcibly removed from their homes and families and imprisoned underground? She recalled, at that moment, something that the doctor had speedily mentioned in their brief encounter earlier that day. It felt like the conversation had taken place an age ago. *Wasn't it night time yet?* The lifestyle underground didn't need to be governed by the cycle of the solar system. As she pondered the implications of the drug programme that Dr O'Hara had suggested was taking place, she didn't immediately notice the package being slid beneath her door. Suddenly, it was given a shove, resulting in a whooshing sound as it slid along the tiled floor, the thin bundle eventually resting a few feet inside the room.

After a moment's hesitation, she realised that the sender had taken care to ensure that the package was received in private. She moved to clutch it from the floor, anticipating the door being opened by one of the officials at any moment. Sitting back on the bed, her eyes darted between the brown A4 envelope on her lap and the entrance to the room. She held the pillow tilted above the envelope, hoping that she would be able to conceal her delivery almost instantly if required, and took a few seconds to allow her heart rate to normalise. As she focussed on drawing steady breaths into her lungs, she noticed a bend in the middle, indicating it had been stored at half its original size for a period.

She slid her forefinger along the seal at the top of the

envelope and removed the contents. Her eyebrows rose, creating delicate wrinkles on her forehead, as she studied the device in her hands. She placed it alongside the envelope and removed the roughly torn sheet of paper. As she studied the wording that had been scribbled using rouge lip liner, the gap in her understanding was bridged.

'CAUGHT YOUR EYE EARLIER. ALL DRUGGED EXCEPT ME. CONCEAL THIS AND WEAR IT WHEN YOU HEAR THE CLUNK INSIDE THE VENT. I KNOW OF ANOTHER ENTRANCE. HOPE YOU GET BROUGHT TO BIG BRIEFING LATER, TALK THEN. ACT MERRILY DRUNK BUT DON'T OVERDO. DESTROY THIS. JODIE.'

*

An hour later, they had covered every millimetre of their quarter-mile quadrant, and DCI Robson had already decided to extend the search without further consultation. He turned the moment he heard his colleague scream, but saw no one. His instinct was to break for cover and he leapt behind the nearest prickly gorse bush. He heard the cursing from the man on the ground twenty yards away and shone his torch in the direction of the sound.

Edging towards the dark heap, he saw the man was now holding his ankle in his hands instead of his rifle. The sound of boots could be heard as the nearest pair from the search party arrived in reaction to the commotion. Jack listened to the discussion.

"What happened, Gary?" asked one of the newly arrived

team members.

"My foot went down into a fucking hole, I think."

"Hmm, could be a warren hole." The soldier offered, shining his torch onto a nearby patch of ground. The third man, who had been assessing their fallen colleague's injury, looked up and offered a diagnosis. "Looks like it's broken to me, let's get him back, we'll take a side each."

Robson was a good hundred yards away and out of earshot, by the time they realised the injured man's partner was no longer there.

After another five minutes, Robson felt like he was the only life form on the moor. The wailing gale threatened to overpower an unmistakable sound, but he had definitely heard it. *Running water*. He allowed his senses to lead the way and his feet nearly gave way on the clay as he arrived at the bank of a stream. He decided to follow its course, and by the time he found what he had been looking for, he had ventured half a mile from the heavily guarded bunker entrance, where the commander was currently barking instructions to the construction team, which had arrived on site with their monstrous machines of excavation.

The gradient of the stream's descent had increased and as the water progressed on the course that it had carved for many centuries, the grassy banks gave way to an undulating rock formation. Jack lay on his front and shone his torch into the thin crevasse where the natural stream disappeared into a man-made construction. He couldn't be sure of the shape that appeared to be outlined by his flashlight, until he managed to squeeze through the gap in the rocks. However, no matter how long he stared at the metal portal, he could find no means of gaining access. He leant forward, resting both his outstretched palms on the cold metal and began to feel desperate exhaustion, as he wondered how much time they had left.

*

It had only been a matter of minutes since the noise had died down from the cheery gathering outside, when Inspector Wilson heard the clunk inside the air ventilation system that she had been furtively warned of. She felt panic as she heard the door to her room being opened and fumbled with the mask, quickly shoving it between the mattress and wall. She had another second to control her breathing, remembering to feign a drunken expression just as the large man entered to invite her to the big event.

She realised she had overdone her 'inebriation' as she looked around and saw only the mildest indication of stupor among her fellow inmates. Indeed, the overwhelming characteristic on display was one of vacancy, and she adjusted her demeanour accordingly, hoping that it wasn't too late. Perhaps the officials would put her initial drunkenness down to the fact that she was a newcomer to the drug.

She watched the attractive woman guide a small child in her direction and deliberately gazed around the group, avoiding eye contact, while keeping her oncoming ally within her field of peripheral vision.

"Isn't this exciting?!" Jodie beamed towards her.

The nearest to them overheard the remark and agreed in

rapturous unison. In their preoccupied state of glee, nobody noticed the young mother lower her voice, as she turned her head slightly to smile at no one in particular.

"After the briefing, follow me."

Wilson responded with a gormless nod, as the group were herded towards the Town Hall.

CHAPTER 64

The emergency Cobra meeting had been brief. The group of people forming the inner sanctum of government, along with the security service personnel, had all left the meeting with solemn looks. They had walked with purpose as they departed the splendid building at Whitehall and ducked into waiting armoured vehicles, acting out the one protocol that none of them had ever wanted to follow.

The Prime Minister looked out on to the streets of the capital, which were well-lit in the darkness of the spring night, wondering at how the city streets were never entirely devoid of people, and whether that would be likely to change in the coming hours or days. The meeting had been the most alarming that any of her cabinet had ever experienced, and as they acknowledged that they appeared to sit on the brink of a nuclear attack, the motives of the perpetrators, or indeed their targets, were still not understood.

Their allies had been notified of the situation. Even those

with whom they shared slightly colder relationships had been briefed of the imminent danger. During the meeting, they had unanimously agreed that the government should take all available action to prevent an unthinkable chain reaction. One by one, almost all the nations on the planet duly raised their threat levels to second highest, in response to the alert from the British. The joint terrorism analysis centre had already adjusted the threat level for the United Kingdom to 'critical', the maximum possible, signifying that an imminent attack was expected. They weren't to know that the immediate lethal danger existed more for those other nations than it did for the British Isles, which would suffer the secondary consequences.

*

Inspector Wilson hadn't needed to dig too deeply into her acting skills to fulfil her stoned performance. The obscurity of the extraordinary oration from Noah did not prevent her from understanding what was about to occur, for she had already had the privilege of her own one to one briefing, delivered without the blandishments. The crowd had delighted in the speech and the ovation at the end seemed to sate the appetite of the orator. His people were now fully on board and the final part of the strategy would be executed.

Now, Noah and his officials had to undertake a task that ostensibly none of them wanted to, but which had long ago been agreed necessary in order to realise their ambitions. Emma caught sight of Jodie in the distance, as she returned to the town square to join the others in the big celebration, after putting her daughter to bed. Nobody felt like sleeping that night and the officials did not wish to suppress their elation – they had other duties to fulfil.

A jovial gathering sat around outside the cafe, sipping drinks. The loud conversation and laughter made Emma shudder at the thought of how, with the assistance of a few chemicals and the delivery of a well-planned indoctrination programme, this group of otherwise rational and intelligent people were prepared to unconditionally support their new leader in blind reverence. The key seemed to be to avoid explicit description and thereby shield them from the true horror of the plan.

Having taken her place on the edge of the square, she was sure she had avoided suspicion and began to meander away from the group in the same direction in which Jodie had left a couple of minutes earlier. She allowed her eyes a few seconds to adjust to the contrasting darkness, eventually making out the faint outline of another person as she stepped into the shadows.

*

Wilson responded as soon as she was beckoned, and eventually crouched in the corner of the corridor alongside the shadow.

"This has to be quick – it didn't take them long to work out that the doctor was missing earlier. This door leads to a longer corridor. It takes about fifteen minutes to walk quickly to the end. If you walk up the steep slope at the end for a couple of hundred yards, there are two rooms at the top of the incline, I think for storage. But, inside the second door on the left, the room resembles a cave. There is a small, sturdy-looking door with a large lever. It must lead to the outside. I didn't try it because I came up here on my own, after the doctor had been caught. Rebecca was sleeping, and I didn't want to risk us being separated by raising an alarm."

Inspector Wilson understood that it wouldn't be long before their absence was noticed.

"If I go along there now, will you cover for me for as long as possible?"

Jodie nodded, her eyes watering in relief as the police officer before her accepted the task. She felt her shoulders rise perceptibly as the burden was shared.

"Yes, I'll think of something to tell them. If you run, you might be able to get to the exit in ten minutes."

"Good. Thank you. Go back to the others now, be careful not to be spotted as you return."

Their brief embrace represented instinctive comradeship. Jodie quietly rushed back towards the group, while Inspector Wilson inched through the door and paced along the dark corridor as quickly as she dared in the pitch dark. Twelve minutes later, she stood breathless at the bottom of a steep incline, and her nervous system informed her that she had not fully recovered from her leg injury. The route up ahead was dimly illuminated, with occasional bulkhead lighting on either side. She caught her breath for a moment, shutting out the growing pain from her lower left limb. Then her athletic frame loped another couple of hundred yards before she stopped to place her hands on her knees, her lungs feeling short-changed in the claustrophobic, damp air, away from the air conditioning of the main living quarters. She walked through the doorway, in accordance with her new ally's instructions, and as she studied her surroundings beyond the paraphernalia that had been dumped inside the room, she evaluated the rocky perimeter and saw for herself how Jodie had concluded that the door before her must lead to the outside world. Wilson was certain that the woman's analysis had been correct. It was the way that she had recently been brought in to the facility.

*

Exhilaration ran through Noah's body like an electrical charge as he gave the command, his senses tuned by his nervous system. Two of his officials departed to shepherd the community back to their rooms. The party was over. The final checks would be made to confirm that the facility was in full and permanent lockdown before the battalion currently swarming the land twenty metres above their heads would be given a whole new problem to concentrate on. He and Thorpe exchanged knowing glances before turning their attention to the operator sat before the control desk.

"Status please, Mikey?"

"All indications are normal, Noah. Our brothers and sisters are ready, and are in full lockdown."

"Perfect. Enter the activation code and prepare to dispatch the rockets when instructed."

"Affirmative."

The ponytailed operative opened the control panel, leaving the key still inserted in the protective front cover. He flicked the switch and watched the panel spring into life, before punching the six-digit code. Five seconds later, the LED screen blipped *CODE ACCEPTED – ACTIVATION SUCCESSFUL.* The three men appeared mesmerised as they watched red LEDs illuminate inside all six of the buttons to the left of the control desk. Noah dabbed at wet eyes as he watched a decade of meticulous planning come to fruition.

*

Deep inside Steep Holm island, one of the secret service's top computer engineers followed the armed personnel deeper underground. Earlier, they had discussed simply taking out the communications hub that had been discovered on the island. However, the team of technological experts had unanimously agreed it was conceivable that such an action could irreversibly trigger a missile launch. The system protecting the six silo entrances had been as sophisticated as anything he had ever come across, but all six doors had finally opened after they had hacked into the CPUs to override the electronic defence system. Neither he nor his five colleagues who had entered the other silos had reckoned on the sight that each now beheld, as the radio clipped to the chest of the captain buzzed into life and a voice echoed into the vast chamber. The commander had hurriedly left him clear instructions before he departed on the helicopter earlier. Shoot on sight any potentially hostile foe and above all, disarm the arsenal.

"Sir, we have a problem."

"I know."

Even the ultra-professional firearms experts were distracted from their concentration by the sight of the colossal rocket heads protruding from the earth below. In the distance, they all noticed the small, yet menacing, red LEDs blinking in each of their respective chambers. They gazed wide-eyed to the heavens, as each roof opened above to allow the lunar glare into the six vast caverns.

"Get the commander on the phone – tell him we're too late and I am ordering a full evacuation."

CHAPTER 65

DCI Robson focussed on steadying his breathing, in an attempt to remove the audible pulsing in his ears. He tuned his hearing to the faint rattling sound coming from inside the handleless door, and moved swiftly to place his flashlight to shine towards the rocky crevasse from the moor. He stood with his back to the wall, tucking himself into the rock face as far as possible to position himself flush with the entrance. The rattling intensified before a clunk could be heard. Jack held the gun steadily as he pointed it alongside the rock wall towards the door, determined not to miss his chance. Before making his move on the slim figure that seemed to move cautiously into the opening, he waited to see if an accomplice was in tow. He took a brief opportunity to glance into the dimly lit entrance from which the dark figure had emerged before deftly moving towards his prey. His command carried authority.

"Freeze!"

He held the gun four feet from the back of the head. Hands

were slowly raised high above head. The compliance of the dark outline before him pleased DCI Robson and gave him the confidence to instruct his captive to slowly turn, enabling a potential identity to be confirmed. The body was a mere silhouette against the light emanating from the torch located immediately behind it, and only an outline of the face could be determined. Arms remained above head, but the outside of the figure's left foot seemed to connect with the side of his head at lightning speed. Two seconds later, another light was directed into Jack's face as he lay on the ground. His muddled sight refocussed momentarily, sending a cerebral communication to some distant location inside his brain which registered that he was now peering into the barrel of his own firearm.

*

Thorpe remained the only calm presence in the control room as they were informed that everyone had been accounted for and were tucked away in their respective accommodation, with the exception of their newest arrival. The angry look on Noah's face was so seldom on view that it was a troubling image indeed to those who had delivered the news, and they were glad when Thorpe took charge of the situation.

"She can't have got far, there's no need to panic. The facility is hermetically sealed."

Despite the reassurance, Sir Geoffrey's tone retained its menacing edge.

"I want her found before we release the missiles. I need to know that the troublesome girl hasn't done anything to compromise the bunker before the blasts are initiated."

"I'll take care of it myself, Noah."

Charlesworth appeared visibly assured by the statement and nodded to his dear friend.

"Do whatever you have to do, and report back as soon as you can, Christian."

Thorpe led the small group of men from the control room, each equipped with a firearm and not in any doubt of their instructions when they encountered the missing female.

*

As Inspector Wilson peered into the face of the felled man, she hadn't expected to experience the urge to embrace her assailant. Her head was a cacophony of emotions as she registered the unexpected sight. The overwhelming desire to kiss the man on the ground at that moment felt wholly inappropriate, given their precarious circumstances.

"Jack!"

"Huh?" came the confused groan.

"I-I didn't know it was you!"

Impulse suddenly overwhelmed free will as she knelt and placed her lips against his to form a tender, passionate seal. Jack caught the familiar scent, which reinforced the identity of Emma's voice and took pleasure from her warm, moist lips in a prolonged, ardent embrace. The intoxicating sensation provided a hidden surge of strength, enabling him to wrap his arms around her. He suddenly burned with desire, yet tried desperately to resist the painful urge to proceed. It was Emma who had the strength to pull away.

"Are you alone, Jack?"

"Yes. But the others aren't far away. If you can keep the door open, I'll call for reinforcements."

An awkward barrier between them grew, tangible even in the darkness.

"Jack, there isn't time. I managed to get away because they are preparing to launch the missiles from here, right now!"

"Fuck. Is Thorpe here?"

"Yes, but he's part of it."

"I know."

"It's more than a bunker, Jack. There's an underground town down there and they're planning to live there for a long time. And it's not the only one. They think they're going to initiate Armageddon."

He struggled to his feet and stumbled behind Inspector Wilson as she returned inside the open hatch. Pausing at the door, he went to the nearest heavy-looking storage container and slid it outside to prevent the door from closing. Seconds later, he was racing down the steep slope behind Emma, barely feeling the connection between his feet and the mortar surface, while the bulkhead lights circled above his throbbing head.

*

Bob and Louise held hands, while Jacob Miller stood just behind them. All three peered through the rock at the two detectives, the scene conveniently illuminated for them. The emergency entrance had been breached. Louise shivered as she placed the radio to her ear and prepared to inform Noah of his new guests, while she and Bob moved into the opening.

Jacob followed the couple through the emergency exit and bent down to grab DCI Robson's makeshift doorstop. *This door won't be opening again.*

*

By the time they reached the door at the end of the dark corridor, sweat was running down his temples and DCI Robson felt a desperate craving for rehydration. Wilson indicated to the doors ahead, as he collapsed into a crouch and battled to regain his breathing.

"Jack, listen. Once we're through these doors, we will be into the lit areas within about a hundred yards. It's likely that they'll be looking for me by now. I think I should go ahead and you follow five minutes behind."

She handed him his gun.

DCI Robson fought to think logically, as his left temple continued to thump in response to the roundhouse it had experienced only fifteen minutes earlier.

"We'd be better together."

He knew as he said it that his decision had been influenced more by his feelings for his partner, than any strategic benefit.

"No. It's odds on that they're looking for me by now. Our only chance of maintaining the element of surprise is if I go alone. They don't know that you're here."

"Okay, but you take the gun."

"No. They can't find me with that. You just need to keep

your distance. Give me a five-minute start. Listen, after around a hundred yards you'll be out into the square—"

"Square?!"

"There's no time for details, Jack. They will most likely want to have me secured in my room. I am in No. 6 Charles Street. It branches off to the right at the opposite end of the square to where you'll arrive. But don't try to rescue me first unless you've managed to acquire a key. The passageway leading from the square immediately to the left of mine is Parliament Street. There are typically around five of them who are armed, in addition to Charlesworth and Thorpe. Some will be looking for me, the others are in the control room at the end of that street. I don't think we have much time to stop this."

"Emma … "

Their bodies remained facing each other, as they watched one another in silence, their eyes burning with passion and fear. Their mutual expressions rendered any form of speech unnecessary, but Jack mustered a simple sentence, releasing her in pursuit of their objective.

"Be careful."

Robson watched her rush towards the dim light in the distance. His eyes remained fixed on her lithe figure as she gradually disappeared through the ever-decreasing gap in the swinging doors, which swung behind the woman who had awoken such strong emotions in him – feelings that he never thought possible to experience again. What confused him most was that his usual feeling of guilt didn't seem to arrive. He concentrated on the timer on his wrist.

Jack bolted when he heard the first gun shot, clattering both swing doors against the wall. Only four minutes had elapsed since Emma's departure when he reached the deserted town square. He looked at the clock in the centre of the square and shuddered when he noticed the date: *01/01/00 New Era*. He heard distant shouting coming from the alleyway on the left of the square and stood for a second, crushing the urge to follow. A few minutes later he was prowling along Parliament Street, passing the building marked as the Town Hall and arrived outside the bland-looking doorway, with the simple sign 'Control Room' identified on the front. After checking the phone and replacing it inside his pocket, he held the gun cocked for action.

Sir Geoffrey Charlesworth and Michael Knight both swung around in unison as the door swung open and a familiar voice commanded them to move away from the control desk. DCI Robson was careful to maintain a safe distance as the two men inched towards him with their hands on their heads, as instructed.

The apparent surprise on Sir Geoffrey's face was short-lived and Jack fought against the unease he felt from the lack of fear in his opponent's eyes.

"Chief Inspector Robson. I hadn't counted on you joining us! However, you'll be an asset to our little community down here."

DCI Robson couldn't resist a mocking snarl at the man who had been responsible for nearly ending his and his partner's lives, but he kept his voice steady.

"I think we can say that your community has come to an end, Mr Charlesworth."

Jack was quick to notice Mikey edge his hand down his side towards a holster.

"Put that fucking hand back now, pal, or you'll lose it!"

Sir Geoffrey gave an irritating chuckle as Mikey flinched and obeyed the command.

"Jack, Jack, we must educate you in our peace-loving existence if you are to become a permanent resident down here…"

Somewhere inside, he knew that Charlesworth was stalling, but still he couldn't resist sticking the knife in.

"Peace-loving? I'm just trying to decide which of your philanthropic actions is the most likely to earn you a nomination for the Nobel prize. Hmm, let's see, kidnapping? Murder? Or fucking holocaust?!"

Charlesworth abandoned his jovial visage and sighed.

"Chief Inspector. We *are* philanthropists. We never wanted casualties, but we also vowed that, should the necessity arise, we would be prepared to take strong, and perhaps undesirable action to protect the future of our people. I'm very sorry about the boat accident, Jack, but I saw your face that day on the island and I knew you would never let it go … "

"*Our* people? And what about those that you've seen off? Your dear friend, Barry, and your butler – if they were your friends, then I fear for your enemies."

"It has been most regrettable, Jack. Poor Barry just became lazy at the last minute, leaving such an obvious trace by using his own mobile telephone. We knew he would crumble when questioned, he was never up to the uglier side of our work. That blasted phone has caused a lot of unrest. If only Barry's brother had handed it over when requested … "

"And what had your butler done to upset you?"

"DCI Robson, this really isn't getting us anywhere. Carl was never meant to be a part of it. But he had discovered some confidential information, shall we say. It's just lucky for us that he decided to confront me first, rather than report his findings to you. How ironic loyalty can be."

Robson felt anger growing inside and couldn't resist the remonstration.

"Mr Charlesworth, what exactly are you supposedly protecting *your* people against?"

Charlesworth sighed, as though he were losing his patience with a petulant child.

"Against the elite order, if you like, Jack. Humanity has never been in such a precarious position as it is right now, ironically, in this time of supposed peace and civilisation. The enlightenment has been and gone. Ostensibly, slavery has been abolished for generations and prejudice is officially regarded as a heinous crime. At least in terms of political correctness, of course. But how we have all become indoctrinated, such that we accept whatever piece of propaganda that aligns with our misconstrued beliefs, and would see our fellow humans suffer at the hands of a corrupt few."

DCI Robson almost found himself inspired by the oration and saw for a moment how this man had managed to cast a spell over his people. He didn't interrupt. Sir Geoffrey was building up a full head of steam.

"How ironic it is that the general population would have such an appetite for the proposal to begin dismantling years of post-war toil, the objective of which had been to ensure that the world would live in equality and that we might be empathic beings. And how perverse that those supporting the proposal to turn back the clock and embark on the development of a nationalistic state should do so in the naïve and selfish belief that this new world would protect them from all that they feared. When in fact, as history has shown us, we all took part in building the monster from which there seems no means of escape. In the name of free speech and free will, we are all accomplices to building the empire that would for evermore seek to prevent the principle of freedom on which it was supposedly founded."

Robson was incredulous.

"Has it ever occurred to you, Sir Geoffrey, that you have yourself become the tyrant that you seek to protect your selected people against? And the fact that you have thought to award yourself the privilege of choosing those who will live – doesn't it remind you of certain other fascist rulers in our recent past?"

He searched the tall man's face, which had become passionately animated for a time, but now reverted to its default impassive state. The eyes revealed nothing. The silence remained for ten seconds. *Touché.* It occurred to Jack that he may have hit a nerve, until he noticed four guns pointing at him and realised that the conversation was over.

The DCI's fingers tensed around his firearm and he felt his own blood boil at the sight of the red liquid trickling from his partner's nose, as she stood next to Thorpe with her hands bound behind.

"Another example of your peaceful ways?" he hissed.

Thorpe intervened.

"I suggest you drop your weapon very quickly indeed, Jack."

He followed the Superintendent's advice, not having the stomach to challenge the supposed man of the law on his reasons for acting as a double agent for a terrorist. As he lowered the firearm, he stumbled slightly as he recognised the harbour master and two of his new CID colleagues standing alongside the Superintendent.

Charlesworth took command.

"It was a thrilling conversation Jack, and very similar to the one I had with your delectable partner earlier. You two have a lot in common you know! But we mustn't allow our plans to be delayed any longer. Christian, are we secure?"

Thorpe nodded in affirmation.

"Mikey, take your position again please and initiate the launch. Ben will have secured the emergency hatch again by now."

"This is a mistake. Thorpe, how can you stand by, for fuck sake, he's going to cause a holocaust!"

"Enough!"

The shout from Charlesworth pierced the room, flavoured with distaste.

"I cannot allow any further interruptions. You have no leverage in this matter, Jack. You can either watch in silence … or not."

He glanced at his gun-wielding servants.

"If either one of them moves or speaks, you shoot to kill, without hesitation. Understood?"

Jack noticed the tension on the faces of a couple of the

armed officials, but despite their apparent discomfort, he knew he couldn't bank on all five armed servants reneging on the order to gun him down if he so much as moved.

"Proceed, Mikey."

DCI Robson and Inspector Wilson watched on in horrified acceptance as the operative leant his lanky frame over the control desk and calmly fulfilled his orders. One by one, he operated the six red buttons, his relaxed demeanour in no way reflecting the impact of his actions. On the screen above the control desk, six separate timers kicked into life one after the other in response to the commands. Each counter came to life with the displayed time – '5:00' – and second by second decreased – '4:59', '4:58'.

Emma gasped as the duration of the countdown suddenly gave unequivocal credence to the confidence on display from their hosts.

"It's over," said Charlesworth. "Please return the officers to their room – we won't deprive them of one another's company, will we? Then all report back to witness our new beginning."

For the first time, Robson was able to decipher the mysterious characteristic in Charlesworth's eyes – lunacy.

The following seconds seemed like a dream. The inspectors were still gazing in terror at the decreasing count on the timers when the bodies flew across the control room, the ammunition ripping the life from them on contact. Mikey wasn't afforded the luxury of seeing his assassin as the single bullet exploded inside his skull and he jerked forward, chest slumped on the control desk. Both Thorpe and Jefferies were punished for their instinctively defensive reactions and both now lay lifeless, with their firearms on the ground beside them. Louise sobbed uncontrollably as her hands were bound behind her.

Noah raised his slender arms above his head, the stains on his shirt revealing that he hadn't been totally immune to the tension after all. While his body composed itself in an urbane gesture of surrender, his eyes expressed no emotion, even as he surveyed the carnage before him, his comrades fallen.

DCI Robson noticed the countdown timers all approaching the two-minute mark as the commander of the secret service took centre stage and faced the fanatical leader.

"Sir Geoffrey Charlesworth, you are under arrest. I need the code to deactivate the launch, sir."

It was an order, rather than a request, but the commander was visibly surprised by the response.

"I'm afraid I can't do that." Charlesworth smiled and put his hand to his lips to blow a kiss into the room. "Farewell, and good luck to all of us … "

The commander moved in closer to negotiate, but found himself looking down at a motionless heap at his feet. Foam emanating from the mouth and nose of the body confirmed that Noah had decided upon his own ending, having digested the pill he had always stashed under his watch strap for such eventualities.

The commander looked to the two timid engineers, peering from behind the row of marksmen, understanding the burden of responsibility that now lay with them. They dutifully responded to the silent command and approached the control desk. The agent knew before he touched the 'Cancel' button that it would be ineffective, but went through the motions. Jack moved alongside him as the screen flashed into life: *KEYPAD LOCKED – INVALID COMMAND*. The room looked on at him almost sympathetically, wondering who he was intending to call on his mobile phone. A hoarse murmur came from the bloody-nosed woman at the back of the room. "The codes … "

The commander, using only eye contact, yielded to DCI Robson's request to try out a desperate idea. Jack entered the six-digit code on the phone. The counters continued to decrease, the first now reading forty-five seconds. Everyone in the room was surprised at their disappointment, not realising how much hope they had invested in the well-intended chief inspector at that moment. All optimism had now left the building.

The commander was already on the secure line, requesting a connection through to the Director General. It was time for the world to prepare. His eyes were fixed on the most advanced timer while he waited for the connection. He watched the display change to '00:09' as he began to brief the Director General.

The commander couldn't see the display on the control desk from where he stood, and continued the discussion using the agreed codewords. It took him a couple more seconds to detect that the mood in the room had gone through a transition. All eyes were fixed on the counters, not daring to look away. The figures ranged from seven to twelve seconds, but the counters had stopped moving.

The commander apologised to the Director General and issued a clear message to disregard the previous communication.

Robson locked his gaze on to Wilson's moist eyes. This time he didn't obey the inner voice that told him to look away, and not feeling his feet against the tiled floor, they came together in an unashamedly long embrace.

CHAPTER 66

One hundred and twenty miles away, also underground, an assembly of parliamentary representatives had received confirmation that the immediate threat had been nullified. The Prime Minister had somewhat awkwardly briefed her global counterparts accordingly, but would face stiffer questions from them later. As they left their bunker to resume daily duties, both she and the cabinet also knew that there were those implicit in the conspiracy that had comfortably evaded identification on shores far away from their little island.

The head of the country felt every gramme of the weight of her duty, as she filled her lungs with cool spring air, walking, jadedly, from the protection of the bunker. She reflected privately on how close they had been to the brink. At that moment, the perpetual grind of the daily job and the responsibility that it brought was in clear perspective. She knew only too well of the corruption that scourged the planet she and like-minded rulers were determined to regulate. The challenge that she and her colleagues faced was to ensure that everyone was pulling in the same direction, which meant that even those entrusted with the most confidential information had to be held accountable. She knew that she would have to give assurances to the world's powers that her government would learn lessons from this episode. However, she would also remind them that the organisation nearly responsible for bringing them down, despite their collective might, had slipped under all their radars and made fools of the global intelligence community. Action would be seen to be taken immediately, beginning with accepting the resignation of the most obvious scapegoat. The Home Secretary had always claimed to be close to the ex-UN weapons inspector, and his appraisal of the man had been close to deification.

Beware of false prophets, who come to you in sheep's clothing but inwardly are ravenous wolves.

She made a point of relishing one final breath of fresh air, inhaling deeply before getting into the armoured car, and appreciating the natural beauty of her surroundings like never before. She and her family would have to make more of an effort to escape from the soulless city more often. She began to shake her head as the car sped into formation with the remainder of the convoy and they began their return to the overcrowded streets of the sleepless capital. The burden of knowledge would lay heavy on her for a long time.

She was snapped from her philosophising by her aide, who started to brief her on her schedule for the day, starting with a briefing by the defence minister, in preparation for PMQs the next day. Her government was coming under increasing pressure to reduce its nuclear capability, and the costs associated with renewing their defences were under the greatest scrutiny. If only they knew what she knew. But they never would.

CHAPTER 67

Scattered across the globe, five separate communities awaited the confirmation. their frenzied anticipation aided by the intoxicating effects of the drugs dispensed by their leaders.

As the countdown reached T plus twenty minutes, it became apparent that the mission had been unsuccessful. Communication had been lost with the principal bunker.

The five community leaders engaged in their brief, rehearsed dialogue over the secure transmission system. It would be their final contact for some time. As soon as the conversation terminated, all five centres initiated the procedure. The contingency arrangements would demand patience, but that wouldn't distract any of them from their ultimate objective.

They had lost their leader but would not waste time mourning. Agreed protocol dictated that they would also have to sacrifice more lives, with immediate effect. The bunkers had to be de-commissioned straight away, and nobody outside the inner sanctum of knowledge could be allowed to carry any memory of them.

The dream lived on, and would continue to do so until their goal was realised. Noah would have been proud.

EPILOGUE

2 weeks later.

The sun had risen early but now sat hidden behind wispy clouds, high above the voluptuous late spring foliage from which birdsong could be heard. Many found the grounds of the chapel a spiritual haven, particularly at that time of year. It being so early in the morning, they had the graveyard to themselves, which was the way both Jack and Jasmine preferred it.

Jack placed a tender hand on his daughter's shoulder as she set down the spray of spring flowers on the tribute to her mother. In the early days following the accident, he had felt compelled to say something, to make everything all right. He berated himself for his inability to read the mind of his one remaining, precious commodity. The past few weeks had reminded him that nobody really controlled anything.

It was a watershed moment, the day it dawned on him that his greatest and wisest offering was to impart love to his child.

The same way that he had when her mother was alive, which had made them all so happy for a time.

The little girl rose in her blue floral dress, and placed a small plump hand in his. He lowered himself into a crouch for the embrace that followed. They strolled hand in hand from the scene in silence, as they had done in recent times, respecting one another's private thoughts. Jack had never wanted to confront his and found such moments difficult, but he had a question to ask this time. He sought a blessing.

He had spent the past few nights pondering whether Isabelle would have approved of the meeting. He was still apprehensive about the certain guilt he would feel when they collected their visitor from the station later that day, regardless of how excited Jasmine had been at the prospect.

Jack snapped back to the present abruptly, suddenly aware of the noise overhead, even though it had been building in a crescendo for a short while. He gazed to the sky as the helicopter chugged gracefully over them, beginning to evoke painful memories. Behind the aircraft, the clouds parted to once again reveal the great orb of light. Over his shoulder, he noticed the solar rays appeared to illuminate one epitaph in particular.

Smiling, Jack lifted Jasmine off her feet as she giggled.

THE END

TO THE READER

Dear reader,

I do hope that you have enjoyed ARCAM.

If you have, I'd be very grateful if you could leave a review of the book on Amazon. As a new writer, such reviews are incredibly important, both creatively and in terms of sales.

To do so, just visit the ARCAM book page on Amazon, scroll down to the Customer Reviews section and hit the *'Write a customer review'* button.

I very much look forward to your feedback!

Best wishes,

Jason Minick

ABOUT THE AUTHOR

Jason Minick lives in the south-west of England. He has a passion for writing, and is a fan of reading many genres.

His debut novel, ARCAM, combines police procedural with conspiracy thriller. It is set in his favourite part of the UK: the south-west of England.

ARCAM is the first book in the DCI Robson series

Jason lives with his wife, Emma, and his three children, Lucy, William and Sophie. The family share their home with two very small dogs, Digby and Tizzie.

To learn more about Jason, please visit:
www.jasonminick.com

You can also connect with Jason on social media:
🐦 **Twitter.com/JMinick_Author**

ACKNOWLEDGEMENTS

I would like to express my gratitude to the people who supported me in the production of this book.

To Jon Turner, my editor and proofreader – thank you for your professionalism and frank input, it has been invaluable.

To Mark Thomas, my designer, for his exceptional work in the presentation of this book, and for his advice and assistance in getting the book to market.

The area of North Somerset and the Quantocks has given us many happy memories, as a family. Personally, it has also provided me with the inspiration I needed to finally write, having for some reason suppressed the urge that has been evident ever since writing my first story at primary school.

I'd like to thank all those that work hard to protect the natural beauty of this area, with a special mention for the volunteers that are charged with the stewardship of Steep Holm island, which, for me, provides such an enchanting interruption in the view across the Channel. The literature that I've used as research has been of much use, and I beg forgiveness for any use of 'artistic license' in the portrayal of these places – all in the name of a good story!

To you, the reader – thank you for reading this book. I hope that it brings you enjoyment, and may we meet again soon, through this phenomenal medium of story-telling …